THE GODDESS & THE WOODSMAN

(2023 revised edition)

Goddessverse Fantasy Series
Book 1

CORALIE MOSS

Pink Moon Books

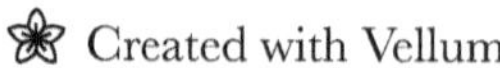 Created with Vellum

Dedicated to the forgotten and disremembered,
and all they have to teach us.

———

Contents

Glossary

Author's note: *The mythological figures populating this book originated primarily from Celtic, Northern European, and Greek sources. I took creative liberties with each figure's depiction, after researching and musing on the roles I wanted them to assume within this story, and the stories to follow.*

Habonde: Celtic. Goddess of the Hearth; of abundance and prosperity. Her symbols are fire and ale.

Baubo: Greek. Bawdy, sexually liberated, this Goddess of Mirth is the embodiment of enjoyment.

Hestia: Greek. Goddess of the Hearth. One of the original Olympians and sister to Demeter and Zeus.

Brigit: Celtic/Irish. Goddess of Spring, the dawn, fertility. Connected to wells and rivers.

Hekate: Goddess of the wild places, childbirth, and the crossroads. Associated with magic and witchcraft. Gatekeeper between worlds. Associated with Demeter and Persephone.

- **The Lampedes:** Torch-bearing underworld nymphs who accompany Hekate.

Astrape: Greek. Goddess of Lightning. Sister of Bronte. Together, Astrape and Bronte were Zeus' shield-bearers.

Demeter: Greek. Goddess of Harvest and Grain. Mother of Persephone.

Persephone: Greek. Queen of the Underworld. Daughter of Demeter. Wife of Hades.

Scáthách: Irish/Scottish. Warrior. Martial arts teacher. Resides on the Isle of Skye.

Epona: Gallo-Celtic (and Roman). Goddess of Horses.

Airmid: Irish. Member of the Tuatha Dé Dannan. Goddess of Healing. Enchantress.

Bé Chuille: Irish. Member of the Tuatha Dé Dannan. Daughter of Flidais. Witch and enchantress who could control trees, rocks, and grasses.

Creirwy: Welsh. Daughter of Ceridwen. A beautiful maiden.

The Lake Maidens: Welsh. Female fairies who live within rivers and lakes.

Minthe: Greek. Nymph. Lives in the Underworld and is associated with the River Kokytus, and mint. Beloved by Hades (before Persephone).

Hades: Greek. God of the Dead. King of the Underworld. Brother of Zeus and Demeter.

Zeus: Greek. King of the Gods. Rules from Mount Olympus. God of the Sky; of Thunder.

Mnemosyne: Greek. Titans. Goddess of Memory. Caretaker of the underworld's River of Memory.

Non-mythological characters:

Rhys, the Woodsman: He and his brethren are caretakers of sacred trees. He is connected to Hekate, and cares for the yew tree that acts as a portal for the goddess' travels between the underworld and Habonde's croft.

The urisk: Figures from Scottish folklore akin to brownies.

- **Finnock (Finn):** Head of Bone Fire Croft's urisk clans.
- **Jillian (Jilly):** Finn's primary wife.
- **June Bug (Junie):** Finn and Jilly's daughter. Age 15.
- **Kila and Lila:** Finn and Jilly's twin daughters. Age 8.

Fergus: An owl shifter who lives on Bone Fire Croft.

Bailoch: Satyr. Manages the stable on Bone Fire Croft, along with his husband, Bodhi.

Bodhi: Satyr. Manages the stable on Bone Fire Croft, along with his husband, Bailoch.

Habonde's acolytes: Eilidh, Fia, Leith, Lilidh, Kenna, Maisie, Iona.

Moros: Works as a ferryman in the underworld. Son of Charon (Greek). Named for his uncle, Moros.

Siggi: One of the Woodsmen.

Pym: One of the Woodsmen.

Other mythological figures mentioned:

- **Atalanta:** Greek. Virgin goddess allied with Artemis.
- **Caer:** Irish. Shape-shifts between human and swan.
- **Brizo:** Greek. Goddess of the Sea. Prophetess via dreams.
- **Odudua:** Yoruban Earth Goddess and mother of Yemaya.
- **Hedone:** Greek. Goddess of Pleasure, esp. of a sensual nature.
- **Ceridwen:** Celtic/Welsh. Goddess of rebirth, transformation, inspiration. Enchantress. Mother of Creirwy.

Content Notes

The Goddess & the Woodsman is a contemporary adult fantasy set in the modern world. The characters within these pages were inspired by figures from Greek, Irish, and other mythologies. This book contains references to and scenes of trauma involving fire and loss of life; memory loss; explicit sexual intimacy between consenting adults; pregnancy (a minor character).

THE GODDESS & THE WOODSMAN

Part One

Chapter 1

I DROPPED my willow laundry basket between lush clumps of
Hart's tongue fern and directed my attention to the frog sunning
itself atop a nearby rock.

"You want to know how obscure I've become?" The sheep-
sized amphibian gave no indication it was listening. "No? I'm
telling you anyway. There is not a single mention of me in one of
the most extensive references for goddesses and mythological
heroines ever compiled by a non-Magical.

"Not. A single. One."

Taking hold of a freshly washed sheet, I shook it out, careful
to avoid dragging the corners across the ground, and draped it
over the clothing line. A rare sunny day graced these Scottish
hills, and I preferred the smell of air-dried bed linens to those
tumbled in a machine. Plus, hauling the heavy basket up the hill
and tossing wide swaths of wet cloth in the air made for a decent
upper body workout.

"You're probably dying to know how I discovered this
oversight, aren't you? I did an internet search. Multiple internet
searches. I plugged in your name too. And you know what I

found?" I continued, turning to face my companion. "You, who deserve your own URL? It's always 'Demeter this' and 'Demeter that' and 'Oh by the way, Baubo lifted her skirt and the goddess laughed.'"

The frog's corpulent torso rippled in the heat rising off the rock, revealing the naked human form of my dearest friend.

"Consider yourself in illustrious company. I do." Baubo pressed her hand to her stomach as she pushed herself up to sitting. "Goddesses the worlds over who have been co-opted, subsumed, renamed, and/or annihilated. Now, tell me why you called me here. A troubled tone underlies your complaining and it's not like you to wallow in self-pity."

Baubo's seemingly carefree personality masked a sharp wit and sharper mind. Serendipity herself must have whispered my need for counsel in my bestie's ear and urged her to pack her bags for an impromptu visit. Pinching a wooden clothespin, I secured the sheet to the line, smoothed the wrinkles, and unburdened myself of the truth. Or most of it.

"I've been having unsettling dreams."

"Have you consulted with anyone?"

I had considered asking Caer, a local goddess, to enter my dreamtime with me—until I'd discovered she was in the ninth month of her swan year. Her transformation back to her human form was months away and I didn't speak waterfowl. "I thought of scrying for Brizo to see if her oracles would be willing to provide me with their interpretations, but—" I shook my head. I'd lost contact with the Goddess of the Sea and Dreams, as I had with many of my immortal sistren, and hesitated to reach out with what felt like a selfish request.

"I'm no oracle, Habonde, but I'm here and I'm listening and I'm fairly good at parsing out messages." Baubo coaxed a turquoise damselfly off her knee and onto her finger, initiating a staring contest. I surveyed the laundry yet to be hung, and the bare spaces on the clotheslines, and decided she was right. For someone I'd been friends with fewer than two hundred years, Baubo knew me better than others I'd known much, *much* longer.

I pivoted to face her and squinted.

"In each dream, I am on my knees, in my garden, with my cultivator in my hand." I found myself moving my arms through the air as I had whilst dreaming. "I loosen the soil, the tines hit something solid, and a carved figurine rises from clumps of dirt, sucking in oxygen like a babe taking its first breath."

Startled at the sensation of plant matter and crumbly soil, I realized I had dropped to my knees and sunk my fingers into the fragrant, tangled stems of thyme and yarrow covering the ground. A damp sheet smacked my cheek and stuck, momentarily blocking my view. "Each dream segment ended the same way: the figurine came to life, looked me straight in the eyes, and walked away."

I rose and swiped my green-stained fingers across the shabby dress I'd pulled on before leaving the house, lost to the memory of seeing representations of the Divine Mother and other archetypes from European pantheons arising from my garden's fertile soil, night after night.

"What do *you* make of these signs? Because even without my opinion, or that of your local oracle, you must know these are no ordinary dream fragments." Baubo eased herself back onto the rock. Though I was tempted to follow her example, I took my time cleaning dirt out from under my fingernails and hanging another sheet before I shed my dress. I gave the comfortably shapeless garment a swift flick, lowered it next to Baubo, and joined her on the sun-warmed rock.

"The divine is waking and the world needs to know?" I offered, in belated response to her question. The ensuing silence from my right led me to imagine I'd put her to sleep with the type of generalized statement more suited to bumper stickers and political buttons. Further lazing would likely lead to more soporific musings—unless I shared what confronted me at the end of each dream, when I would return my gaze to the freshly dug hole and see bones, mostly finger bones and toe bones, bathed in the moon's light, taunting me with their mysterious origins until I re-covered them with the soil I'd disturbed.

And every morning, I awoke in a cool sweat.

I would share the rest later. Pushing off the rock, I brushed bits of moss and grit from my hands and resumed my task until every sheet and pillowcase hung straight off the crowded lines. A protracted groan startled me out of admiring my handiwork.

"I need a cool drink, a full pen, and a pad of paper," my companion announced. "You are going to enumerate each of these dreams, and I am going to record every detail until the message you have been sent is as clear as the waters of that river I hear."

Still on her back, and still with eyes closed, she waved her hand in the direction of the wide stream that meandered south and west from its origins in the Lake of Secrets beyond the northern border of my croft.

"I have all that at the house." Gathering my dress, I tossed it over my shoulder and swung the empty basket at my side. My stomach rumbled. "Come on you old hag, let's lunch first then work."

MY RAMBLING HOME was my sanctuary, in every sense of the word. It had started out in the fourteenth century as a squat stone structure with a single room and a roof of bundled thatch. I'd commissioned two additions in the mid-eighteen-hundreds: separate, two-story buildings set at a slight angle to one another and connected by a covered walkway, with slate roofs, walls constructed of more refined stone, and suites for guests.

One had to travel further back in time, to the Early Middle Ages, to find the original foundation of the central fireplace anchoring the massive kitchen. As a goddess of the hearth and ale and other of life's necessities, blessed be, I had been worshipped for centuries in nearly every home, my communal fires tended night and day by my acolytes as the wheel of the year turned. Hestia Herself had lit my first fire with a log carried from her temple.

I had not been publicly worshipped in three, maybe four hundred years, and I blamed my diminished stature, incompetent memories, and atrophied magical abilities on that prolonged lack of attention, of… of devotion. I'd fought against the encroaching religious movements and lost, forcing me to come to terms with the world's ever-changing norms and embrace modern technologies as they arrived. Though perhaps not as whole-heartedly as other immortals.

Someday, *someday*, I would remember, I would *be* remembered, and I would—

Enough. I drew a clean, crisply ironed housedress of sky blue and white striped linen over my head. Letting go of an ancient, intractable sorrow, I rolled the sleeves up past my elbows and opened the stove's firebox. Flames reached for the stems of dried wheat and pieces of split wood I fed to the banked coals.

Why could I not form a cohesive theory about the bones I'd seen in the hollows left behind by the figurines' rising? An itch started in the center of my spine. I rolled my shoulder blades and tried unsuccessfully to reach the bothersome spot.

"Give me a scratch, will you?"

Baubo dragged her fingertips here and there until I moaned in relief. "You're hesitant to have a deeper look, aren't you?" she asked, patting the soothed area to signal she was done. "I would be too, my friend. I would be too. Some memories are best left buried under soil and ash."

I sucked in a sharp breath as the image of dirt-smudged bones filled my vision. Profound grief blossomed within my chest, and just as quickly faded. Mourning had first brought Baubo and I together. She had lost a beloved human to old age; I'd lost several structures on the croft to fire, along with my ability to recollect the weeks and months surrounding the tragedy. I hadn't been able to lay my fingers on the singed edges shrouding those memories these past many decades, no matter how hard I tried.

But that was then, and this was now, and perhaps the nighttime visitations were an invitation of sorts.

"I fear if I don't have a closer look, my dreams shall only get wilder and more insistent until their meaning is as obvious as the nose on my face." Hands shaking, I reached for an apron and approached the wooden counter. "Blanch those tomatoes, would you? I have a hankering for gazpacho."

Baubo knew when not to push. She also visited enough she knew her way around my kitchen. While she fussed over the tomatoes, I dealt with my disorientation by grounding myself in mundane tasks, like preparing cucumbers, onions, and garlic cloves, and de-seeding bell peppers.

"Tomatoes are done." A bowlful of peeled and cut Brandywines and Black Krims landed at my elbow with a dull thud. "I'll pick some fresh dill."

The screen door bounced against the doorframe. Pulling the food processor from the shelf below the moveable cutting block, I funneled dripping handfuls of vegetables into the hopper, processed the ingredients, and added olive oil, vinegar, and a hefty pinch of fleur de sel to the resulting cold soup. Baubo held a clump of rinsed dill and chives over the salt-fired bowl and snipped at the ends.

"Enough?" she asked, popping a few purple chive flowers atop the mixture.

"Perfect. Let's take this outside."

We each made three or four trips between the kitchen and the long table I set up every summer beneath the vine-draped pergola. Once we finally sat and spread our napkins on our laps, I noticed Baubo had liberated a pad of paper and a jar of pencils and pens from my desk. Sneaky goddess. I tore off a small hunk of bread, dipped it into my soup, and offered it to the earth below and to the sky above before popping it into my mouth. My lunch companion did the same, then lifted her spoon and held it in the air between us.

"Bon appetite," I said, tapping her utensil with mine.

"Bon appetite."

I'd barely gotten my first flavor filled bite into my mouth when Baubo opened the pad to a clean piece of paper and uncapped a fountain pen.

"Tell me about these dreams."

Chapter 2

I DRIZZLED an extra spiral of olive oil on top of the summer
soup and buttered a slice of baguette, an evasive tactic but one I
needed to gather my thoughts. Once Baubo got going with her
questions, my perspicacious friend would keep going until she'd
exposed every who, where, why, when, and how for her keen
appraisal.

Bright red juices flecked with greens and whites from the
herbs and vegetables soaked the floating bread, pulling the
hapless bite toward the bottom of the wide bowl. I knew the
feeling, and quickly dipped my spoon under the bread and lifted
it to my mouth. Baubo scooped and chomped, constantly
shooting glances across the table. With my mouth watering in
anticipation of the next bite, I asked myself when had the rising,
wordless figurines begun to invade my dreamtime? And which
was the first?

"Well?" Baubo finally asked. "Out with it."

"The Venus carvings came first, night after night, one at a
time. Brassempouy. Willendorf. Dolní Vûstonice. Mal'ta,
Monruz, and others from the European continent and islands,

made from mammoth tusk and calcite. Oolite. Limestone. Or molded of clay." My fingers curled inward in response to the visceral memory of cradling each figurine in my palm before it grew, its limbs taking shape, and walked away.

"They looked newly made," I added, recalling the feel of their smooth surfaces against my roughened skin. "And when I mentioned this nightly phenomenon to Odudua, she said she, too, had been having dreams of a similar nature." My friendship with the Yoruban Earth goddess had been made easier with the advent of the internet, a phenomenon we both found amusing.

"And what of our sistren from India, Asia, Oceania, the Americas and other parts of Africa?" Baubo's words probed at my memories. I closed my eyes and rested my hands on my lap.

"The Ancients have walked through their dreams as well."

Her spoon clattered against the side of her bowl. "Oh my."

"We've been exchanging emails and texts," I continued. "Even letters and notes by post and raven. Oshun. Bat. Ninmah. Xiwang Mu. Kojin. And others. All of them confessed to having similar dreams and experiences." My eyes opened slowly, fixing on the tomato juice-stained apron covering my lap. Insight flashed within my head, only to scatter in the afternoon breeze like feathered drifts of milkweed seeds. "Something's stirring. I just don't know what it is."

"Did no one offer any insight? Did *none* of the figurines speak?"

"Not one." I mentally rifled through the messages I'd received from other immortals who were equally as mystified. "We've looked to the positions of the moon and planets, consulted ancient texts, and searched for omens, and found nothing that would presage this worlds-wide arising."

"Have you seen anything trending on FlittR?"

That sentence made no sense to me. I told her so, and she informed me FlittR was a social media site for Magicals. Thus enlightened, I resumed scooping up spoonsful of soup and watching birds gather dusky purple grapes from the arbor overhead. Baubo rapped her knuckles on the wood, sending utensils and dishes rattling and startling the birds.

"A gathering *must* be called, Habs."

"I agree." I'd sensed the need for the dreamers to do more than share their concern as more and more messages filled my inbox and crowded the surface of my oak desk.

"We would need a site large enough to hold us all."

I couldn't stop the nervous snort-giggle in response my friend's suggestion. The logistics of bringing together goddesses and other mythological figures would be an enormous undertaking. If it came down to hosting an in-person event, I had the hectares to pull it off. Though getting every individual here, along with their partners, offspring, and retinues would take an obscene amount of coordination *and* cooperation. And food. So. Much. Food.

"Let's start with video conferencing," I suggested. "It will give everyone a chance to speak, share their experience, offer insight."

Baubo rolled her eyes and fell backward off her bench, landing with an "Oof!" on the cushion of herbs I planted in lieu of grass.

"Very dramatic. I know you secretly adore modern technology." I buttered another hunk of baguette and waited as my friend waved her bare, tanned legs in the air and processed the idea of setting up a meeting between the matriarchs and their attendant personalities.

"We would need a talking stick," she mused, shaking her feet and setting the bells around her ankles to tinkling. "Or a cursor. A talking cursor. Something. Some of us are wordy bitches."

Covering my mouth with my napkin, I silently agreed.

· · ·

BAUBO STAYED with me the rest of the day, continuing to ask question after question, taking notes about the dreams and *hmm*'ing over hand drawn maps of my lands she'd found stuck in a drawer in the library. Frazzled we seemed no closer to an actionable plan, I suggested we watch the sun set from the top of the hill. I had to tromp up there anyway to take down the dried laundry before the evening air dampened everything. Once twilight rose, I fully expected my friend would avail herself of the orchard portal and depart for her own home, though I'd given her a permanent suite of rooms adjacent to mine once it was clear we adored each other's company.

"You go on and get your sheets," she said, handing me the empty wicker basket and shooing me toward the door. "I'm going to dig up a fresh nubbin of elecampane."

I almost asked, "Why?" though I suspected I knew what she had mind. Elecampane was revered as a portal plant by pagans, faerie folk, and other Magicals seeking to leave their body and travel from one plane to another for short periods of time.

"Something greater is afoot," she added. "I shall guide you on an ancestor journey. I've brought my bodhrán."

An ancestor journey. I hadn't undertaken one in ages. Engaging with the specters of the unrested was oft times painfully draining work, though the afterlife was occupied with more than just unsettled ghosts. Heat spiked in my elbows, finger joints, and the crown of my head, as though the radiant ones were pointing out that I was long overdue for a visit.

"If you're up for drumming, I'll change my bedsheets when I get back and then I'll be ready."

Knowing what the next few hours might entail, it did me good to walk the uphill path alone. I watched the sky change colors as I emptied the clotheslines, folding as I went, then hefted the creaky basket atop my head. I took one last, long look at the distant horizon and listened—for birds quieting, for nocturnal beasts rising, for the nearly inaudible *plip* of the sun winking out of sight.

There. Another day done. I followed the narrow footpath to my back door and set to readying myself for the work ahead.

"DRINK THIS."

Baubo placed a porcelain cup of grassy tea on my bedside table. Her curt instruction reminded me we'd shared this ritual this before. I finished braiding my hair into one long plait and debated whether to wear a light sweater over my nightgown.

"And chew one of these," she added, tapping a saucer dotted with bits of peeled root.

I drew a pale blue shawl over my shoulders and perched on the side of my bed. The scent of sunshine rose off the sheets and a delicate perfume wafted from the vase of flowering jasmine I'd added to the crowded bedside table. Perusing the saucer's offerings, I chose a pea sized slice of rhizome and lifted it to my nose.

Inula helenium—commonly known as elecampane—smelled, to me, of grandmothers. Though I couldn't recall my own, I'd tended the bedside of many an old woman. Those walking close to Death and the Afterlife carried a discernible smell. It wasn't necessarily unpleasant unless the dying were afflicted by certain diseases.

"Chew, my dear. Put those molars to good use. We've a long night ahead."

Obediently, I rolled the piece of root on my tongue to waken my salivary glands before moving it between my teeth. Bitter. Pungent. Woody. I chewed slowly, sipped at the cooling tea, and lit the beeswax candle. Cupping the glass votive holder between my hands, I held it over the floor and addressed the soil and rocks below the uneven floorboards.

"Great Beneath." I spread my toes and waited for my body to become a taproot; my limbs its secondary and tertiary roots; my hair, its feathery rootlets. When I felt myself transformed, I spoke again. "I ask that you support the journey I am about to begin. Blessed be."

Returning to my corporeal form, I raised the candle toward the beam and plaster ceiling. Light bathed the entire room in gold.

"Great Beyond." In my mind's eye, I became a nightbird, a great owl, wings spread as I soared through the blue-black sky above the thatched roof. "I ask that you watch over me as I travel to places beyond this realm. Blessed be."

Lastly, I drew the candle toward my heart, careful to avoid the messy tendrils framing my face. "Great Within." I brought my awareness inside of my body, passing through skin, soft tissue, curved ribs, and into my heart. "I ask my inner Oracle to share her wisdom with me as I embark upon this journey. Blessed be."

Invocation complete, I carefully placed the candle back on the table and lay on my mattress at Baubo's request. She drew up the top sheet to cover my chest before settling into the armchair in front of the window.

I swallowed the masticated bit of root and closed my eyes. As I sank into the comforting support of my wool-stuffed mattress, Baubo's drum filled my ears and stepped its way into my bones. Beat by beat by beat, my awareness retreated from the familiar surroundings of my bedroom and entered an otherworldly waiting room filled with a wolfish gray fog. I placed another piece of the root between my back teeth, adjusted my shawl, and chewed as I waited to see who, or what, would appear.

Da-da-*dum*, da-da-*dum*, the bodhrán beat on and on and I realized Baubo had been murmuring this entire time. Tuning into her voice, I repeated the invocation to the ancestors silently along with her.

Wise and loving ancestors,
Meet me where I am.
Wise and loving ancestors,
Lead me to my past.

Wise and loving ancestors,
Guide me back again.
Wise and loving ancestors,
Bring me to my hearth and home.

———————————————

Chapter 3

———————————————

BEYOND THE FOOT of my bed, the crackled backside of the oval mirror standing in the corner softened into a tarnished, silvery haze. My limbs relaxed. I knew this doorway, had passed through it and back many times. Relieved, I secured myself to the drum, letting its steady beat became a cord of sound connecting me to my friend and to my home.

I let go. My physical body remained comfortably ensconced in soft, cotton sheets. My non-tangible form rose face-up, floating past Baubo and through the mirror feet first. The hem of my nightgown fluttered around my ankles. Cool air pebbled my skin. Loose hairs tickled my nape and forehead, and the weighty length of my braid trailed behind my body.

Where are you taking me?

My question was met with silence, the kind that stretched on and on, sending rooty, wraithlike fingers into the past and the future. Nothing unusual. Sometimes, the ancestors chose to not respond. Sometimes, they chose to not show up. Half the challenge of meeting the immortal shadows was getting comfortable with the accompanying lack of sound. That, and allowing my tether to run as long as the journey required. Baubo could drum for hours and never tire, never lose the beat, and I trusted she would not let me go or leave me stranded.

I finished chewing the second piece of root and swallowed. As the noise inside my ears quieted, sonorous voices rose out of the darkened surroundings.

We are taking you, to you.

What do you mean? Were we making a stop at the Waters of Self-Reflection, a fabled lake said to show that which the viewer most avoided examining within themselves? Or was I being escorted back to my bedroom's oval mirror? Whatever the ancestors meant, not following their directives was not an option. To resist ensured being sent back. No refunds, no return ticket, and no guarantee they would answer the next time they were summoned.

Open your eyes and watch, the voices continued.

Open your ears and listen.

Open your heart and feel.

Open your mind and remember.

Open your mind. I winced. It felt like the bones of my skull were shifting, the cranial sutures widening. Pressing my hands to the sides of my head wasn't the solution. Neither was curling in on myself like a pill bug. I panted through the sensation, spreading my arms away from my sides and turning my palms upward, forcing myself into a state of openness and receptivity.

I inhaled. Oxygen spread my ribs, expanded my lungs, and enlivened my beating heart. Someone, or some… thing, some force, palmed the backs of my shoulders and tilted me until I floated upright, legs dangling. They… it… pressed down, forcing my bare feet to settle on stone. Icy cold needled my skin. The body-less presence landed behind me, holding my head between its hands.

Watch.

Cool, bony fingers forced my eyelids open, stretching my skin over my cheekbones and forehead. Shapeless garments from ages past molded around barely discernible body parts, then dissipated and re-formed until figures began to emerge out of the shadowy mist. Their silvered hands held candles and torches with licking blue flames, and buckets of glowing, sapphire coals. Illuminated by the bluish light, other cloth-draped arms carried colorless bundles of hops, rye, wheat, and oats. The figures moved toward me, which brought more of their features into focus. Eyes like those cool, blue coals; cloud colored hair worn down or drawn back from their face; skin in death-tinged shades from mercury to pearl white. Passing to my left, each figure looked me in the eyes and exhaled a name, *their* name, without moving their lips.

Habonde

Habondia

Abondia

Abunciada

Abundantia

Abundia

Hestia

Hestia's frigid fingers grazed my elbow. The hands holding my head forced me to pivot, to hold the goddess' indecipherable gaze until she passed. Unlike the others, she continued walking until she disappeared. I was again pivoted to face forward. The figures that remained formed a circle with me in its center, the glow from numerous blue flames illuminating the vast space. In unison, they stopped and fixed their faces toward the darkness they'd stepped out of.

A pinprick of light swayed in the distance. A gap opened in front of me. As the light came closer, it grew in size and intensity and gradually, another figure emerged. Taller, more substantive than the preceding ones, clad head to toe in a golden, long-sleeved gown and adorned in fiery accessories, she paused in the space made to receive her.

Triple circles of bright orange flames circled her upper chest, wrists, and ankles. A crown of fiery arrows and brilliant red flowers topped her head. As one, my aspects exhaled her name, me included.

Brigid.

She floated to a stop. A bristled boar with bronze-tipped tusks nestled against the side of her leg. She patted the beast's head and urged it to sit.

I waited. *We* waited. My eyes adjusted to the goddess' resplendent presence. Baubo's drumbeat continued to reach my ears, while the faint scent of burning resin filled my nose. Brigid raised one arm. The movement of her lacy sleeve created comet tails and falling stars as she gestured behind her. Another figure moved through the lightless space, clothed and armored in deepest black but for flame-bright hair and burnished skin.

Hekate. Goddess of Crossroads and Queen of the Witches. Light Bringer, Moon Mistress, Keeper of the Keys. She arrived, accompanied by a lion to either side and followed by a retinue of nymphs bearing lamps and draped head to toe in sheer black gauze.

My knees quaked and my heartbeat stuttered at the unsubtle reminder my lineage included Brigid and Hekate. The Ancient Ones embraced, and the Mistress of the Underworld's lions chuffed as they lowered their massive bodies to the ground. Her nymphs raised their blackened metal lamps and set them on their heads, then walked behind the row of figures already circling me.

Hekate faced Brigid. The glow from the one highlighted the features of the other. "You called."

Brigid tilted her head in my direction. "She is the one who called."

"Speak," Hekate commanded. Her voice stirred the bronze

snakes twined around her waist into action. They lifted their heads and separated. One spiraled around her thigh; the other circled her breasts in a figure eight before settling itself like a reptilian stole across her shoulders.

Bravely, I set one translucent foot in front of the other. The closer I drew, the more I noticed details of each goddess' physical appearance I could not have discerned from a distance. Brigid's pale blonde hair, most of it frizzed and knotted, was in need of a good brushing. Her once elegant gown showed wear and tear, with patches covering worn spots in the fabric and embroidered sections trailing loosened threads.

The lions' ribcages stood out against patchy, untended fur. Even the nymphs appeared drawn thin, with hollowed cheeks and dark circles under their eyes. When I dared bring my gaze to fully to meet Hekate's, I clamped my hand over my mouth before I could stop myself.

"Go ahead, say it. I look like something the cat dragged in." One of her big cats coughed, and she crouched to rub its head.

"You do look a bit travel weary," I offered, noting the dents and dings in her armor and the dried mud caking her boots. "I've asked you here so I could speak to you of my dreams and receive your wise counsel, but I wonder if the two of you would prefer to come with me, perhaps refresh yourselves with a good night's sleep in my humble home, partake of plentiful food and country air?"

Hekate's brief smile read more melancholic than interested. "Brig? What do you say?"

"I would spend a night and a day amongst my sistren." Brigid stood a little taller. The movement loosened petals from the roses in her crown, sending them floating downward to disappear like dying embers in the blackish murk cloaking our feet. "And once we've rested and bathed and accepted our offerings, Habonde can explain why she's pulled us away from our pressing duties and cast us as sundry interpreters."

"And what of our companions?" Hekate asked, indicating the boar, the lions, and the silent lamp bearers.

"There is more than enough room for them," I assured her, reaching out my arms. I, too, was a goddess, with a willing staff of many dozens and magic at my disposal. I could—and I *would*—bring these two with me. Between Baubo and the house elves, the stable masters and the urisk, brownie-like faerie folk living on my lands, guest rooms and animal accommodations would be readied in record time. No detail was too small to ensure Brigid and Hekate were comfortable.

Only, I forgot this conversation, this entire encounter, was happening within a separate realm. The Queen of the Witches signaled her lions and her followers. The Goddess of the Wells tapped her boar's head and it stumbled to its cloven feet. Hekate took Brigid's hand and the entire lot of them—the beasts, the nymphs, my ghostly aspects—faded into the darkening mist.

"We shall see you in two dawns' time, Sister Goddess."

Two dawns' time. Hekate's parting words gave me a little over twenty-four hours, which meant I and my croft's inhabitants had our work cut out for us, even with the help of the land's ambient magic. With a rising sense of urgency, I knew it was time to leave. Retreating from the place of the ancestors required I tug on the threads connecting me to Baubo—and that she respond as promptly as a hungry fisherfolk with a trout on its line. It took three gentle pulls, and a sharper fourth, for her to change the rhythm she beat on her drum to one that would beckon me home.

Chapter 4

BANGS AND CLATTERS ricocheting off my kitchen's walls
jerked me upright. On my bedside table, the beeswax candle
burned low in its glass holder. Baubo's bodhrán and stick had
taken the place of her ample butt on the armchair's cross-stitched
cushion. I wiggled my fingers and toes and scratched at my scalp.
I was back, and I wasn't at all rested and ready for the
multitudinous task of readying my home for the arrival of two
goddesses, their beasts, and their companions.

"Babs, are you there?" I swung my legs over the side of the
bed and stood, impatient to get started. "Have you seen my
broom?"

She popped her head into the open doorway. "You going for
a midnight flight?" she asked, and disappeared.

"A midnight wha—?" I snorted. I hadn't flown in ages. "No, I
need my broom for sweeping floors. We're about to have a lot of
guests."

"In the middle of the *night*?"

"In the middle of the wha—?" I raised the window higher
and stuck my head outside. The sky was filled with stars. "Oh.

No. In the morning," I yelled. Secretly relieved I hadn't overslept, I clasped my fingers together, stretched my arms overhead, and twisted side to side. More cupboard doors clicked open and banged closed, accompanied by muttered curses.

"Is there something I can help you find?"

"Where do you keep your stash of chocolate?"

"What kind of chocolate?" Woozy, I wiggled my chilly feet into sheepskin slippers, traded the shawl for an ankle-length robe, and shuffled across the worn floorboards.

"The good kind. I'm famished from all that drumming, and I want to make cocoa."

"What time is it?" I opened the pantry and withdrew an airtight tin of seventy-five-percent cacao fèves from one of the perpetually cool lower cupboards.

"Bedtime. And what's this about guests?"

I plopped the heavy container on the counter. "I'll make us cocoa. You get out that paper and pen you were using earlier and sit down."

"Uh-oh, sounds ominous."

Reaching overhead, I unhooked a saucepan from the pot rack, plucked a wooden spatula and wire whisk from the cracked crock stuffed with utensils, and checked the woodburning stove. "Cow or oat?" I asked, opening the refrigerator and surveying the bottles on the door. Baubo *moo*'d.

I set to measuring milk and weighing out fèves. "Brigid appeared. As did Hekate. They didn't look so well, they looked —" I stirred the mound of melting chocolate with the broad side of the spatula and settled on a single word. "Unkempt."

"*Hmm*. 'Unkempt'? That surprises me. Were either accompanied by their attendants?"

"Brigid came alone, though she had a large boar at her side. Hekate arrived with two lions and maybe eight, ten nymphs. The lions' fur looked moth-eaten, and the nymphs could have used a bath and a change of clothes and a week's worth of sunshine and nourishing meals."

"How dismal." Baubo *tsk-tsk*'d. "Did you gain any insight about the connection between your dreams, and what you saw tonight?"

"I literally just woke up," I reminded her, "and I'm waiting for all my pieces to return."

"Cocoa will help with that."

"Cocoa helps with everything." Steam from the milk rose, warming my cheeks and disbursing the scent of melting chocolate. I stirred in turbinado sugar, watched the mixture darken, and added a pinch of salt. "Off the top of my head, I'd say the Goddess wants to rise and walk this earth in all her forms as she has in ages past. But goddesses like us and others we know are—"

Insight hit me like lightning striking a rock, splitting it in two and revealing its crystalline interior. "The goddesses are worn down. Brigid. Hekate. Others around the world that I've been communicating with. They're exhausted, and because most of us are no longer worshipped as… as fervently and devotedly as we were in the past, we're running out of an important fuel source with which to replenish our powers."

I lifted the heavy saucepan, set it to the side, and faced the kitchen table. "But worship is not the only missing element, my friend, and that is where you and I and all the dreams being dreamt by our sistren come in. I think I'd already given up when you and I first met, given up on humans, given up on the power of communal ritual. Given up on myself."

Baubo peered over the tops of her reading glasses at me. "Do you have marshmallows? Because processing your profound thoughts this late at night requires marshmallows. *And* booze."

Chuckling, I frothed the cocoa, poured a demitasse to honor Hestia, and filled our mugs three-quarters full. I added a finger of cherry liqueur and a chunky hand-cut marshmallow to each, left Hestia's atop the stove, and joined my bestie on the loveseat's saggy velvet cushions. Lifting our mugs, we toasted.

"Where do we even start?" I whispered, savoring the soothing richness of the combined flavors of chocolate, cherry, and cream.

"You know me, I'm the one who cracks a joke, then rolls up her sleeves and gets down to business." Baubo doodled on the paper balanced on her thigh and sipped, doodled and sipped. I waited for the punchline until my mug was empty.

"So, where's the joke?"

She shook her head. "Sometimes, there is no joke. You said Brigid and Hekate are coming here tomorrow?"

"Day after. Hekate said, 'two dawns'."

"They'll need accommodations to bathe and sleep." She looked up suddenly. "Is there a crossroads on the croft with a portal for Hekate to travel to and from the underworld? And what of a well for Brigid?"

"No crossroads, just one long lane in and out and lots of footpaths. Unless we count the spots where the footpaths cross." Baubo noted my input, followed by a big question mark. "There are at least two uncapped wells," I added, "neither of which is goddess worthy. The others have been modernized or capped. And you're familiar with the portal in the orchard."

"Very familiar. It does the job for travels on this plane, but where Hekate's concerned, I—" She lifted her shoulder in a shrug. "We're going to need a miracle. And maybe some heavy machinery."

"I'll sound the horn for Finnock in the morning." Finn was the unanimously elected leader of the urisk clans and my appointed groundskeeper. He would have a clearer idea of the status of the croft's natural and magical resources. "Oh, and there's more I haven't shared."

I collected our mugs and filled them with water to soak.

"Brigid and Hekate were preceded by goddesses directly related to me. Ones I had forgotten. Hestia came last, then departed without a word."

"You contain multitudes, my friend."

"As do we all," I agreed.

"The long life of a goddess is filled with more versions of our original iteration than any one of us can recall."

"True, true. But it's the disremembering of those versions that bothers me, as though I've given up on myself every bit as much as the humans have."

Baubo rubbed between my shoulder blades and tugged on my braid. "Speaking a thing brings you closer to figuring out how to fix a thing. We should sleep. There's nothing we can do tonight, and the sunrise is sure to bring an insight or two."

I BRUSHED my teeth and returned to bed. Night air had cooled the sheets, prompting me to pull on wool socks and another blanket. For the first time in many nights the remainder of my dreamtime was blessedly undisturbed. I slept like the dead and woke to the sound of repeated knocking. Once I ascertained the noise wasn't coming from inside my head or the kitchen, I threw off my covers and raced to the side door. If I'd misheard or misunderstood Hekate's "two dawns' time" and she and Brigid had arrived already, I was toast. I would never live down the impertinence or paucity of welcoming the two wearing nothing but a simple nightgown.

Throwing the same lacy blue shawl over my shoulders, I opened the door, quickly shielding my eyes from the morning's blinding sunlight. A male figure, taller in height and broader in shoulder than the locals, took a step back, and another, until he was standing on the pebbled walkway, not the wooden stairs, and removed his hat.

I blinked hard. Gazing at me was a woodsman. But not just any itinerant woodsman looking for extra work on my croft, one of THE Woodsmen, males from ancient lineages whose magic was intrinsically bound to trees. Though I didn't know *how* I knew this bit of information. His button-down shirt boasted no insignia, his pants were free of sawdust and wood chips, he carried neither awl nor axe.

I just *knew*.

Birdsong swelled, the stone fruit tree near the corner of the pergola offered its ripest fruit, and I curtsied to the Woodsman like I was one of those plump, juicy plums just waiting to be plucked. The shawl slipped off my shoulder, taking my nightgown for a ride and flashing more of my skin than was comfortable. A slow grin spanned his face, and he pivoted on the heel of his leather-soled boot, giving me a moment to collect myself, as well as a view of his backside.

His very muscled backside and the drop-shaped patch of sweat soaking the center of his linen shirt.

"Are you Mistress Barleywine?" he asked, scuffing the side of his leg with his straw hat. His bronze and leather bracers fit his forearms snugly and the metal's gleam found echoes in the tips of his near-black hair.

"*Ms.* Barleywine but call me Habonde. Please." I readjusted my gown, then crossed the shawl over my breasts and tied the ends behind my waist. "You may turn around."

His grin, the one that heated my lonely, neglected nether regions, had not only stayed on his face, it had deepened. It took every ounce of self-control I had to not smile back.

"I apologize for surprising you so early on a summer's morn, but I received a summons to tend to the yew trees and this is the location the Brethren of the Woods and I were given."

"The *Brethren?*" I squeaked, my eyes rounding at the thought of more of his ilk wandering my croft.

"Yes." He gestured vaguely behind him with his hat. "They're back there. Somewhere."

"But there are no yews on my land, haven't been for—" I wracked my brain to recall when the last of the sacred trees had been cut by city-dwellers for the sake of "progress."

"Oh, I beg to differ, Ms. Brandy— Habonde. There's a healthy one just over that hill."

"And I, too, beg to differ, Mr.… I'm sorry, I didn't catch your name?"

"That's because I haven't properly introduced myself. I'm Rhys. No 'mister,' no last name, just Rhys." His grin widened, revealing a mouth full of healthy teeth and deep crinkles at the outer corners of his eyes. He swiped his forehead with a handkerchief, bringing my attention to his luxurious hair. My fingers twitched to feel its texture, to remember— I shook off the discomfiting sensation I'd felt his hair before and chalked it up to a swell of hormones.

"And who sent the summons?"

"And good morning to *you*," Baubo interjected, elbowing me aside. "I'm Baubo Elefsina, Habonde's best friend." She arched an eyebrow at me, then returned her attention to Rhys. "I see we have at least one Woodsman to feed. Did Hekate Herself summon you, and have you brought others of your kind?"

"And good morning to you, Baubo Elefsina. Hekate did, and there are three of us in total. I believe you'll find the others at the yew we raised. I was just coming to introduce myself and inquire about our lodgings." Rhys set his wide-brimmed hat back on his head and crossed his forearms. I refused his biceps' invitation to give them a squeeze. "If you haven't any rooms available, we can build tent platforms. We brought our own wood."

"I bet they did," Baubo murmured.

I tried to nudge her aside, but she stood her ground. Stubborn goddess. "I think Baubo and I need to confer. I'm not sure where we're going to house and feed everyone. Could you give us an hour or so to figure out the logistics?"

"Any chance a man could get a cup of tea while he waits?"

Rhys seemed not the least bit inclined to leave the pebbled path. Baubo elbowed me back. "He could get a lot more than a cuppa with those eyes," she whispered.

I pulled on her apron strings and tugged my mouthy friend behind me. The Woodsman's warm, brown gaze had already gotten an eyeful.

"Of course," I said. "I'll make a pot and set out mugs for you and the others."

Tipping his hat, Rhys smiled again. "If you'll hand me a basket, I'll pick your plums. I noticed a few ripe ones on my way in."

"You do that, and I'll make a fresh tart," Baubo shouted from the kitchen.

"There's a stack of baskets under the pergola." I waved my hand toward the outdoor sitting area. Stepping inside, I closed the screen door and met Baubo in the kitchen. "And don't you say a word about my plums!"

Chapter 5

CACKLING, Baubo fanned herself with one hand and gathered the makings for tea and pastries and other breakfast foods with the other. Still floaty and unmoored from the night's journey, the morning's hasty awakening, and the Woodsman's disquieting presence, I filled the kettle, set it on the stovetop, and added a log and a sprig of wheat to the fire.

"I'm going to get dressed while the water heats. I'll make my own coffee."

"Better strap on your breastplate if you can find it. Rhys seemed rather charmed by your chest."

"It's been a long time since I flirted with the likes of a Woodsman. I feel a bit rusty," I admitted, laughing as I passed the wide-open kitchen door and spied Rhys plucking fruit and depositing each plum into the basket hugged against his side.

"There's a cure for that," Baubo shouted.

"Shh!" I hissed, tearing my eyes off the man's graceful movements. "Our guest will hear you."

Baubo harrumphed, and I fled for the sanctuary of my bathroom. There was no good reason for me to act like a nervous virgin; that ship left port centuries ago. I splashed cold water on my face to cool my heated cheeks. Droplets rolled down the front of my throat and between my breasts and I closed my eyes at the sensory memory of prior lovers' touches. A visiting naiad had inadvertently become stuck when her river's banks overflowed, trapping her in the wide stream meandering through my land. She'd met the dryad living in one of the old oaks, one thing had led to another, and the three of us had enjoyed months of frolicking while waiting for her river to settle within its banks.

How long ago was that?

I had no idea, though I could ask the dryad whether our shenanigans had left a timestamp in the oak's annual rings. Smiling to myself—and thinking I should clean my bathroom ahead of our esteemed visitors' arrival—I shook cleanser into the sink, found a rag, and scrubbed the porcelain bowl, along with the chrome-plated drain cap, faucets, and spout.

Reminiscing about past intimacies proved distracting. Any more scrubbing and the plating might come off. I moved on to the bathtub and the toilet, where the bubble of warmth popped.

Why could I recall my summer with the dryad and the naiad with such clarity, while other memories eluded every attempt at capture? My knees sagged and I sank to the floor. And why the persistent dreams? Why the visit from the myriad versions of myself forgotten in the altered priorities of modern times? Why Brigid? And why Hekate?

Hekate. Why did the ancestors take me so far back in my lineage that she had manifested? Had she come to me as Mistress of the Underworld and Keeper of the Keys? Was a journey to the underworld in my near future?

Had she come as Goddess of Crossroads, here to signal I had choices to make?

Or had Hekate returned as Queen of the Witches, Light Bringer, Moon Mistress? Was there a greater message in all these visitations, beyond what Baubo and I surmised? And what of Hestia? Why had she come, yet continued on? She had been the only specter to touch me; the only one that seemed self-aware.

I don't have answers to all the whys, I whispered, rinsing the tub with the help of a drinking glass and watching undissolved bits of cleanser swirl around and around and down the drain. *I just don't.* My temples throbbed with a tumble of questions, and I'd managed to soak the front of my nightgown. Dampened fabric molded to my breasts and thighs, and when I stood in front of the oval mirror in my bedroom, I looked like a version of the very same Venus figures I'd dreamt of. Thick-thighed and curvaceous, yet I lacked the power contained within those carved bones and stones.

Power. I stepped closer to the mirror. The silver paint on the other side had long since crackled and chipped, and truth be told I rarely spent time looking at myself. I kept the antique out of sentiment and inertia, and because finding a reliable portal mirror had become nearly impossible. But in this moment, in my nearly sheer wet garment and messy braid, I could have been Brigid or Hekate as I'd seen them in the night.

Threadbare. Untended-to. Tarnished.

Why me?

The edges of my silhouette softened. Behind me, a long row of Habondes, hazy figures my shape and height, lined up. One by one they floated forward, passing around my shoulders and head and dissipating in the sunlight streaming through the leaded glass windows.

"Habs, are you okay?" Baubo's concern penetrated the solid wood of my bedroom's closed door.

"Ye-es?" Goosebumps pebbled my arms as more ghostly iterations passed through and around me.

The knob rattled. "I'm coming in."

Baubo hesitated at the threshold. Her figure filled the

doorframe along with the scent of vanilla extract, custard, and plums. "What's going on?" she asked, leaning in to sniff the air. "Why does it smell like bleach and ash and why are you all wet?"

My disheveled state activated her protectress mode. She bustled into the room, lifted my quilted silk robe off its hook, and had me out of my gown and into the rose-dyed garment in seconds.

"I think the elecampane root's still active," I offered by way of explanation, or excuse.

"Come. I know how you like your coffee. You're not leaving my sight until I know your head's on straight and all your bobbles and bits are back."

Letting Baubo care for me required far less effort than resisting. Plus, it gave me time to find the boundaries of my physical body. She placed a steaming cup of espresso in my outstretched hands, popped the lid on a jar of light cream, and poured out the perfect amount. I stirred my coffee, closed my eyes, and sipped.

"I brought tea to Rhys. His men should be joining him soon. They'll be hungry and though cooking's—"

"—not your job," I said, finishing her sentence and making my friend laugh. "Thank you for stepping in. I know you'd much rather be out there sunning yourself and trying to get a rise out of our fabled guests."

"Been there, done that, and I hope to do it again." Baubo winked. "Finish your coffee, get yourself dressed. And no detours! We've twenty-fours to prepare for the goddesses' arrivals and we're going to need every second of it."

I did as she asked, then washed my cup and set it on the drying rack. Baubo placed two large cast iron frying pans atop the stove and filled them with sliced tomatoes and zucchini, pale yellow squash blossoms, pinches of fresh tarragon and thyme, then poured whisked eggs from a bowl to just below the rims.

"Frittatas coming up in twenty minutes." She slid the pans into the oven and turned her attention to gathering plates and utensils. "I cooked. You clean."

TWENTY-FOUR HOURS TO prepare for Brigid and Hekate's arrival was a gift. The two could have accepted my invitation to return with me or exercised their divine rights and been accommodated within minutes, a feat which would have pulled every last bit of magic from me, the soil, the plants and trees and stream, leaving us nothing in reserve.

Between me, Baubo, the three Woodsmen, the other Magicals on my lands and anyone the goddesses might send ahead, we had enough resources to create simple, acceptable places for them to sleep, eat, and bathe, and meet with their local followers should they wish.

I dressed in a lightweight, long-sleeved T-shirt, and a pair of worn denim overalls, after securing my assets into one of those insufferably challenging "sports bras" and my generous backside into the most utilitarian cotton underpants in my drawer. I didn't need the constant feel of silk caressing my skin, reminding me there were Woodsmen visiting my lands.

Which got me thinking about Rhys' probable expertise with handling tools and shaping wood. Returning my robe to its hook, I bit the padded sleeve to stifle my groan and bounced my forehead against the back of the door.

Why me?

And why *now*?

<hr>

Chapter 6

<hr>

I MADE it a habit to only blow the croft's sounding horn when absolutely necessary. By late-morning, with the dishes done and Rhys and his equally striking cohorts long gone after polishing off both pans of frittata and most of the tart, I deemed it absolutely necessary. The call would alert magic folk from all over my land to gather at a preselected meeting spot to receive further instructions.

Extreme emergencies—potentially devastating weather, enemy invasion, rampaging gods—required me to use both magical and modern means. We hadn't had a situation like that in so long, I made myself check the expiration date on the commercial air horn stored in the cleaning closet.

It was good for another two years. I left the can on the shelf and selected the more traditional bull's horn, threading its mouthpiece through the hammer loop on the leg of my overalls. Trailing my fingers through the upright stems of sage, lovage, and rosemary bursting out of pots and urns, I walked toward the back gate. Baubo huffed alongside me, a toolbox in one hand and a basket of snacks in the other. Not knowing which skill set I'd be using, or where I'd be needed, I'd brought along my own notepad and fountain pen.

"Can I carry anything for you?" I asked.

"I'm good. Did Rhys happen to give you the location of the yew tree?"

"Just over this hill." We retraced our steps to where I'd set my drying lines and sure as day followed night, a mature yew commandeered the dip on the other side of the low hill.

"Would you look at that. I wonder if it's permanent?" Removing the horn, I lifted the tapered end to my mouth, wet my lips, and blew once, twice. Three times would put too urgent a spin on the summons. Within moments, answering calls sounded from the urisk and the birds.

A gentle tug on my pant leg alerted me the first wave of help had arrived.

"M'lady?" As usual, the leader of the urisk clans beat everyone else. Taller by inches than most of his ilk, his head, topped with an ever-present brown felt hat, reached me mid-thigh.

"Finnock, thank you for getting here so quickly."

"Rumor has it we're to dig a well?" Finn tilted his head back, a challenge written into his craggy features. How he'd come by that bit of information within hours of my ancestor journey was a mystery I'd never solve.

"In a day, if you please."

Grumbling met my ears. I raised my hand to quiet the land-loving folk forming loose clusters behind Finn. Them complaining on hearing my request, followed by a few rounds of bargaining, was a longstanding tradition between us, and one I didn't have time for today.

"Brigid Herself will be here at sunrise tomorrow." Finn and his helpers gasped. I continued. "Her presence is a great honor for all of us. You will be compensated with coin and, should your work please her, a blessing." Holding the horn between my knees, I quickly scribbled a reminder to ask Brigid for that favor.

"There's more," I added. "Hekate is coming too. Three Woodsmen have arrived and are tending to the Goddess of the Crossroads' yew tree, which you'll see behind you. They have brought cut lumber which can be used to build any structures requested by either goddess."

I continued to point downhill, giving the news time to sink in.

"M'lady. I have a suggestion." Finn's gravelly voice assumed a more balanced, take-charge tone.

"I'm listening."

"I shall send my dowsers to confirm, but I've a hunch the best place to dig a fresh well for Brigid Herself would be closer to the stream. With the willows and oaks providing shade, the location would be the coolest and quietest place to situate our guests."

Our guests. I pressed my lips together at his proprietary remark. I'd already planned to situate *our guests* closer to the stream. The area was flat, the community of dryads living amongst the trees hospitable to one and all, and it was far enough from my house and gardens I could maintain my privacy. But I didn't mention any of that.

"Excellent suggestion as always, Finnock," I said, biting back a smile. "I trust you will coordinate with the dryads and the Woodsmen about boundaries and protocols for temporary housing?"

"As m'lady wishes."

Dozens of urisk swarmed down the hill, Finn at their center. More would come once news spread that Brigid and Hekate were arriving. The group split, with the majority veering toward the stream, and a few heading toward the lush, dark green canopy provided by the yew tree's outspread arms.

The meadow surrounding the tree's location appeared healthy and unaltered, meaning whatever magic the Woodsmen used hadn't pulled water or nutrients from the soil. "I think it's time I visit the yew."

"I think you're right." Baubo set down the wooden toolbox and scanned the view below. "You know, I don't think I've seen a finer-looking man on the croft since my first visit. The way Rhys looks at you, I'd say he's yours for the asking."

"He is… handsome," I agreed.

"So, what's stopping you?" Baubo nudged the side of my leg with her basket.

"The same thing that always stops me," I answered, hoping to shut down further inquiry. It wasn't that I didn't like sex or didn't want to have sex. One dryad in particular continued to let me know he and his partner would welcome me back into their treetop bed any time, any season.

Shrugging, I added, "Before you start nagging me to book a therapy session with Hedone—"

"Ooh, now there's an idea! Our favorite pleasure-promoting goddess has a new book out. *And* it's illustrated." Baubo nudged me again. "I hear the pictures are very detailed."

"She sent me a signed copy and I'll read it when all this is over. Now, tell me what you're planning to do with those hammers and hand pies."

Baubo tapped her chin. "I was going to offer to my carpentry skills, but that was before I saw how many urisk you've got and how eager they seem to please. I'm thinking we might consider expanding the guest list. Others will hear of our preparations and wonder why they were not invited."

"But this is different." I sank into a crouch. I had a feeling the quiet, idyllic life enjoyed by those who called Bone Fire Croft home was about to get exponentially complicated. Finding a quiet corner in my library and tucking into Hedone's book seemed an enticing alternative. "You and I know that what's happening here is in response to something specific, to me and my dreams."

My companion wagged her head side to side. "Other goddesses don't."

"Which 'others' are you most concerned about?" I asked, though I suspected I already knew which names Baubo would evoke.

"Demeter."

"Crap."

Demeter had her fingers in everything of an agricultural nature and her displeasure at being left out of the loop could, and likely would, do more than affect the health of our crops and orchards. Plus, there was her closeness to Hekate, and Hekate's to Demeter's daughter, Persephone, to consider. "You're right. We'll have to invite them."

"Them?"

"Demeter *and* Persephone. It's summer, which means no one has to negotiate a trip to the underworld to fetch the Queen."

"And if Hades accompanies them?"

"The more the merrier?" I shrugged. Though I would raise a glass to Persephone and Hades on hearing they'd reached an amicable solution to their marital issues, I didn't have the bandwidth to update myself on the constant stream of rumors surrounding the King and Queen of the Underworld's troubled relationship.

"But what if Zeus catches wind of this gathering of goddesses?" Voicing my greater concern sent icy rivulets up and down my spine. The uncontrolled entitlement displayed by the Olympian Sire was one reason I, and others like me, had resorted to dimming our shine. "Because as far as I'm concerned, Zeus is not allowed *on* my land or in the air *over* my land. Period."

"Got it." Baubo opened her arms wide, pulling me up to standing and into an embrace. "I'm sorry," she whispered, pressing her cheek against the side of my head. "One of the brothers is welcome. Another is not. Hopefully neither will deem it necessary to impose their presence."

"One is *conditionally* welcome. And I see Jillian's at the stream. Would you ask if she wants help setting up for lunch and tea?" Jillian was Finn's wife and usually managed the meal-planning aspects of gatherings on the croft. "Oh, and should Hades show up, we've got to make it clear he is *not* welcome to attend or observe any of our goddess gatherings."

"No gods, noted."

The only males wanted at this time were those who came ready and willing to help. The last thing I needed was unnecessary conflict and posturing. I steered my thoughts away from the anxious direction they were heading and watched Baubo disappear into the low-lying brush collaring the sides of the wide stream.

I followed another of the paths stamped into the grasses before veering toward the new tree. Time to check in with Rhys, then return to my home. Baubo's mention of Demeter, Hades, and Zeus had me imagining worst case scenarios and I would need help keeping my croft's boundary lines strong and those within its borders safe. I planned to contact my friend, Astrape, and get her on the payroll. Long a part of Zeus' entourage, she'd broken with the god and now hired herself out as an independent security contractor.

Once I had that and everything else sorted for Brigid and Hekate's arrival, I'd get to work on a deeply personal task. I was the only one fit to undertake clearing a particular site of centuries of debris, and I had been avoiding the job far too long.

MOVING into the shade provided by the yew's outermost branches, I entered a world where the ancient behemoth's multiple trunks melded into a warren of dark passageways.

"Habonde. I'm glad you're here." Rhys' voice moved out from the trunk's hollowed threshold, followed by his head, shoulders, and an arm. He waved me over. "I imagine you're wondering how we managed to bring this living giant to you."

"Yes, I am," I said, picking my way across the unfamiliar roots. "I assume you used Woodsman magic?"

"In a way." He took hold of my wrist and guided me into the dark. "Watch your step. Let me know when your eyes have adjusted."

I inhaled through my nose. Yews and their needles had no distinct smell, at least not that I could discern. It must have been Rhys' natural scent filling the small space. I didn't mind it, not one whit, and though I was grateful the dark cloaked my interest, today was not the day to start crushing on the Woodsman or inquiring about his relationship status.

"Do you live on the croft by yourself?" he asked, releasing his hold on my arm. The bands covering his skin from his elbows to his wrists glowed warmly in the low light, and his facial features remained in shadow.

So much for avoiding personal questions.

"Yes, and no," I answered, addressing his silhouette. "A few of these hectares have been mine for hundreds of years. The size of my holdings grew as farmers and townspeople picked up and left this area for the cities. I bought parcels as they came available." I stared upward. The velvety dark gave no indication how high the tree rose overhead, and I wasn't ready to share I was perpetually single by choice. "Why do you ask?"

"I'm curious, is all. My men and I are based on the Shetland Islands, though it feels like we're rarely home."

"You three live together?" Rhys being in an amorous partnership would make this so much easier.

"In a manner of speaking. There are more of us, some with

spouses and children. We have a tradition of living in community. Makes it easier to share life's ups and downs."

"Sounds idyllic. Baubo's my best friend, as she mentioned. Probably the closest I have to family. I've no partner, no children, just the land to manage."

"And what of the Magicals on your fertile acres?"

I sensed the twinkle in Rhys' eye. Where I'd hesitated to get personal, he was jumping right in. "There are mostly the urisk clans and dryads, and a few naiads. Other waterfolk live in and around the stream, and a few owl shifters have built aeries. The more humans left, the more room there was for other Magicals. I have made it my policy to welcome one and all."

He *hmm*'d. "That circles me back to this tree. My crew and I tapped into the magic that was here and pulled the yew out of the roots below the very ground we're standing on."

"I have no memory of ever seeing this tree." Awed, I rubbed my hands along the trunk's inner surfaces, marveling at its age and size. "Will it stay after you've gone?"

"It could. Though that depends somewhat on how long we're here, and how much magic we're able to channel into its root system. A tree this size requires a constant source of magic, likely more than your croft can provide without affecting every other inhabitant." He pushed his hair off his forehead and gazed around. "A smaller version of it should stay once we're gone, especially if you grant Hekate access beyond this gathering. For now, it will function as her portal in and out of Scotland. I assume she and her attendants will want to set up their tents under the tree."

He lightly touched my shoulder. "Come. I don't want to keep you, and I have more work to do."

Feeling emboldened, I paused. "Would you care to share a pint of local ale at day's end?"

"Thought you've never ask."

Chapter 7

I LEFT Rhys to his tasks and detoured to the stream. The flutters
in my belly mimicked the looping paths of insects going about
their business among the field grasses and wildflowers. I felt a
little nauseous, a bit unsettled in my skin, and I thought I could
pinpoint exactly why.

Rhys.

It could also be that what I was feeling had more to do with
everything I was currently dealing with, rather than any one
Woodsman, and the best cure for this kind of unnamed
discomfort was to stay on task—just like Finn and his horde of
helpers. They appeared to be well on their way to sorting the
gifted lumber, having placed five piles in a wide horseshoe
amongst the tallest trees. Judging by Finn's enthusiastic
gesticulations, once the platforms were built, the tents going atop
them would be angled to face the stream. The largest staked-out
area, likely the site of Brigid's personal tent, anchored the center
of the U-shaped formation. Behind it, another crew waited,
shovels ready, while more urisk hauled in stone on low
wheelbarrows and skids from Goddess-knew where.

The agitated butterflies in my belly doubled.

"Finn! You didn't take down one of my border fences, did you?" I had to yell to be heard above the noise produced by such industriousness. I would be in trouble with the local historical commission if any of the ancient property markers and sheep fences had been moved or altered, their stones "borrowed." Even if it was in service to Brigid Herself, we couldn't exactly use that explanation with the mostly nonbelieving humans populating the nearby towns.

"Surely you know me better than that, m'lady." Suddenly, Finn was in front of me, accompanied by two urisk-folk wearing tool belts over their work attire and equally indignant frowns on their faces. "Takes the right kind of magic to get the land to give us a few rocks. Lucky for you, I've got the touch." He rubbed his fingers together and grinned at his companions.

"I *am* lucky, Finn. Carry on."

Patting my flighty heart, I continued onto the path following the stream. Dappled sun and cheery birdsong serenaded my walk home, while hearing from both Finn and Rhys that living magic lay underfoot reassured me for the work ahead.

I wanted to reach out to Hestia before tackling my project, and before contacting Astrape. Entering my kitchen, I opened the heavy door to the stove's fire box and knelt on the hearth's flat stones.

Hestia, mother of the sacred flame,
Mother of the hearth,
Receive my humble offering.

I fed stalks of dried grain, their drooping heads heavy with the weight of seeds, into the low flames one by one.

Hestia, heart of my home,
Heart of my croft,
Receive my endless devotion.

Sitting back on my heels, I waited for Hestia's face to appear within the rising flames. I added more grains to the sounds and smells of popping seeds and called her again.

Hestia, draw near and bestow us your light.

Draw near, and join our gathering.

Draw near, mother in spirit, and sit by my side.

When it was clear Hestia would not be showing up, I closed and latched the door and moved on to the next task. Leaving the kitchen, I headed for the secluded area at the far end of the pergola and stopped in front of the former birdbath I now used to communicate with a chosen few. Every time I uncovered the wide, shallow bowl and set its round top to lean against the base, birds would flock to the overhanging branches and scold me for keeping the clear water to myself.

Today was no different.

"I'll ask Finn to carve another one for the likes of all of you," I promised. "But he's very busy right now and this one is mine. These waters took a long time to spell just so. No bathing!"

I closed my eyes and calmed my breath and pictured Astrape's face. Using my first two fingers, I traced her signature lightning bolt emblem across the surface of the water.

Astrape, I seek thee.

Astrape, I reach thee.

Astrape, I summon thee to my home.

I repeated the call two more times before opening my eyes. Holding onto the birdbath's carved rim with both hands, I leaned over the water and searched for my friend.

Her features rose from the bottom of the stone bowl and blended with my reflection. An alarming whitish material covered her face like a sodden paper mask and her eyes had been replaced by pale green circles. I might have shrieked before asking, "What happened to you?"

"A vacation happened to me, Habbba-dabba." Astrape's voiced bubbled to the surface. "I'm at a spa in Upstate New York and the closest body of water was this hot tub. Lucky for you there's no one else here and I could answer your summons."

"But what's that stuff on your face?"

"Cucumber slices and a bentonite clay masque. The clay's supposed to draw toxins out of my pores and help heal scars." She lifted one of the cucumber slices and smirked. "Gonna take a wagonload of clay to fix *my* scars but hey, the aesthetician has great hands, and no one knows I'm here. Except you."

I zippered a line across my lips. "I hate to take you away from such luxuries, but I need your skills, and I need them tomorrow." I gave Astrape the pared down version of Brigid and Hekate's impending visit, along with my concerns about Demeter and Persephone should they accept Baubo's invitation. "If Zeus shows up, I won't have the bandwidth to deal with him *and* host the gathering."

Astrape replaced the circle of cucumber and sank below the surface of the water. Bubbles tumbled out of her mouth. I hovered my face closer to the birdbath.

"Astrape!"

A string of curses burst in my ear and her face nearly bumped into mine. She removed the cucumber slices and opened her eyes. Rivulets of water zigzagged through the clay, making it appear she was crying. "And you think *I* have the bandwidth to deal with Zeus and possibly my sister? You do know she and I are estranged?"

I did know. Bronte, thunder-bearer and Astrape's twin, had chosen to remain aligned with Zeus after a series of altercations forced the sisters to choose sides.

"I apologize for my assumptions, my friend," I said, pressing my hand to my heart, "and if this request causes you pain, I will find someone else to guard my borders, my workers, and my guests."

"You would be hard pressed to find anyone like me, so I shall do it. But you owe me, Habonde."

Relief loosened the tension from my arms. I would give up Astrape the guardian if it meant I could keep Astrape the friend. "I shall gladly owe you, and I shall see you are returned to your spa once this meeting is finished, and all have safely left my land."

"I may decide I need to hire other freelancers."

"Hire as many as the job requires."

The thunder-bearer nodded and sank out of sight. Watching her leave brought tears to my eyes and a tremor to my hands. She had been through so much—we *all* had been through so much—and in this moment, I regretted reminding a sister of past events and current conflicts.

I replaced the cover on the birdbath and detoured into my kitchen for a glass of sweetened currant juice to clear my throat. Astrape mourned the break between her and Bronte, my request had irritated an unhealed wound, and imagining I could mend the sisters' relationship was pure hubris. Fire was my element, the hearth my altar, and I was far more apt to burn things down or bury them underground.

Holding that self-reflection foremost in my mind, I headed outdoors, passing through the front gate and stepping onto yet another narrow dirt path. This one led me southeast toward the primary site where Finn and the caretakers deposited cut brush and trimmings. The hulking, spidery thing waiting for me had to be twenty feet across, if not more, and its tangle of clippings and pruned-off branches rose higher than my head. I marveled at its current size and gave thanks for Finn and the urisk and all the others who loved this croft as much as I did. Without their constant care, more of my land would resemble this brambly mass.

I unrolled my sleeves and pulled a pair of heavy leather work gloves from a back pocket. Stepping closer, I considered what approach I should take to clearing the pile. I needed access to what lay underneath, and I didn't have time to take it apart piece by piece and transport it to another spot. Also, chittering squeaks and chirps informed me the pile had become home to numerous creatures. Their nesting spots weren't mine to destroy.

"You're not thinking of setting fire to that elegant mess, are ye?"

Startled, I spun fast and nearly planted my face against a feathered chest. I must have missed Fergus' noiseless landing. "No. Too many small birds and rodents live there," I reassured the owl shifter, pointing at the mound. "I do need it moved, though. Permanently. Do you have any idea how to keep it intact *and* get it out of here in the next thirty minutes or so?"

Fergus rustled his wings and assayed the pile before making a complete circuit of its perimeter. "With a few adjustments, my parliament and I should be able to lift the entire pile at once," he said, after returning to my side. "Where would you like this resettled?"

"Somewhere safe for its inhabitants, but out of the way of the other projects near the stream, which you'll see once you're in the air. And thank you," I added.

"My pleasure."

Fergus whistled for his crew and returned to contemplating the pile. I tromped down a dusty footpath to one of the old tool sheds erected in useful spots throughout the croft's rolling hills. This structure had walls built of rounded stones and a thatched roof with a deep overhang. A wheelbarrow leaned against one wall, while rakes, shovels, and other gardening tools hung from hooks attached to the rafters. I set the wheelbarrow upright, noting the handles had splintered with age. I wouldn't have been able to use it if I hadn't brought gloves. After the coming gathering was over, I would ask Finn to check all the sheds to see that all communal tools were oiled, sharpened, and repaired or replaced.

Guiding the loaded barrow toward the clearing, I plotted how to approach my task. Birdsong and mouse chatter reached my ears, growing louder as I walked into the sunlight. I looked up in time to witness four sets of strong wings beating steadily against the air as the brush pile broke away from the ground and surged upward. Four more birds took off, positioning the net held in their talons below the rising debris.

"Huzzah!" I hollered, waving my arms, hopping up and down and dodging falling twigs and dried leaves. It wasn't often I witnessed a brand-new sight involving Magicals, and this qualified as an unmissable event. I watched the eight owls until the pile disappeared, until the only thing left to do was address what had been uncovered.

I chose a metal rake from among the tools and tied a bandana across my forehead before beginning to clear the debris littering the uneven ground. With the sun high in the sky and the temperature rising, I knew I would sweat buckets. I considered removing my shirt, and decided to keep it on once I saw the size of some of the thorns left behind.

After two rounds of raking, the second with a finer tool meant for grasses, but before starting to dig, I walked a spiral toward the center of the cleared area. Trees and buildings had likely come and gone from this section of my land, and though I could no longer count on them to mark what I was searching for, just being here tugged at the threads of memories.

Retracing my steps back to the pile of tools, a familiar feeling settled over my shoulders and dormant magic stirred beneath the soles of my boots. I traded the rake for a pickaxe and pressed its pointed tip against the dry soil. Lifting the tool overhead, I widened my stance and let gravity bring the tool down to meet the ground. The tip bounced before skidding between my feet. It took an embarrassing number of swings to figure out where to position my hands on the thick handle and how high to swing, and when I couldn't get it right, I caught myself muttering at the inanimate object. Which didn't help. What I needed was a song, something basic to give me a rhythm I could work with, and up burbled a sea shanty.

We're… running down a stormy sea
And rolling through the thunder
Way, haul away, well, haul away, Joe
It's… every man aloft my boys or we'll be driven under
'Way, haul away, well, haul away, Joe
'Way haul away, we're bound for better weather'
Way haul away, well, haul away, Joe

That would do. I lifted the pickaxe and brought it down in time to the cadence inherent in the lines. By the time I'd completed a second verse and chorus, I'd found my rhythm. As I sang, taking liberty with subsequent verses, I aimed for the hard packed soil and pebbles. Once I'd broken up the surface layer, I dumped the tools out of the wheelbarrow and loaded it up with the largest of the loosened chunks. Those I deposited at the outermost part of the clearing, load after load. I continued wielding the pickaxe until I consistently hit stone, not dirt. Switching techniques, I kicked at the flat bits with my boots, uncovering hewn stones all a similar size.

What I sought was close, and every cell in my body vibrated with that surety. I fumbled with the broom, brushing lightly, tentatively before sweeping it back and forth as though my life depended on it. A spiral pattern appeared, guiding me toward the innermost ring framing a bowl-shaped indentation roughly two meters across.

I had to stop. Catch my breath; pull myself together; refrain from reaching for implements long destroyed and acolytes long dead; rid my ears of the ringing of the priest's hammer as he pounded iron nails into the freshly sawn planks covering the drowned ashes.

Those pieces of wood had long since rotted away. Bits of oxidized metal littered the broad, earthen bowl. I fell to my knees, peeled the scarf off my head and the gloves from my hands, and pressed my palms and forehead to the blackened dirt. Dead embers formed a solid, uneven layer and I knew what I would find once I broke through the hardened crust: a hearth, *my* hearth, the stone-lined vessel that cradled flames for hundreds and hundreds of years until the day a man in religious robes entered the village. He personally doused the sacred fires kept alive by generation after generation, stripped my acolytes of their duties, forced them into heavy robes, and ordered my name to go unspoken.

Blessed be, I whispered, my lips hovering above the ground as my tears flowed. *Blessed, blessed be.*

Chapter 8

I WORKED FOR HOURS, unsure where I was in time. I went from singing sea shanties to recalling snatches of planting and harvesting songs as I dug and shoveled , swept and wept. Later, as treetops obscured the sun and the temperature began to drop, I noticed I was shivering in my sweat-soaked clothes, and I finally forced myself to stop and survey my work.

The cleared hearth wasn't perfect, but it would do. For the first time in over eight hundred years, the flames that once fed household cooking fires would have a place to burn again. The spiral pathway would guide practitioners to the heart of the hearth during rituals, and, with the help of the stonemasons amongst the croft's talented faerie-folk, a new altar could be built by August's First Harvest.

I longed to unlace my boots and walk the spiral barefoot, hair adorned with seasonal flowers and grains, body clothed in the appropriate gown, head and hands meaningfully adorned in precious metals and gems. I longed to feel the sense of community and belonging flowing between the fire ritual's observers, and from them to me and me to them in a continuous, living loop. I longed to feel the energy build, energy I, as Goddess of the Hearth, would feed back into the wood and flames.

I will feel all that again. All that, and more.

Turning my back on the fruit of my labor, I cleaned the tools as best I could using my gloves, wheeled the barrow back to the shed, and headed home.

I will feel all that again, I repeated to myself. *All that, and more.* All I needed was— I paused on the pathway. There was no simple answer, no short list of what it would take to resurrect the old ways that had kept my fires thriving and kept me *alive*, not just… *surviving*.

Voices raised in volume as I rounded the corner to the rear garden. Fairy lights generated by real fairies lit the grape vines and wild rose hedge in pulsing shades of lavender and pink. Under the pergola, Baubo shifted in her seat and raised a tankard in my direction.

"Where have you been?" my bestie asked.

"Digging in the dirt." My smile cracked the dried muck coating my cheeks. I went to swipe my face and stopped when I noticed more dirt embedded in my sleeve. "That beer looks good. I'm going to grab a shower, then I'll join you."

Finn mumbled something into his ale and Baubo *cackled.* "Rhys is washing up right now. He and the other Woodsmen insisted on manning the grill tonight and making us all dinner."

"And man the grill they shall," Finn added, draining his glass and knocking it twice on the table. "We've worked up quite an appetite this day, haulin' stone and cuttin' wood and hammerin' pegs 'n' nails. The teenagers be organizin' side dishes. I'm sure one of 'em shall show up here soon, beggin' for donations."

He waved goodbye before disappearing into the lowering light.

"'Man the grill'? We don't have a grill." *Uff,* my overalls were also coated in dirt. More concerned with who could build us a grill on extremely short notice, than with Rhys' presence, I undid the clasps on the straps and the buttons at the waist and worked the pants over my hips and down my legs.

"Your Rhys assured me they've already concocted something temporary by the stream. We're to do a trial run tonight to make sure everything's set for tomorrow."

"'*My* Rhys'?" I snorted. Baubo covered a grin by draining her tankard. "I'm so hungry, I'd eat anything cooked for me by anybody," I admitted. Exhaustion threatened to claim what was left of my legs, and I debated leaving the overalls right where I'd shed them. Baubo gathered the ceramic mugs and shooed me toward the house.

"Go on. I've bathed. Get cleaned up. Put on a dress. I'll pick up your things and toss them in the washer."

"Leave everything for me. I should shake off the dirt first." Taking the handle of the screened door, I paused. "What do we have to contribute to this impromptu feast beyond the novelty of seeing me in a dress?"

"Rhys said you promised him your best ale, and I'll send Finn's younger ones to see what's ripe in the garden."

"Then my best it is. Oh, have the older ones bring a keg or two up from the root cellar."

I opened my bathroom door to a blast of warm, steamy air hitting me in the face, along with the scent of a soap that was not my soap and a male voice singing the same sea shanty I had been singing earlier.

Somewhere between Baubo telling me Rhys was showering, and me peeling off my stinky, sweaty shirt, bra, and underwear, I failed to notice that it was my bathroom that was occupied. I grabbed a towel, wrapped it around my torso, and slunk out backwards and into the hall.

Of all the bathrooms in the house, why was Rhys in *mine*? A nervous giggle escaped out of my mouth.

Baubo. Playing at matchmaking.

A wilder woman than me might have taken the earlier interest she'd seen in Rhys' eyes and invited herself into the generously sized shower stall. I'd once embodied that wild woman, but something about Rhys' gaze and his utter sense of ease in his own skin turned me into a modest house mouse. I sat on the hall bench, closed my eyes, and tried to remember if I'd seen anything of the Woodsman's naked physique through the steam.

No. Though it turned out, all I had to do was wait another minute before the door opened and a very clean, nearly naked man stepped out.

"Habonde. I didn't know you were here."

Semi-nudity suited the Woodsman. I stood a bit too quickly and had to renegotiate my towel's positioning. Rhys gazed at me appreciatively as wafts of steam curled around his neck and waist as though wanting to pull him back under the shower.

"You don't remember me, do you?" he asked, after a very long pause.

I searched his face for something familiar. "I— I'm afraid I don't."

"We've shared a bath before."

Time slowed. We'd shared a bath? When? And had we shared *more* than the same body of water and a bar of soap? "Just the two of us? Or was it one of those communal things?"

"It was quite private. Just the two of us. You liked it when I massaged your scalp."

Time more than slowed, it came to a screeching halt before reversing direction. I remembered the Woodsman untangling my braid. Separating the three thick strands and guiding me under the water.

Keep your eyes shut and tilt your head back, he'd said, and I had willingly followed his instructions, the scents of vetiver and sandalwood filling my nostrils. He'd brought me a wad of dried vetiver from India and showed me how to use it to dry brush my skin before I bathed.

I lost myself to the memory of his strong fingers, to the care he took working soap into my hair, all the way to the ends. How he'd gathered the waist-length strands together and squeezed out the excess water.

"As much as I would like to reminisce, I have workers in need of a feast," I said, returning to my senses and retightening the towel. All business, I walked past him, entered my bathroom, and started to close the door. "Baubo mentioned something about you and your men grilling for the lot of us? There's more to do to prepare for tomorrow and if I know Brigid, she'll be here at the break of dawn."

Poised at the threshold, Rhys held himself so still, I could see droplets of water riding the waves in his hair, glistening like pearls. I almost grabbed his wrists to stop him from shoving his hair off his face.

"Then we shall reminisce another time. Perhaps over that ale you promised," he added.

"I would like that." I made no move to close the door.

"I would like that too, Habonde."

I handed over his pile of clothes and his vambraces, leaving me with the scent of vetiver; leaving me wondering what other memories lay stored inside, and how many of them featured the Woodsman.

Chapter 9

I TOOK Baubo's earlier advice and pulled a dress from my closet. Pale green and patterned with white and purple wood violets, its construction took me back to the prior century, when women's clothing was designed with darts and pleats and other ways of highlighting curves. I liked it because the top half cradled my chest comfortably without me having to wear an undergarment, and the bottom half swished around my calves when I moved.

"Habs?" Baubo called.

"Be right there." I cracked the door open so she could hear me. "I just need to comb out my hair."

"A passel of Finn's boys already came for the ale. All we have to do is show up."

The mirror over the bathroom sink was still fogged over. I swiped it with my hand and sucked in a breath. The face peering out from behind wide, drippy swathes wore a lush crown of wild pink and red roses on her head. A loose white gown exposed most of her neck and shoulders and her hair was down. At first, I didn't recognize her as me, and the vision faded before I could get a lock on which iteration had chosen this moment to appear —and to appear in color.

Was *that* the Habonde that had enjoyed bathing with Rhys? And when had all that lush hair and dewy skin dried out? Inspired, I pumped generous dollops of lotion into my palm and applied it to my arms, neck, and legs.

"Is everything okay?" Baubo asked, opening the door wider while knocking.

"No." I rubbed the last of the lotion into my fingers and the backs of my hands. "But I'm going to do something about it."

"About what?"

Good question, and one I desired to answer. "About the fact that I've managed to forget most of my lives and I'm not entirely comfortable with what I've become."

"And what is it you think you have become, my friend?" Compassion radiated from Baubo's entire being, and I considered if it would be better if we postponed the festivities and shared a heart-to-heart.

"Forgotten. Disremembered. And not just by those I once served. By *me*." I couldn't stop the swell of self-pity pulling the corners of my mouth into a petulant frown.

Baubo grabbed my hand and sniffed. "If it's any consolation, you smell good enough to eat. Give me some of that and tell me more as we walk. We both need food, and you need to thank Finn and the others for the efforts they put in today."

"You're so very right."

"I know."

I stuffed a couple of shawls into my bag, one in mulberry purple and the other a dark green with long fringe, and slipped a pair of sandals on my feet. Baubo had chosen a silky maxi-dress patterned in shades of yellows and oranges.

"Now it's my turn to tell you, *you* look good enough to eat," I teased, following her out of the house and handing her the green shawl. "Here. In case it gets chilly by the stream."

"Thank you. With any luck at all, I shall be devoured by night's end." She flung out her arms and twirled through and past the gate. "We have a mission, Habs! A mission, and honored guests—some of whom are *very* handsome—and the urisk and the dryads especially are happy to see something fresh and new happening around here."

"Are you insinuating life on the croft has gotten a bit dull?"

"A *bit?*" She shook her head and looped her arm through mine. "The goddess is alive, magic is afoot, and we're living in the thick of it. Now, tell me more about what's rising to the surface."

I slowed our pace. This would be my last opportunity to have my best friend all to myself before dawn brought Brigid and Hekate to the croft. "I keep seeing past versions of myself, especially when I look into mirrors or when I'm on the verge of falling asleep or just waking. And earlier today I—" I hesitated before sharing why I'd finally done something about the out-of-control brush pile. "I uncovered my hearth. That's where I was all afternoon."

Both of us slowed further as the weight of history bore into our bones.

"Was it the hearth I heard locals speak of when we first met, the one that was shut down and disappeared into myth?"

"Yes. It would have been too risky to rebuild it right away and over time, it became a dumping site for the groundskeepers. Fergus and a few other owl shifters helped in the clean up by lifting centuries' worth branches and leaves and vines," I continued. "They kept it intact so the creatures living inside would not be disturbed. Once they flew the pile away, I raked up the debris that was left and started chipping at the dirt. I eventually uncovered rings of gray stones. And I found a bowl of near petrified ash in the center."

My footing faltered. "I started to remember the old days, the old ways. I remembered my acolytes, and what it was like to welcome them in, darling things, so innocent and eager. I remembered what it was like to feel their magics, to imbue them with the importance of their work as they moved through their training. I remembered the ceremony of carrying the first lit logs into every new home built in the village, or to welcome a new family into our town.

"I remembered, Baubo, even the horrible parts, when the priest came and… and destroyed what he and others like him had no right to touch."

She clasped my arm. "I sense there is more. Go on."

Shudders wracked my chest. Words broke apart on their way out of my mouth. "I cried for what's been lost, for the precious lives, for the traditions, for the rituals that connected us to generations past. And I cried for myself, I got… I got *mad* at myself. And now I have to fix this, and I know it's going to demand everything from me."

I sucked in a deep breath and stood taller. "If I hadn't seen Brigid and Hekate with my own eyes, seen the toll all this burying and forgetting has taken on those who are so strong, so ancient, I might think my mind was making this all up. But they need help —we *all* need help—and I'm going to do something about it."

Laughter and delicious smells floated our way. Baubo stopped a few steps shy of turning the corner on the path that would funnel us right into the heart of the celebration. "*We* are going to do something about it. But first, we are going to feast and drink and dance. Maybe even dally with a dryad or naiad or Woodsman or two. And tomorrow, as the sun rises, we shall honor the dawn, welcome our guests, and get on with turning the messages in your dreams and your mirrors and your heart into reality."

"Thank you." I squeezed Baubo tight. "Merry meet, my friend."

"Merry meet, merry part, and merry meet again."

$$—————————————$$

Chapter 10

$$—————————————$$

THE ENERGY BUBBLING through the lively party happening on the banks of the stream pulled me in and spun me around. Before I gave myself over to the festivities, I thanked every Magical in attendance for the work they'd done, whether it was building or baking, hauling or digging. Finished with that joyful task, I accepted a mug of ale and met the merry fires and happy faces, though the face I wanted most to see was focused on the newly assembled stone-sided grill. I drank while I danced, sipping from communal mugs, and let my troubles rest.

Rhys found me once his cooking duties were over and invited me to share the plate he carried. My eyes widened at the array of vegetables roasted in olive oil and herbs, at the bread and the goat cheese, the bowl of ripened cherries, and the bottle of wine tucked under his arm.

The Woodsman had already laid out a thick quilt at the base of an unoccupied tree. I sat, he handed me the platter and had the elderberry wine uncorked before he realized he'd forgotten something.

"Be right back," he said, propping the bottle against my leg. I nibbled on bread, admiring his stride while watching him walk away, and return, and accepted the ceramic mug he offered. "Can I get you anything else before I sit?"

"You can tell me how you finagled that bottle of wine from Jillian." Finn's wife guarded her wine-making techniques ferociously, doling out bottles only when she deemed their contents ready, and only to those she thought would appreciate the care she took with each blending of grapes and other fruits and berries. "Oh, and I could use a fork."

Rhys pulled utensils wrapped in a napkin from a back pocket and presented them with a flourish. "Jilly offered the bottle to me with the caveat I share it only with you."

Grinning, he lowered himself onto the edge of the quilt, untied his boots and removed his socks, and placed them on the grass.

"You've accomplished in less than a day what takes years for most," I commented, noting how quickly he had inserted himself into the croft's social rhythm.

He leaned his back against the tree and crossed his ankles. "Then I'll consider myself a very lucky man. And that is a very beautiful dress."

"I clean up well." *And I might have chosen it for you.* Stretching my arm forward, I drew the platter between us. Rhys unrolled his napkin while surveying the options. He tore the hunk of baguette apart and proceeded to layer both halves with grilled vegetables and thin shavings of aged goat cheese. I accepted the half offered to me, and we bit into our dinners looking out over the crowd.

The silence between us felt comfortable, easeful. I finished the first slice, declined a second, and chose a cluster of cherries from the platter. When I sat back, Rhys' shoulder was right there. I took advantage of his warmth and leaned my weight against him as I ate the fruits one at a time and spat the pits into my palm.

I was hard pressed to recall the last time I'd watched my

people gather for an event of this size. A few of the adults rounded up the children and, to loud protests and a few tears, had them say goodnight before herding the littles home. I wasn't the only one happily buzzed from the camaraderie; from the wine and ale and dancing; from the abundance of joy swirling through the air. Add to all that the novelty of picnicking with someone who took pleasure in seeing my needs were met… I could get used to having a Woodsman at the croft.

"This needs to happen more often," I murmured, tossing the cherry pits into the trampled grass.

Rhys dribbled wine onto the ground before filling our shared cup and offered the first sip to me. "Do you not celebrate the festivals along the turning wheel?"

"I do privately," I said, savoring the fruity red. "Or with Baubo if she's around and so inclined. Some time ago, I can't recall when, the public rituals just stopped." I let that admission sink in, and I appreciated that Rhys didn't rush to fill the silence with suggestions about what I could do to improve my goddessing. Though I might have let all manner of things slide, my dreams, my journey to the ancestors, and today's efforts at my neglected hearth meant the time for apathy had passed.

Rhys pressed a cherry to my lips. "There's a ritual the Woodsmen perform," he said, tugging at the stem until the fruit popped into my mouth, "one that would feed magic directly into what is already here and amplify its power."

His rumbly voice lulled me into relaxing against him even more as I bit the fruit in search of its pit. "And what ritual is that?"

"It is one we've practiced before, my goddess," he murmured, nudging my shoulder. "More than once. At times, we kept the energy we created to ourselves. Done with a different intention, with more preparation, we could take the power raised by the joining of our bodies and gift it right back to your land."

My beautiful dress started to feel tight, restrictive. I undid the top two buttons, allowing night air to cool my overheating skin.

"Tonight, would be the perfect night for ritual," Rhys added, perhaps taking my actions as an invitation—which they weren't. Though I may have engaged in public displays during past rituals, I was far from contemplating stepping into that role again. Vague memories of long ago events threatened to ruin my growing attraction to the Woodsman. I leaned forward and reached into my bag for my shawl.

"Did I suggest too much, too soon?" Rhys asked, as he refilled our shared cup and offered it to me. I settled the drapey wool loosely over my front, took a sip of wine, and handed the cup back.

"I got a little lost inside my head, is all."

"And what did you find on your travels?"

"It's been a long while since I shared my body with anyone and when you spoke of ritual sex and raising magic, I—" I shrugged. Rhys' confession had knocked me off kilter. "I'm hesitant to explore what that would look like at this point in time."

"You have a history with these rituals."

I couldn't tell if he was asking a question or making a statement. "My memories are foggy at best."

"Perhaps they stay hidden to protect you."

"Perhaps."

"Then let's take that off the table and talk about us."

"Us?" When did Rhys and I become an "us"?

"Would you like to know what I recall of our first meeting?"

"I would. And you could start by telling me how long ago we had this 'meeting'."

He chuckled softly. "Ahh, Habonde. It was at least two hundred years ago, in the early years of the nineteenth century before

Queen Victoria began her reign. A handful of my brethren and I traveled by carriage to Bone Fire Croft. We'd heard stories of your Beltane celebrations and decided to experience the magic for ourselves. When you emerged from your tent in your white gown, with a crown of flowers wreathing your head, I— I was speechless. I used every trick I could think of to get you to notice me."

Chill bumps rose on my arms. "I had a memory earlier today," I shared, "of wearing a white dress. I had wild roses in my hair. I don't remember what happened next."

"You chose me," Rhys whispered. "After the first part of the ritual finished, you chose me to be your consort and you led me into your tent. I was bursting to pleasure you."

"And not just do your duty to the Goddess?"

"Ahh, but it *was* my duty to pleasure the Goddess, to pleasure *you*. I remember the feel of your skin. Smooth like silk, warm like firelight, and your hair the red of embers."

"And the crops that year were plentiful?"

"Ay, they were, grains and fruits and nuts to last through to the next spring."

I fumbled in the dark for the cup of wine, only for the contents to splash out as I miscalculated the distance to my mouth. Rhys wiped my wrist with his napkin, helped me hold the cup steady as I finished what was left.

"Is there anything you need from me before I float off to bed?" I asked, licking wine off my lips. Opening a sliver of distance between our bodies, I readjusted my shawl around my shoulders.

"Tonight, no."

"You don't ask for much, do you?" I turned my head to see reflected firelight dance in his pupils and the corners of his lips curl upward.

"Come the end of this business with Brigid and Hekate, I will ask for many things, Mistress Barleywine. For now, promise me you shall sleep soundly."

"I promise." I turned slowly onto my knees to face him. He tossed the cup onto the grass and clasped my face in his hands, bringing my forehead to his.

"If you were the wise woman I know you to be, you would keep your promise and get plenty of rest. Because I aim to worship you again and, once I start, sleep will be the last thing on your mind."

His words threatened to work on me as my pickaxe had broken through the hardened crust of my hearth. I almost kissed Rhys. I wanted to—his parted lips suggested he wanted me to—but I couldn't. Some fuzzy lesson or oft-repeated admonishment about kissing being the deepest of intimacies held me back. Instead, I sank onto my heels.

The Woodsman blinked away a flicker of disappointment. "Go."

I stood, gathered my bag and sandals, and adjusted my shawl. Rhys sank against the tree, one knee bent. "Goodnight, Rhys."

"Goodnight, Habonde."

Part Two

Chapter 11

DISTANT BIRDSONG gently alerted me morning was heading westward toward Bone Fire Croft. I tossed the covers off and swung my legs over the edge of the mattress. My feet found the hooked rug that had been there for years. Pale light shimmered along one curved side of the mirror. Though the rest of the furnishings sat quiet, their mass shadowed in bluish black, the light hitting my front side added a pearlescent sheen to my skin.

What would Rhys' body look like in the same light? And what would our bodies look like, together? With the birds' voices changing every few minutes, I set thoughts of Rhys aside and turned my attention to covering my curves. Rummaging through my underwear drawer, I found a compromise between sexy and utilitarian. High-waisted bell bottoms were making a comeback, or so I'd read somewhere, and as I owned multiple pairs of originals, it would be a jeans kind of day. I buttoned up a clean pair and clicked on the closet light.

I chose a white-on-white embroidered blouse with a modest scoop neck and sleeves that came to my elbows and tucked the bottom part into my jeans. My feet were tough year-round, but who knew how much terrain I'd have to cover this day. I went for durable sandals, the waterproof kind worn by hikers who enjoyed fording through streams. After giving my hair a thorough brushing, I pulled it off my face and into a high ponytail.

Had I continued to train and keep acolytes, one of them would have helped with the next part of my morning routine. I didn't, so it was up to me to choose the appropriate adornments. Too much jewelry, and it could appear I was trying to outdo my guests. Too little could send the message I didn't care.

I reached for a moonstone teardrop set in silver to wear on my forehead, strung it on a leather thong, and tied it under the ponytail. Rings could get scratched if I was called upon to use my hands, and earrings had a way of getting tangled in my unruly hair. I opted for a pair of matching silver cuffs and slid one on each wrist. I liked their weight and filigreed edges, and when I stopped in front of my mirror on the way to the bathroom, I admired the symmetry between the shimmering gem resting on my third eye, and the grounding presence of the cuffs.

At the far end of the hall, the guest bedroom door creaked open and bare feet padded past the bathroom door as I brushed my teeth. I found Baubo in front of the kitchen sink, filling the kettle for tea and coffee. Her hair was caught up in a messy bun atop her head and I didn't recognize the T-shirt trying and failing to cover her butt.

"Blessed morning to you," I said. I couldn't wait for her to recount her nocturnal adventures.

"A blessed morning to you. How did you sleep?"

"Like a log." Feigning disinterest, I entered the pantry and perused the selection of large and small thermoses. "Are we making tea for just ourselves, or for a small army?"

"Don't you want to know how *I* slept?"

Gotcha. Grinning, I stepped back into the kitchen. "Baubo, how did *you* sleep last night?" I asked, raising my volume. A deeply masculine grumble sounded from far down the hall. "Or maybe I should ask, how did you *all* sleep? Or *did* you sleep?"

"Someone had to see to the other two Woodsmen," she said, body parts jiggling as she walked the heavy kettle to the stove and fed another log to the fire below.

"And?"

"And let's just say the apples hanging from the trees in your orchard will ripen early this year."

I guffawed, thanked her for taking one for the team, and planted two big stainless-steel thermoses on the counter. "Will you make it through this day without a nap?"

Baubo snorted. "What do you take me for, an amateur?"

"Never!"

I opened the back door to get a feel for the weather and returned for my herb knife and a bowl. "I think it's going to get warm early in the day. I'll cut fresh mint for iced tea. Would you get the dried hibiscus flowers soaking?"

Herbs I used frequently grew in the large pots and urns lining the walkway. I cut a generous amount of two different mints and brought the bowl to Baubo.

"You off to greet our guests?" she asked, unsuccessfully stifling a yawn.

"I am. The tents should be up and ready to house everyone, the stream is cool and clear, and I've hired the older daughters amongst the clans to act as attendants should the help be requested."

Baubo shook her head. "I hope that's enough."

"It has to be, for now, and if I must assist them with their baths or whatnot, then I shall." I leaned against the doorframe and admired the lightening sky. "I miss training acolytes. I wish I had the means to—" Not knowing quite how to finish my thought, I shrugged and stepped onto the first flat path stone.

"The means to what?" Baubo asked.

I waited there, sun warming the top of my head, until I had the words just right. "To resurrect what I once had. Though I have no idea if there's any interest in reviving past practices. No idea at all."

I mused on my wish, and my doubts, as I meandered up the hill. Dawn's light poured over the horizon, illuminating the trees and grasses and flowering heather in its path. Raising my arms, I spoke my desires to the wide-open, cloud-adorned sky. "I wish to see my lands, and the lands beyond, become a place where the Goddess is again welcomed and never forgotten. I wish my lands to be a place where others find respite and community. I wish to share my knowledge of our ancient ways."

A quiet chorus of leaves fluttering and seed pods shaking floated up the hill from the direction of the stream and the yew tree, warming my heart. I kissed my fingertips, touched the ground, and went to see if either goddess had arrived.

RHYS MOVED out from beneath the shade of the massive yew's long and twisted lower limbs. I took in the entirety of him: the way the polished bronze bands on his forearms caught the sunlight; the supple leather boots and the muscular legs in tight black pants; the belt wound twice around his hips; the dark brown shirt clinging to his muscled arms and torso; the knife sheaths strapped to his thighs.

The Woodsman had dressed to greet the goddess he served and every item adorning his figure look like it relished its role. In my white blouse, I was day to his night. Though everything around us brightened when he smiled.

"Good morning, Habonde."

"Good morning, Rhys." I stepped closer, noticing Hekate's insignia embroidered in copper thread on the left side of the shirt, a subtle reminder of the primary reason behind Rhys' presence on Bone Fire Croft. "I hope you're not expecting your men to join you this early. When I left my house, they were still in Baubo's bed."

He shook his head and laughed warmly. "They need not be here for Hekate's arrival. I suspect she will be tired and ready to bathe and eat and rest. I will see to her lions' care and assist her Lamp Bearers with setting up their lodging should they require it."

I stopped a good foot shy of his chest and stared into his eyes until their warmth emboldened me to address his earlier offer. "You spoke of us feeding magic back into the earth. Before we discuss that further, I have a project of my own I could use your help with."

"Is it urgent?" he asked.

"Hmm, not urgent per se, but with you, Brigid, and Hekate here, I think the universe is sending me a message."

"And one must heed the messages."

"One must," I agreed. "And when I'm ready to share the details, how do I reach you?"

Without hesitation, he wrestled a wooden ring off his left hand and presented it to me. "Turn it thrice. It acts like a beacon. And what if I have need of you?"

Smiling as I pocketed the ring, I took the short, curved knife I used earlier to cut the mint and sliced a curl from the end my hair. Rhys opened a deerskin pouch hanging off his belt and tucked the hair inside. "Let a few strands loose into the air and speak your desire." Feeling coy, I added, "Your message will get to me. Eventually."

A shift in the energy in the air alerted us of an imminent arrival via the one of the portals. "I've got to go—" we said simultaneously. All business, Rhys returned to the heart of the yew tree. I hightailed it toward the river, where tent platforms and the freshly dug well awaited. I was excited to see everything in the daylight.

Outside the curved row of platforms, teams of urisk tended to three fire rings. Huge copper pots had been set directly atop the logs. Steam, thick and fragrant with lavender and other herbs, rose above the simmering water. It did not escape my notice that Finn himself, and every one of the urisk, wore a uniform of sorts consisting of natural linen dresses, or pants and shirts, and pale gray linen aprons.

Though it would have been simpler to invite Brigid into my home and give her the second story suite reserved for honored guests, I approved their efforts. The Magicals on my lands and nearby areas were eager to be of service, and I couldn't say no when Finn had sent a crow to deliver his note suggesting a lavish bathing area for the goddesses while I'd been clearing the area underneath the brush pile.

We have the pots to heat the water, three tubs, and plenty of tarps. 'Twould be no effort at all to make a space for Brigid Herself to bathe in private.

I'd readily agreed and okayed him sending a team to purchase the special Turkish linen towels the goddess preferred, along with an assortment of locally milled soaps, shampoos, and scented oils. Combs, brushes, and scissors were on the list, too, and if I knew the fairy-folk, they'd likely snuck in a few extras.

Astrape appeared from between two of the tents. Her long legs ate up the ground as she approached. I barely had time to catalog the many weapons she carried when she clasped my arms above the elbows.

"Greetings, Habonde. I've brought a small team with me, and I've brought a warning."

"Greetings, Astrape." I returned the formal gesture of welcoming. "A warning?" I repeated, as I kept an eye on the well for the burst of bright, golden light that would precede Brigid's arrival—or had in the past.

"Zeus advances." Astrape released me and loosened the drawstring on one of the pouches looped around her hips. Cupping the bottom, she reached in and withdrew a few tubular sections of rough, irregular, finger-sized rocks. "Fulgurite," she said, placing them in my palm. "Fossilized lightning. It rattles like bones when any of the thunder gods are near."

One by one, I held up the pieces to the sky. A few were hollow; some had greyish crystalline linings. Had Baubo and I piqued the god's interest by simply speaking his name? Could Demeter or Persephone have said something?

Astrape released my arm. I returned the fulgurite to her pouch. "My sister remains at Zeus' side. Should he show his face here, and she is with him, I will protect you and your guests against him, but I will not do anything that would directly harm her."

"I understand. And because we know the boundaries and portals between our worlds grow weaker, I need you and your team to secure all ways in and out. No one wants a rampaging mad man sniffing at their borders."

"Forewarned is forearmed," Astrape assured me. "I will do my best to see neither he or nor his avatars disrupt your gathering. None of us need the kind of upset Zeus' followers delight in inflicting."

"I agree." The glow I'd been watching for had just started to peek over the top row of stones. "Brigid's coming and I must go."

Chapter 12

THE BRIGHT ONE ROSE, enveloped in light and dressed as casually as I'd ever seen her in what looked to be a terrycloth bathrobe, a matching turban fastened with a rhinestone and turquoise brooch, and cat-eye sunglasses. She clasped both my up-stretched hands and stepped heavily from the stone to the raked ground, stumbling slightly as her foot slipped in its kitten heel slipper.

Stunned into speechlessness, I reached for the large handbag slung over her shoulder. She sighed as I relieved her of its weight. "Could we dispense with the prayers and pomp and just get me to a bath?"

Where Astrape's grip had been firm, steady, Brigid's hold on my forearm was almost frail. "The water is hot, and our attendants are eager to serve you as they will serve the others traveling with you."

Frightened eyes darted up to meet mine. "Oh, Habonde, could I ask that you alone assist me?" she whispered. "Can you spare yourself? I'm afraid I'm… well, you'll see. I am not myself, and I do not wish for others to witness their goddess at less than her best.

"And please, after all this time, surely we're on a nickname basis," she added.

"Of course, I will care for you, Brig. I understand your desire for privacy, and I will inform the urisk-folk."

"Could you have one of them wait here for my boar? His joints are arthritic, and he loathes portal travel."

"Of course."

As I led her from the well toward the platform with the bathing tent, Finnock waved his extensive network of family and friends into two lines. I signaled them to lower their eyes. We walked between lines, with Brigid accepting their murmured wishes for her good health. At the end, I spoke quietly with one of Finn's wives about the boar, and the change of plans.

"I shall station my most competent girls outside the tent," Jilly assured me. "They can pass whatever you need through the opening and ne'er set eyes upon our Lady until she is ready," she whispered back.

"Thank you for understanding."

I closed the tent flaps behind us and marveled openly at how the urisk had transformed the simple structure into a lush spa fit for a beloved goddess. Brigid approved, passing her hands over stacks of towels piled atop gleaming wooden benches, and *ooh*ing at the vases of field flowers. Pausing at a bowl of soaps, she lifted one after another to her nose before handing a bar to me.

"I like this one."

She set her sunglasses on the live edge oak table curving around three sides of the deep copper tub and shrugged out of the bathrobe. I unclasped the brooch holding the turban in place and loosened the towel wound around her head, gasping as long strands of brittle golden hair fell away with the cloth.

"It's bad, isn't it?"

Pressing my lips together, I refrained from answering and helped the naked goddess into the steaming water. Bending her knees, she lowered herself slowly. I placed a towel behind her head and shoulders. Bony fingers clutched the tub's rounded rim, and a soft sigh escaped her mouth as she leaned back.

I pulled up a low stool and waited. The moment her shoulders relaxed, I asked, "Brig, what happened?"

"Modern life happened, Habs. May I call you Habs? I've heard you and Baubo refer to each other as Habs and Babs and Habonde takes more energy. I must conserve what little I have."

"Yes, call me Habs and I have many things that might give you a boost, starting with soaking in this bath and getting herbal tonics and nourishing food into you."

Brigid's eyelids closed and she nodded. I hurried to the front of the tent and stuck my head out. "Junie, could we have a plate of soft scrambled eggs, lightly toasted bread, and a selection of fruit preserves? And is there any of that turmeric elixir your mother makes?"

June Bug, Finn's oldest daughter, ran to deliver my request. I brought Brigid's handbag over to the tub and pulled up another three-legged stool. The Bright One and I had history—we shared the same geographical region, for starters—but I doubted she'd ever been so utterly and unconcernedly naked in body *and* demeanor in my presence.

I chewed at my upper lip.

"Is there anything in your bag you need?"

"No not yet," she said, rolling her head side to side. "Would you wash my hair? And—" She paused and looked away. "Thank you for serving me as wholly as you serve the hearth."

"It is my pleasure." Supporting the back of her neck with one hand, I filled a copper cup with water and poured it over her head, wetting the top. I bit back the response on my tongue, the one where I confessed my hearth-keeping days faded long ago.

"Slide forward. That way most of your hair will be in the water."

She followed my request with a low moan of pleasure as I worked shampoo into her roots, gradually drawing her upright to get more into the rest of her hair. She curled forward and propped her arms on her knees. I balled together the long, floating hairs and dropped them into the woven trash basket. Brigid didn't need to see any more evidence that something was wrong.

"I've never run so low on magic, Habs. *Never.* Not even during the Reagan and Thatcher years. Keeping up with all the requests for my aid or intervention or to show up for this or that celebration, without being able to recharge fully, has just… drained me. I don't know what to do."

"It's a challenging situation, isn't it?" I offered.

"It is. We have fewer who follow us, so when they ask for help, we can't say no. Yet because we have fewer and fewer with every turn of the wheel, we're unable to reap the benefit of their belief, their faith."

I massaged more shampoo into her hair, then started the process of rinsing it all out. Once the strands squeaked, I shook the bottle of thick conditioner, poured it into my palm, and worked from the ends of her hair upward. That done, I curled the mass of it on top of her head.

"I have an idea forming," I said. "You're not alone in your feelings and something must be done before you and I and every other goddess disappears from collective memory."

"What is your idea?"

Words tumbled from my mouth as the concept brewing in the deepest recesses of my psyche found its way into the light. "I think we should set up a place where goddesses like you and me and those like us around this world and others can take a break from their duties and just… recharge and replenish and not have to worry about a thing."

Brigid didn't respond right away. I deflated a bit, then dove back in. "Though I suppose there would be consequences if we just up and walked away."

Brigid snorted. "For some of us, the consequences could be catastrophic. For others, not so much."

"But what if we had a competent substitute take our place?"

"Like, goddesses doubling up on their workload?" She shook her head. "That sounds like the opposite of what we need."

"What if we had proxies?" I came up with the idea of a proxy in the moment and it sounded like an apt description.

"Where am I going to find a proxy, Habs? Now you're just grabbing at straws."

"We would train them, Brig!"

"'We'?" she asked, rolling her head to shoot me a skeptical look.

I waved my hand near my face. Ideas were assaulting my brain like mayflies. "We start a school, a… a training program. It would take some time to get it up and running, of course. A year perhaps. But during that year we could all work together, share our duties and responsibilities. Then when our proxies are ready, we could truly retire from the world for a bit."

Resting my forearms on the edge of the tub, I sat back on my heels.

"And where will you find these eager trainees?" she asked, breaking her silence just as June Bug's short arms sent a tray through the front of the tent.

"I'll tell you over breakfast, which has just arrived." I took the tray, thanked the red-cheeked adolescent, and set the plates and utensils on the narrow board designed to span the width of the tub.

Brigid sat up taller and took a deep sniff of the food. "This smells delicious."

"Swallow the elixir first, then eat. The conditioner needs to stay in for at least fifteen minutes. Would you like coffee or tea or hot chocolate?"

She closed her eyes again and lifted her face. A melancholy smile played along her lips. "I would love a mug of sweet hot chocolate flavored with lavender buds and topped with whipped cream." Opening her eyes, she looked at me. "Would that be too much to ask?"

"If a mug of our finest cocoa will bring you even one step closer to regaining your health, I will gladly fetch it."

I returned to the front of the tent, placed Brigid's order, and added a mug for myself. "I'll have scrambled eggs too," I added, "and a shot of the elixir."

Here I was, talking to a goddess about taking better care of herself, while my own stomach growled with hunger. As I waited, and Brigid pondered the array of toast toppings, I showed her the selection of garments stacked inside a chest. She selected an ankle-length dress embroidered along the sleeves and at the hem with pale green vines and leaves. I shook it out and hung it on a wooden hanger.

June Bug slid a second tray between the tent flaps and called, "Hello?"

"Thank you, Junie."

"You're welcome, Mistress Barleywine. And the Woodsman asked me to tell you the Goddess of the Crossroads has arrived and is bathing in her tent."

Holding the tray to the side, I peeked out. "Which tent is hers?"

"It's not here, it's over there." June Bug pointed in the direction of the yew tree. "The Woodsmen helped us carry water to fill her bath."

"Has she ordered food?"

"Ay, she has. My sister is seeing to her." She lowered her voice. "We drew straws. I was verra happy to see I was to serve our Lady."

"She is glad to have you," I whispered. "Could you have someone help you bring two more buckets of hot water?"

Chapter 13

BRIGID PRACTICALLY PURRED as the added heat of the water enveloped her body, and returned to picking at her plate and admiring the mug of fancied-up cocoa I placed in front of her. Downing my shot glass of turmeric, fresh ginger, lemon juice, and coconut oil, I perused the baskets of beauty products and found almond oil for the bath. I added it in and swirled it around with my hand.

"Hekate is here. She's bathing as well. Are you feeling better?"

"Much. Whenever I close my eyes, I can recall days past, the ritual of attendants bathing me, dressing me, all of us walking out together to hear requests, grant boons…" Her voice and gaze wandered upward, to the tent's peak where someone had hung a posey of vines. She absentmindedly dropped crumbs into the water as she brought a triangle of toast to her mouth.

"And what comes next?" Brigid corralled the soggy bits of bread and placed them on the tray.

"We're expecting Demeter and Persephone. Possibly others. Yesterday, I placed a summons to Astrape to guard the perimeter of my lands. I— I spoke with her right before you arrived. She has read the signs and thinks Zeus may try to crash our gathering."

Brigid drained her mug, leaving the space above her upper lip coated with a film of cocoa. I handed her a washcloth and gestured to my own face. "I won't allow him to interrupt us," I continued. "I've spent too many hours counseling Magicals and humans who've been victims of his… appetites."

"And yet many whom we call sisters were born—or reclaimed—as a result of those appetites."

"True." And one of those co-opted offspring, Persephone, would likely join us. "It's the sense of absolute entitlement flowing through the majority of his actions that galls me. How can someone be so, so… impervious to societal change?" I rocked back on my heels before standing. "I would like to not speak or hear his name mentioned again in the coming hours and days."

"I second that. Shall we rinse my hair and get me dressed?"

I collected the glasses, mugs, and dishes, set both trays outside the tent, and did the same with the empty buckets. Waving June Bug over, I requested she bring me the mixture her mother had prepared at my earlier request. When I had explained to Jillian what I wanted, she'd suggested chamomile and mint for their scents, and lemon juice for brightening Brigid's light gold hair.

"I've called the first session for ten this morning," I informed the goddess, as I slowly poured the special rinse over her head and rubbed it into her hair. "That will give you time to settle into your tent, have a walk or a nap. I know the urisk clans and the dryads and others who've worked so hard to get everything ready for you would appreciate seeing you up and about."

She squeezed the excess water out of the strands and stood. Bathwater sluiced down the pinkened skin on her arms, breasts, and belly. "I do not need to be reminded of my duty, Habonde, and I am well aware of your desire to keep the peace amongst the Magicals who make their homes on your land."

Chastened, I hurried to appease her. "I'm so—"

"No apology needed. I admire your dedication to those you've taken under wing. Perhaps more than one future attendant or acolyte walks among them?" She stepped out unassisted—already her limbs looked plumper, her spine straighter—and accepted my offer of the first towel.

"I have my eye on a handful." I did, I realized, starting with Junie and her sister.

"Good." Brigid straightened, wrapped the second towel around her torso, and dismissed me with a nod. "I can dress myself."

Relieved she felt better, and only slightly annoyed at her change in tone, I reached for the tent flaps and turned. "June Bug is the name of the young woman who brought us our breakfasts and the extra water. I feel confident leaving you in her hands."

"June Bug," Brigid repeated. "How charming."

I updated Jillian, let her know I was off to check in with Hekate, and reminded her of the ten o'clock session.

"We're ready," she reassured me, "and thank you for trusting Junie with all that responsibility. She is near to bursting with the honor."

On my way to the yew tree, sounds of hand-sawing and hammering reached my ears. I veered in their direction and found Rhys' two brethren cutting leftover bits of lumber. Teams of urisk elders supervised their younger ones on making low benches with curved seats, suitable for the coming gathering.

Surveying their industriousness brought me back to times past when gatherings were a far more common occurrence on the croft and guests often purchased the seats and other handmade items from the urisk before leaving.

I sensed the building of a storehouse was in my future, as was a consult with an architect. If my proxy-training idea took off, we'd need dorms to house the trainees, a dining hall with an industrial kitchen, meeting rooms— I had to stop in the middle of the path to jot down my ideas and settle my overactive imaginings. A project this size entailed much more than ordering nails and lumber and a six-burner stove. There were environmental considerations, for starters, and our gardens and orchards would have to be expanded.

Which circled me back to Demeter. Her support for this project was critical, yet I would have to make it clear that her ex-husband and his cronies would be allowed no part in our endeavor whatsoever.

I ducked below the yew's overhanging branches and entered an encampment filled with two of the natural canvas bathing tents, and others that must have arrived with Hekate's Lamp Bearers. Their tents were narrow, with double peaks, and made from a nearly sheer red fabric. Lit from within, they resembled glowing embers, giving this group a more subdued feel than the cluster near the stream.

I approached one of the nymphs and asked for the whereabouts of the next goddess I wanted to see. She pointed to the closer white tent.

"Hekate?" I patted the sturdy canvas. "It's Habonde. May I come in?"

"Enter."

I had to reach between the flaps to undo the ties. Inside, Rhys lounged on cushions alongside the two lions. All three looked well-fed, sated even. A sharp sensation flamed inside my chest. Did Rhys' relationship with Hekate include physical intimacy? And was that *really* any of my business? For all I knew, the man simply adored large cats.

Re-tucking my shirt into my jeans, I quickly decided that whatever defined Hekate and Rhys' relationship wasn't my concern and directed my voice to the curtained off area to my right. "Do you have everything you need?"

"Fresh roe deer meat for my lions. A quiet place to rest and hot water for all. Yes, Habonde, you've done well. I've lost count of how many days it has been since we last stopped and simply—" Her voice wandered off, replaced by a splash. "I might never leave."

Rhys rolled to his feet, his mellowed gaze searching for mine. "Hekate, I'm off to replenish the hot water."

A satisfied "*Mmm…*" floated upward from the vicinity of the tub. I curled my hands around Rhys' bronze armbands. He twisted slightly and held my silver cuffs. The thrum between us strengthened as he leaned in, kissed one cheek, and the other, and faded when he let go and picked up the empty buckets.

I smoothed the loose hairs falling into my face and watched the Woodsman exit the tent. "I've just come from seeing to Brigid's bath," I said loudly, "which seems to have helped her as well."

"We gather at ten?" Hekate asked.

"Yes."

Walking sideways, Rhys re-entered the tent and brought the filled buckets behind the curtain. I couldn't hear the ensuing exchange between him and Hekate. Raising my voice again, I asked if she needed anything else.

"Not from you, my sister. I am happy to be left alone to bathe."

"Then I shall ask one of your Lamp Bearers to check on you and make sure you don't fall asleep."

Hekate's laugh was surprisingly deep. "Good thinking."

Rhys set the buckets by the tent flaps and held one back as I exited. I wasn't expecting him to follow me out, nor was I expecting him to take my elbow and steer me around until we were face to face.

"Habonde. Wait." I didn't resist when he laced his fingers through mine and pulled me a few inches closer.

"Do you have everything *you* need?" I asked. I struggled to keep a flirtatious tone out of my voice.

"Yes, I do. My men do as well, and we are gratcful to you and Baubo for your generous hospitality. Are you busy, or would you have time to meet me under another tree?" he asked, eyes gleaming. We moved imperceptibly closer with every breath and the familiar scent of vetiver filled my nostrils. "Or are there other guests you must see to?"

"No, not at the moment." I swallowed hard and licked my parched lips. Pulling my hand from his, I clasped my fingers behind me and tamped down the urge to unbutton his shirt and rip it off his shoulders. "What about you?"

"I have the desire to see to you, Habonde." He cupped the back of my neck and rubbed the spot below my ear. Heat passed through Rhys' touch, igniting fiery lines down the backside of my body. His caress weakened my resolve. I slid shaking fingers between the buttons on his half-undone shirt.

I shouldn't have done that. Proximity to him burned whatever next tasks I had planned, to a pile of coal and ash.

"Why have we not yet kissed, Mistress Barleywine?"

"Because kissing is intimate, Woodsman," I whispered, holding still as a deer.

"More intimate than me filling you as I did in the past?"

My blood's bright tang wet my tongue. "Far more intimate," I managed to whisper as he danced us into the shadows underneath a wide branch.

"Why did you choose me?"

Disentangling my fingers from the Woodsman's buttonholes, I froze at the rising memory.

My partner in the fertility ritual gazed up with blown out pupils and a smile that spoke of a well-sated lover. Before offering him an answer, I studied the figures moving outside the sheer gauze walls of the tent erected for our coupling. Many centuries past, we would have copulated atop an open altar, in view of my followers. Now, Beltane rituals were reduced to Maypoles and ribbons and lovers claiming each other behind closed doors.

Lifting myself off the man's thighs, I wiped off his belly and mine. Though I participated in this ritual as my duty to the land, I no longer allowed the males I chose to penetrate me. Nor did I allow them to kiss me on the lips. Those greater intimacies were only granted only to lovers. Here, atop the Beltane altar, it was enough that I played my part by seeing to my partner's pleasure and my own and sending the energy we raised into the ground below. From there, roots would take over, spreading the magic amongst trees and flowers, berries and weeds, feeding birds, animals, insects and, eventually, the humans consuming the food produced on these hectares.

Yes, this method diminished the potency of the magic, but I strove to make up for the changes I'd made in other ways.

"Habonde?"

The man's soothing, curious voice pulled me out of the lively underground's enthusiastic response to fresh magic. I pressed my finger lightly to his lips, and answered, "I chose you because of your mouth."

"My mouth? Not this?" he asked, patting his broad, muscled chest, "or my other gifts?"

"I could judge neither, as you were fully clothed at the choosing, and so I listened for the timbre of your voice, the care with which you spoke, and the words you chose to make your case."

"So, you chose me for my mouth and *my tongue." His smile was infectious, and so I smiled back.*

"I have yet to test your tongue," I admonished, rising higher and making to step from the altar and onto the carpet of freshly threshed grains.

"Are you saying you are done with me then?" He rolled onto his side and propped his head on his hand.

"For this night, I am."

"And what of tomorrow night, and the next?"

• • •

UNNERVED BY THE memory of our first meeting and the desire in the question he'd asked, I widened the space between Rhys' chest and mine.

"I'm not ready for this. I want to remember what it is we once shared, Rhys. I do. But this is not an altar, nor is it a day of ritual, and I need to hear you speak what it is you desire."

"I barely slept after you left last night. I want the woman who wears the skin of a goddess. I want the goddess disguised as the mistress of Bone Fire Croft. I want *you*."

Rhys' husky, desire-infused tone almost convinced me to say yes. Muffled sounds of cracking and slithering brushed past my ears as nearby branches curved around us, creating a private place to continue talking. A supportive tree limb met my upper back. Vines rose from behind Rhys' shoulders, twining a fragrant crown of jasmine around his head.

"I think this tree wants me to want you, too, Woodsman."

Rhys wrapped his arms around me and groaned against the side of my throat. Tiny white flower petals stuck to his forehead and brushed my skin, releasing more of their intoxicating scent.

"I have waited so long, but I can wait some more. Though time has a way of meddling with things I desire. And I," he said, his rolling brogue infused with sorrow and longing, "I desire you."

Chapter 14

EVERY WORD RHYS SPOKE, every action he took, conveyed the
depth of his desire for me—and it spun me off kilter. Once the
tree released us, I stumbled backwards, reaching for a branch
rather than Rhys' outstretched arm and choked out a goodbye.
Wobbly legs bore me home. I had to wash his scent off my hands
and face, shake the crushed jasmine petals out of my hair, and
change my blouse, leaving me scant minutes to get myself back to
the gathering ground.

Ever-thoughtful Baubo had left a small pitcher of hibiscus
lemonade in the refrigerator. I poured it into a narrow thermos
and headed out the door.

"Habonde."

Only the fact that I had my hand on the bottle's lid kept me
from wearing the bright fuchsia tea and changing my clothes a
third time. I stopped short and took a deep breath. "Hades. What
are you doing here?"

Garbed head to toe in fashionably wrinkled black linen and
understated jewelry at his wrists and throat, the King of the
Underworld crouched by one of the urns overflowing with mint

and rifled through the leaves. Lifting his fingertips to his nose as he rose, he said, "I hope to visit with my wife. A little bird told me she's arriving later today with her mother."

Confused, I came off the steps. Though I'd long ago stopped listening to the gossips funneling news of Mount Olympus into other immortals' ears, my interest was piqued. "A little bird?" I asked.

"One of Hekate's torch bearers."

"And Hekate does not mind this torch bearer announcing her business and that of her friends?"

"This torch bearer is my appointed liaison. There is nothing underhanded going on."

"And does the torch bearer know you refer to her as a 'little bird'?" I brushed past him on my way to the gate. "I'm in a hurry. And you are not allowed further than this garden, not this day nor tomorrow."

He pinched off a blossoming sprig of *mentha pulegium*, a variety I'd planted to repel garden pests and which was— apparently—better suited to dispelling aphids than major deities.

"Could you spare me one minute, Habonde? I have no intention of disrupting whatever it is you have going on. I am weary of" —he tucked the mint leaf into his shirt pocket and waved a hand in the air, indicating everything, and nothing in particular— "and would much prefer to sit among your peaceful plants. Perhaps avail myself of the fruit in your orchard or a cool drink from your kitchen."

"Speak quickly. Help yourself after."

A more serious demeanor replaced his casual tone. "I am aware the gathering you've arranged is for goddesses only, hence the probable presence of Persephone and Demeter. My brother has been pestering me and my wife to visit, so I took this as an opportunity to leave my duties in the hands of Dionysus for a while and hit two targets with one arrow. Metaphorically speaking."

"Which brother and which targets?" I doubted the sibling in question was Poseidon, though I forced myself to ask for clarity's sake.

"Zeus. He knows something is afoot, something interesting that does not include him, but which *could* include any number of his daughters, former wives, lovers. How he came by this information, I do not know, though I could wager an educated guess."

Zeus had two ears of his own, and a thousand more attached to other heads tasked with doing his listening for him. Gripping my thermos tight, I moved closer to my fellow immortal. "Do us *all* a favor and keep him away. What my sistren are coming to discuss concerns us and has nothing to do with those who sit atop Mount Olympus."

"Is this a moon-cycle matter?"

"No."

"Is this place safe?"

"It is, as long as my guests stay within the bounds of my property. Astrape is here. She has reinforced the wards and will do what it takes to guard us."

Odd. Was that relief smoothing the worry lines creasing Hades' features? "Then I shall do my part as well."

I thanked him and said goodbye. Closing the gate, I turned to make certain the latch was secure. A visibly pregnant figure, clothed in a short, fluttery apple green dress and gold accessories stood framed between two urns.

Minthe. The nymph's banishment to some distant mint pot must have been lifted, and now she and Hades were…? I noted Hades' hand on her ripe belly and the way they both gazed down. Had the two resumed being lovers? Could what I was seeing indicate there was more to their story?

Zipping my lips, I hurried along the path and set thoughts of the denizens of the Underworld aside. I would ask questions only when, and if, their problems became my problems.

Minutes later, I came to the area beside the stream where the white tents had been set up. There was no sign of Finn or his menfolk and everything was quiet. I veered toward Brigid's bathing pavilion.

"Jilly?"

She ducked out from between the flaps and waved me over. "Mistress Barleywine. We're just cleaning up before we deliver morning tea to the gathering and start preparations for lunch."

"Anything I should know?"

Jilly practically levitated as she clutched her hands to her chest and beamed. "Brigid Herself seemed *very* pleased with her accommodations. She asked June Bug to escort her while she strolled along the stream. Junie knows to take her to the gathering at ten o'clock sharp."

"Thank you, Jilly. You've worked miracles in such a short time."

Smiling, she smoothed the front of her immaculate linen apron. "'Tis a joy to be thus occupied, m'lady. I would welcome more days like this."

"As would I," I assured her. "If things go well today and tomorrow, we may both get our wish."

A FREE-FORM CANVAS awning shaped like a giant swan taking flight spread its wings over the small field past the tents. Underneath, the handful of benches assembled by the Woodmen and urisk were stacked beside piles of rugs, quilts, and blankets. June Bug and a couple of her kin bustled around a long, low table. Judging by the volume of tiered plates of sweets and pitchers of teas and fruit waters, no one would go hungry or thirsty between breakfast and lunch.

Astrape walked the outer perimeter of the setup, flanked by her three companions. Armed with long bows and quivers stuffed with arrows, each took up their position at one of the awning's support poles. Though the quartet's presence calmed the worry nipping at my heels, knowing Hades was on the croft along with the pregnant Minthe deepened my concern. Rumor had it the King of the Underworld never got over losing the nymph in a deal he'd made with Zeus. Hearing him confirm Zeus suspected Demeter was coming here formed an added knot in my belly. How much, if anything, should I share with her and her daughter of what I'd seen in my garden?

Astrape's whistle pulled my attention outward. She waved, I gave two thumbs up, and she jogged northward.

Underneath the awning, Hekate relaxed on a familiar silk rug, hand-knotted in shades of red, from rust to pink. Her lions sprawled behind her. The same nymphs who'd accompanied her through my ancestor journey spread out to either side on shared blankets and little stools. Most had plates of assorted pastries in their laps. The pleasure I derived from seeing them relaxing took me by surprise and if I knew Jillian, she'd added herbal elements that provided nutritional boosts to everything she prepared.

Brigid lounged against a stack of pillows in the middle of a round, creamy white rug. She reminded me of a lotus flower, its petals opened wide to the light, its yellow stamen echoed in the goddess' loosely braided crown of tansy and buttercups. Her boar napped in a patch of sun-drenched wildflowers beyond the awning's reach. Without staring too long at any individual, thereby drawing attention to my pointed perusal, I could tell this group was already benefitting from Bone Fire Croft's offerings—and could stand to absorb more of our ambient, nourishing magic.

To my left, the ever-regal Demeter occupied a chair that could double as a throne, her straw summer handbag parked at the chair's side. I suspected the furniture, as with the rugs, had come from one of the rarely used rooms in one of my houses. The Corn Goddess wore a short-sleeved, belted jumpsuit paired with a few pieces of solid gold jewelry. At her elegant feet, garbed in a sleeveless romper with her head bowed and stringy hair hiding her face, was Persephone. She looked up, raised her phone overhead, and sighed. I understood her frustration, but there was nothing I could do—or wanted to do—about our internet's spotty reach. I would, however, bring a bit of cheer to her gloomy demeanor. Though she and I weren't close, the normally put-together Queen of the Underworld seemed to have paid not a whit of attention to her wardrobe or to getting herself anything to eat.

"Junie?" The brownie whipped her head toward me and smiled shyly. "Could you make a tray for Persephone? I know she loves sweet treats and pink is her favorite color."

"'Tis my favorite color too, my lady." She quickly started sorting through the stack of mismatched plates and cooed when she found one decorated with pink roses. "Shall I pour her something to drink?"

"Hibiscus lemonade. Let her know what's in everything you serve to her. I don't want the Queen worrying whether it contains pomegranates. And for Demeter—"

Junie gasped. "I am to serve her *too*?"

Jillian bustled up to the table and patted her daughter's back. "I shall serve the Corn Goddess. June Bug, hand me that vase of poppies. Kila, bring the flowering yarrow to Brigid and add a few of the smaller yellow swamp irises, and Lila—" She perused the selection of flowers in the aluminum bucket behind the refreshment table and lifted a mixed bouquet of blossoming wild pea for her three-year-old twins to deliver. "These will do nicely for Hekate."

I left Jilly and her offspring to their tasks and walked to the center of the circle where Baubo waited, clutching her ever-present notepad to her chest.

"I'm not late, am I?" I whispered.

"It's near ten-past."

"I would have been on time, except Hades showed up at my back door and said he wanted to have a word." I drew my bestie closer. "He's sworn he'll do everything he can to keep the croft a Zeus-free zone. Though I suspect his mind is on other matters."

Baubo leaned against my arm. "Tell me, was Hades alone?"

"Minthe appeared as I left." I lowered my voice further. "Did you know she was pregnant?"

Baubo sighed. "I heard rumor this morning she'd asked for safe haven amongst the croft's naiad clan until the babe is delivered, is all."

"Does Persephone know?"

"She's not spoken a word since she arrived other than to swear at her phone."

"Then I guess we'd best get started."

"The floor's all yours."

"Would you do the honors?"

Chapter 15

BAUBO SHOOK HER CURLY HAIR, lifted the silver bell hanging
from a chain around her neck, and rang it lightly. June Bug and
her younger sisters scurried back to their mother. The lions raised
their heads and blinked. Demeter tossed a tea sandwich to each
and shifted in her chair to face us, while Baubo settled between
Demeter and Hekate on their overlapping rugs.

"Brigid. Hekate. Demeter. Persephone. Thank you for
attending this informal get-together on short notice, and for
gracing these hills with your presence. Though I admit I cannot
recall the last time we all met, a series of events has led me to
believe it was urgent that we gather again.

"Since Beltane, I have been having vivid dreams in which the
oldest extant goddess figurines crafted by mortal hands rise from
the soil in my garden and come to life. I might have swept the
dreams aside, thinking them related to the moon or a rare
planetary alignment—except I wasn't the only one having such
dreams."

I stepped sideways, to the lone remaining bench, and dragged
it forward as I continued speaking. "Goddesses with attributes like

mine started reaching out to me, and I to them, all of us sharing our dreams. And as we spoke of things other than the figures and what they could mean, a common theme emerged. We all confessed to feeling varying degrees of physical exhaustion, and some confided their inner storehouses of magic had drained to perilously low levels.

"We agreed we're at a loss about how we could solve these personal issues while simultaneously seeing to our responsibilities."

One of the lamp bearers raised her arm slowly, darting her gaze between me and Hekate until the Keeper of the Keys nodded her head.

"The seven of us have noticed a similar situation. We've spoken of it amongst ourselves—"

Hekate pivoted on the heel of her hand and addressed the nymph. "And why did you not mention this to me, Lumina?"

Lumina paled. "Our role is to light your path, to—" She lifted her arms, gesturing to everything and nothing.

"I know your roles, and I know of your deep and abiding dedication to performing your duties. But if any one of you is weakened, we are all affected."

"And that goes for you, too, dear one," Demeter chided, extending her arm toward Hekate. "I shall not air the Underworld's current staffing challenges to those not involved, but even I have noticed changes."

"Yet how is it you look fresh as a daisy, Demi?" Brigid asked. Demeter bristled slightly and settled back into her chair's stiff embrace.

"First Harvest is but days away, Brig. As the grain ripens, so do I, and this place" —she swept her arms outward, indicating the fields beyond the awning and the whole of the croft— "this place knows abundance. I felt it the moment we arrived at Habonde's orchard portal, and I have witnessed fruits and grains ripening before my eyes."

"But your daughter appears—"

"My daughter is *my* concern." Demeter turned her attention to me, even as Persephone pocketed her phone and turned to Brigid.

"And my sorrows are mine to sort." The Queen of the Underworld sat straighter and pulled the tray of treats left by June Bug closer, effectively ending Brigid's probing. "Baubo, now would be a really good time to do your thing."

My BFF, who had been monitoring the back and forth between Brigid and Demeter, tugged at her pant legs and grinned. "I would, if I were I wearing a skirt."

Laughter released some of the tension tightening my shoulders and reminded me I was in the presence of peers. "Baubo is at least partly responsible for all of you being here. I told her about my dreams, and she convinced me an ancestor journey was in order. She even dug, washed, peeled, *and* sliced the elecampane herself. Two nights ago, I ingested the root and drank the teas and with the guidance of Baubo's drumming, the wise and loving ancestors brought me face to face with long forgotten iterations of my past, all the way back to Hestia."

Opening my arms toward Brigid and Hekate, I continued. "The ancestors sought fit to also remind me of my connection to others and brought you two into my vision."

Demeter lifted one finger off her chair's armrest. "And why is Hestia not here?"

"I don't know. She was the last of my direct ancestresses to appear, but she did not stay. I tried to summon her to my hearth earlier today, and she did not answer." My growing concern about Hestia's whereabouts threatened to derail what I wanted to say next.

"A possible answer for these widespread dreams and their

uncanny similarities came to me yesterday." My heart beat harder within my chest. Beyond the tent, delicate flowers turned bright faces in my direction. Birdsong quieted. Brigid's boar and Hekate's lions lifted their heads. Even the stream softened the volume of its tumbling notes.

"I believe it is time to reinvigorate the magic in the earth beneath us, in the air and waters around us, and in the sky above us. I believe it is time to resurrect the best of the old ways, to bring them forward and marry them with the best of the new.

"I believe it is time to reawaken the vast knowledge we have stored away, and to teach contemporary Magicals how to serve the Goddess and, by extension, themselves, their families, and their communities." I paused for a moment to let my words sink in. "I have enough land here to build a… a site for both respite and retreat, and for training. Our kin around the world in similar situations are considering doing the same."

"And then what?" Demeter asked, smoothing invisible wrinkles from her attire. "What happens when, say, a fledgling witch or shifter is trained to serve? And what do you think of allowing in halflings, or even those with no discernible magic?"

"Those are good questions. At this point, I can only offer generalities, then work toward specifics. Mind you, I've only just started to sketch out the educational aspects, but I imagine a general program at first, then further specializations as we onboard more instructors."

For me to sell this idea, I had to get better at thinking on my feet and quickly articulating hazy ideas. "Ideally, each student would come out of the program understanding how to serve the Goddess in general, and depending on their kind of magic, their skill, their… interests, they would move on to specializing with the goal to eventually becoming a proxy."

The moment I again spoke the word proxy, I got the tingles, and though the full meaning of their duties would take time to craft, the idea had taken root. "Once we have certified proxies, then goddesses in need of respite can choose their surrogate and leave their duties in their hands." I took a breath, my mind somersaulting with ideas. "For a set period of time," I added, "and with supervision."

"I would need three." Hekate's voice boomed toward me, startling her lions into shaking their massive heads and searching the tent. "With none of them squeamish about staying in the Underworld."

"Good point. Which adds questions around how much time each of us could contribute to training our replacements." I glanced to Baubo and mimed writing. She waved her pen and notepad. I should have known she was on it. She finished jotting something down and looked up.

"Some of the magic we work involves sex," she gently reminded me. "Have you any thoughts on that?"

My mouth froze open as a memory surged forward.

"HABONDE, come quickly. There is a man outside the temple, and he insists on speaking with you and only you."

I gathered my long skirts and followed the anxious acolyte from the temple's antechamber, down the hall lined with flickering torches, and into the open-air vestibule. One of Zeus' henchmen, recognizable by the insignia on his helm and the attitude coursing through his stance, stood gripping a young maiden's shoulder. The girl was on her knees, her gown in tatters, her face bruised and bloodied.

"What is go—"

"This wench was no virgin and when she spoke her lies in Zeus' presence, she was rightly punished. Zeus seeks the return of his payment, or this liar's tongue. I am good with either." The man reached over his shoulder and withdrew a blade from the sheath strapped to his back. "Choose now," he ordered, aiming the blade's wicked point at my throat.

The gold coins in the bowl sitting atop a plinth rose into the air at my beckoning.

"Release her, and Zeus shall have his gold."

The henchman thrust the girl at me. She cried out as her knees hit the stones, then crawled forward and leaned against my leg. Sweeping my arm in front of me, I flung the coins into the air. Curses filled the room as gold rained onto the man's helm and clattered to the floor.

"Cross the threshold of this sanctuary again on pain of death."

The henchman tossed a coin at me and smirked. "We shall see about that."

He left, his heavy feet clomping, his metal and leather armor clanking. I made no move until I knew he was gone, then bent to lift Iona's quaking form into my arms and carry her to the healer.

"I am virgin, Mistress, I am, I—"

"Shh, shh, little dove, I know you are," I whispered. "Like most males seeking virgins for their sexual pleasure, Zeus believes an intact hymen equals an untouched body."

"But you said that has nothing to do with being virgin, nothing."

"And my words are true. Being a virgin means you are whole unto yourself and you, Iona, are whole and strong and worthy."

I transferred Iona to the bed in one of the healer's treatment rooms. "I am so sorry you experienced Zeus' cruelty. He may reign on Mount Olympus, but he is no longer welcome on Bone Fire Croft."

$$\rule{3cm}{0.4pt}$$

Chapter 16

$$\rule{3cm}{0.4pt}$$

"HABONDE, DID YOU HEAR MY QUESTION?"

The memory of Iona and the henchman faded at Baubo's whispered prodding. I pressed my hand to my belly to regain my center. "I did. Given that the political and religious climate amongst humankind has spread its influence into the Magical world, I would be inclined to consult with our sisters in the sacred sex-work trades, and perhaps Hedone, for their input on such matters."

Murmurs of agreement reached my ears. Demeter again raised a single, regal finger. "What do you envision as the next step?"

"What I proposed is simply is the seed of an idea. If anything I've spoken of rings true for you, we could gather again after lunch for further discussions. And please, consider spending the rest of this day and night here on Bone Fire Croft. There are conversations to be shared, there is food aplenty, plus hot baths, cool streams." I almost mentioned the internet was strongest at my home but thought better of it due to the possibility of Persephone running into Minthe. Or Hades. Or both. "If you think of others who should join us, we can utilize the orchard portal to bring them in."

Baubo stood then and stretched, raising both arms. I exhaled my relief at having spoken what I wanted most to say. Demeter and Brigid came to their feet simultaneously and stared at each other. I half-expected I would be forced to run interference when suddenly they embraced and then invited Hekate and Persephone to join them. The four immediately began speaking, their body language inferring the earlier tension was forgotten.

I took my first deep breath in an hour. The rich hum of Magical beings debating a new idea was balm to my ears, right up until a splintering sky silenced every voice. My legs reacted before my head, and I tore out from underneath the awning to the sight of Astrape streaking across the sky atop her winged horse, tossing lightning bolts in the direction of a roiling gray cloud. Her three guards stepped away from the poles, arrows nocked into their bows, their eyes and bodies following Astrape's trajectory.

Running back, I grabbed Baubo's arm and dragged her over to Jilly and her daughters and the other urisk who had volunteered to serve as attendants to my guests.

"Get them to a safe place and keep them hidden." I had to yell over the noises spilling from the sky. The lions and bristled boar added their voices to the uproar.

"We can help. Surround the young ones," Hekate commanded her nymphs. "Get them to the yew tree." Taking each of her beasts by its scruff, she bent to whisper into their ears. She stepped back, allowing the lions to stand guard as the Lamp Bearers corralled the urisk and their children into a tight formation and escorted them away from the field.

"Hades promised he would do everything he could to keep Zeus away," I said, once Hekate and I saw the group was safe.

"Hades is mightily distracted. Did you happen to notice an abundance of mint in your garden this morning?"

"I did." Was this the best moment to mention what else I'd seen in my garden? I decided it was. "You're right about the distraction. I saw Minthe there with Hades."

"Oh, Minthe." Hekate rubbed her forehead. "The fights between Hades and Persephone grow more persistent and every time they reach an impasse—and it is always the same impasse—he seeks the comfort of others, and she retreats to her rooms in House Hades." She crossed her arms and shook her head. "The more I consider this proxy idea, Habonde, the more I like it. I require reliable assistants to work with me in every realm I access. Hades has become distressingly unreliable when I need his help in the underworld, yet he hasn't shared with me what's going on."

"I suspect I saw something I shouldn't have."

"Oh?"

"Minthe is pregnant, and Hades did not seem unhappy."

"Great Goddess, that could explain why the River Kokytus has—"

"Wife!" Zeus' roar barreled its way through the crackling thunder, turning the shocked look on Hekate's face into one of annoyance. "Daughter! I know you are here, and I demand to see you both."

A sickening jolt nearly threw me off my feet. Hekate moved to shelter Brigid. Demeter and Persephone stood shoulder to shoulder. Scrambling to my feet, I accepted Baubo's hand and released her as someone tugged at the back of my shirt.

"Jilly, what are you doing here?"

"I brought you this." She offered a metal and glass contraption equipped with a thick needle and a trigger, and three glass vials filled with a sickly yellow liquid. "It's a tranquilizer syringe. We use 'em on the big animals. Been known to work on drunk humans and pompous Magicals."

Laughing on the inside, I accepted her offering, jammed the vials into my pants pocket, and thanked her. "Get back to safety."

"You don't have to worry about us," she assured me. "There's plenty more what came from."

Outside the awning's protection, Astrape circled above the field, wind whipping at hair and clothes, dark clouds scudding in our direction. One large section of those clouds formed into a horse. Legs pumping, it broke away, its coat and wing feathers changing color from steel gray to yellowy gold as it headed towards the rest of us.

"Hold your ground," Demeter ordered, dropping Persephone's hand and speaking as much to her, as to Astrape and her archers. "And someone get me sugar. That horse has a sweet tooth."

Baubo nabbed a sugar bowl from the refreshment table and offered it to the Corn Goddess. "I'll deal with him," Demeter assured us, cradling the container in both hands. "There is no reason a family spat should put a damper on our time together. Persephone, come."

Elbows linked, the two strode out to meet the King of the Gods and his overblown ego. Or Demeter strode and Persephone reluctantly shuffled alongside her.

"You never know when his bluster is a just a whole lot of hot air," Brigid observed, "or when he's truly determined to get his way."

"I trust Demeter can reason with him." I had to.

"Do you want me stay with you in case you need to use that?" Baubo asked, pointing to the syringe I continued to grip.

"I'm good. Go check in with Jillian."

"You staying here?"

"I'm hoping to speak with Demeter in private, rather than put her on the spot," I said, studying the odd weapon. I decided if Zeus was close enough that I needed to use the device, I'd rather use my herb knife's sharp, curved blade. "Here. Could you return this to the urisk? "

Grimacing, Baubo accepted the handle and the vials. "Residual embarrassment from Zeus' behavior could work in our favor."

Baubo left, holding the clunky syringe at arm's length. Nervous, I wiped my sweaty palms on my jeans and felt the outline of Rhys' ring. The urge to summon him rose and fell. Between Astrape and her three protecting the tent area, and Demeter bravely confronting her ex, there really was no need to get the Woodsmen, or any of the fathers, brothers, and partners amongst the urisk, involved. Much as I loved and appreciated Finn and his ilk, the goddesses and I could handle this interruption ourselves.

Placing my tongue against the backs of my teeth, I issued a trill. A small flock of crested tits landed on the ropes securing the awning to the stakes and waited for me to make my way over.

"Listen in, would you please," I instructed, "to the conversation happening near the great horse."

The birds flew off and landed singly and by twos. Neither Zeus' mount nor the others noticed. Scant moments later, I received my first report. That bird flew off, another landed, and so it went. At one point Demeter, who continued to hold the horse's rapt attention with the sugar bowl, pulled Persephone behind her.

"You bring shame on our house."

That had to be Zeus.

"This is your fault. It will always be your fault."

Zeus again, playing the blame game.

"You forsook your duties."

And the King speaks yet again.

"You forsook our daughter."

That could only be Demeter.

"Father, stop pretending everything's alright. I cannot abide my husband, nor can he abide me."

Go, Persephone!

"This is not the final word."

Yes, it is, Zeus. Time to turn that horse around and hightail it off my croft.

"There is nothing left to save, and the sooner you—"

My jaw might have dropped open.

"Say nothing. Appearances must be maintained."

Sorry, Zeus. Not happening.

"You shattered that facade the day you made your deal with Hades."

Demeter's rage radiated outward, flattening grasses and flowers in its path. Zeus remounted his winged horse, dancing the beast in a circle and trampling the field in a show of displeasure. The birds fluttered up and flew off, and Demeter embraced Persephone.

Baubo sidled up next to me. "For all that we are gifted, some of us lead lives of quiet desperation."

"And some of us are not so quiet." Zeus tossed a ragged thunderbolt in the direction of the oak trees lining the stream, only to roar as the bolt was intercepted by Astrape's sleeker, faster model.

"That poor child is miserable."

I assumed she meant Persephone. "Is it too much to imagine we could use this group to flesh out the proxy-training idea and relieve her of her suffering?"

"It's worth a try."

Grasses and flowers rose up and reached for the Corn Goddess and her daughter as the two made their way toward the awning. Astrape swooped low over the field and landed her horse. The dappled gray beast's graceful legs pounded the ground, and Zeus' former lightning-bearer quickly caught up to Demeter and Persephone. She dismounted and offered the younger woman a hug. Demeter continued on, looking back only once as Persephone and Astrape embraced.

"I am going to the stream to cool off and wash that… that pernicious, manipulative narcissist out of my hair," she announced once she was closer. "Would either of you care to join me?"

I snagged my chance to speak with her alone. "I was thinking the same thing. We can stop at the bathing tent for towels. Baubo, fancy a swim?"

"I think I shall wait for 'Seph. It has been far too long since the two of us had a chance to speak."

"I would appreciate you sharing your wise counsel with her, old friend." Demeter stroked Baubo's arms. "You know how hard it is to change the course of one's life. My fears for Persephone's long term mental health are coming true and the changes she cries for require everyone who truly loves her to adjust their expectations."

"I have only her best interests at heart, you know that dear friend."

"And you are one of the few whose sentiments I trust."

Chapter 17

DEMETER and I disrobed on flat rocks terraced along a section of the stream. Rope swings of varying lengths dangled from branches overhanging the water. Azure damselflies hunted among the shore grasses. A green-haired naiad rose her head above the streams rippling surface, blinked, and made her way lazily toward the opposite bank.

"What an idyllic place." Demeter dangled her legs over the edge of the rock and sighed as she eased herself into the water. "Why do I not visit more often?"

The densely wooded area across from us tugged at my awareness. As far as I knew, the dryads had more or less claimed that area for themselves. "Perhaps because your duties in this hemisphere are numerous?" I answered. "Perhaps because I've neglected to invite you here as often as I should have?"

"I would attend your First Harvest celebration if asked." Sweeping her arms away from her sides, she floated further from the rock and turned to face the sun.

"Then I would ask you now to be my honored guest."

"I accept," she said, laughing lightly. "I shall let you know how many to expect once I know who will be traveling with me."

Curling my toes for leverage, I bent my knees, reached my arms skyward, and dove in. The current slowed in this wider section of the stream. I opened my eyes to see curious fish, another naiad, and Demeter's legs, and when I surfaced, I asked the question foremost on mind.

"What do you think of this proposition of a school?"

"I am… intrigued. And though I know the idea is in the seed stage, I would like to be kept informed."

"Would you consider signing on as an advisor?" I asked.

The Corn Goddess slowly, lazily kicked her legs and waved her arms. The winged insects flying in to investigate the top of her head flitted away. "I have much to consider before I could commit."

"Thank you."

"You know you're going to have to hire someone versed in social media and the mysterious ways of those far more youthful than either of us. And in Persephone's opinion, you have got to do something about your lousy internet and its pitiable lack of bandwidth."

I laughed so hard I nearly choked on the water. "Did you ever think you would hear yourself uttering words like 'social media' and 'bandwidth'?" I asked, once I could speak.

"No. But such is our reality, Habonde. If you create a training program here, you will need to recruit as you once did for your acolytes, from those between six and—" She flicked the side of her hand across the water's surface, sending a floating clump of pond weeds further downstream. "Just how old were your acolytes?"

"The girls entered my temple as early as they wanted—and when I say girl, I include those born as Hekate, or our Baubo, or born into a body with male attributes yet knowing they were other—though usually not prior to the age of twelve, or upon their first moon blood. And always with the option of not continuing."

"Unlike some temples," Demeter muttered.

"True."

The current moved us further apart. Demeter started speaking, and I swam closer to hear, "We rely on the old ways to travel and to communicate. On portals and scrying and talking with the birds. Many do not and will need to be taught."

The scope of developing and implementing a proxy training program grew another limb. Rather than sink into the stream in a parody of drowning under the weight of a project not yet started, I nodded in agreement. "Though we will learn from modern Magicals, too, I would want the emphasis on learning the ways that have been with us as long as—" I realized I had no idea how to quantify the length of my life. "The ways that have served us well."

"Persephone keeps up with all the modern… stuff. Perhaps there is a role here for her."

And there it was, the perfect entry point for a conversation about the Queen of the Underworld's mental and emotional state. "Demeter, I am no mother, though I often felt motherly toward my acolytes, yet even I can see 'Sephie's in pain. Do you want to share what's going on?"

Bugs paused their hovering. The stream slowed to a stop. Naiads surfaced in the cattails, blinking their inky eyes as Demeter closed hers and exhaled frustration, sorrow, resignation. "Could you wave your hand in the air and conjure us some of that ale your renowned brewers produce?"

If Demeter desired ale to loosen her tongue, she would have ale. Facing the shore, I whistled for the crested tits, who carried my request to Jilly. "By the time we swim to the other side of the stream and back, ale will be waiting for us on those rocks. Are you in?"

"I'm in." Nimble as a naiad, she flipped over and set a quick pace. As host, I would have let her win no matter what, only she seemed to be inviting me to compete. Kicking my legs, I followed, never quite catching up even as Demeter struggled through the grasses before touching the shore and turning around. She had toweled off and donned her sheer undergarment before I hauled myself out of the water and onto the rock. A basket of dark brown, pop-top glass bottles waited for us in the shade offered by a thick clump of bracken. I wrapped a towel around my middle and accepted the bottle she offered.

"Slàinte!"

"Evíva!"

"So, back to Persephone," I said, shaking out another towel and stretching my legs into the sun for warmth. Lifting the ale to my mouth, my gazed snagged on the tangle of undergrowth and tall grasses where the naiads liked to hide and, I suspected, observe the croft's goings-on. Beyond, distant hills rose, and for the life of me I could not remember what lay between them, and me.

"My daughter longs for a true love, a romantic love, Habonde, and yet the few individuals she has… dabbled with have not fully understood what it means to be consort, or lover, or… whatever, to the Queen of the Underworld. Persephone's responsibilities are distinct from those of Hades. Who, as we know, is her husband in title only."

I dared to ask if Persephone and Astrape had feelings for one another. Demeter turned sad eyes to me. "If it turns out that is so, I would wish for them an easier union."

Curling an arm around my knees, I stared at the slowly moving water and swigged the ale. Last summers' grains filled my mouth, and I savored every nuanced bit of flavor influenced by the soil, the rains, the sun, and Finn's diligent watch over our crops.

"Astrape would understand Persephone's unique duties better than most," I offered.

"True. Plus, there is wiggle room in Persephone's schedule. She'd have even more flexibility were she to have a proxy." Demeter took a long swallow, covering a burp with the back of her wrist. "For that alone, I would be ready to support this wild idea."

"Would you be willing to bless these lands so that we may produce enough by way of fruits and vegetables and grains to feed ourselves, our animals, and have enough left over to share?"

"What are you inferring?" Demeter's brow wrinkled. "Have I been remiss? Are your crops failing? Because if they are, I would look in the mirror for possible reasons why. From what I have heard, you've allowed nigh on two hundred years to pass since you last invited a consort to join you on your altar."

"You are right. I am the one who has been remiss." I really had to stop offending my friends. Chastened, I assured her I'd misspoken, adding, "I've allowed most of our rituals to slip through my fingers and not bothered to initiate them at the next turn of the wheel. Humans consult the internet for answers, not their goddesses and gods, or even the signs and portents provided by a close watch of the wind, or the weather, or the messages in birdsong and animal movements."

Laying on my stomach, I heaved a sigh, sending the surface of the stream rippling and grasses and wildflowers twisting and fluttering. "I should re-name this place Bone-Tired Croft, for that is what I am and what I should not be."

A breeze from the direction of the tent platforms brought the scents of lunch preparation straight to my nostrils. "Enough," I declared, pushing up to my hands and knees and dropping the ale bottle I'd emptied into the basket. "Baubo accused me of self-pity, and I shall have none of that issuing from my mouth from this moment forward."

Demeter waved her bottle in the air. "Here, here," she cheered. "Open me another will you? I shall avail myself of the sun and quiet for a while longer. The mantle of motherhood weighs on me, and I have needed this moment of respite, my sister."

She shaded her eyes as I pressed a cool bottle into her hand. "I thank you, and I shall join you for lunch once I've indulged myself a bit more."

I dried the damp skin underneath my breasts and between my legs, dressed in my jeans and cotton blouse, and bundled the used towels into the basket with the empties. Looping a finger through my sandals' heel straps, I walked barefoot through the wild grass, along the path, delighting in the dappled sun and Demeter's forgiveness. And for the first time in a long, long time, I closed my eyes, slowed my pace, and attuned myself to the goings-on beneath my feet.

Earthworms, ants, and burrowing bugs. Tubers and bulbs. Roots, so many roots and mycelium, fungi and trees communicating through their underground network. I set down the basket. My feet pulled me off the path, toward an old, old oak with knobby roots at its base and mossy patches bandaging its bark. I lay belly down, rested my cheek on a tuft of moss, and waited.

For what, I had no idea. All I knew was that I had been called to this spot, in this moment, on this day, and the longer I gazed at the sporophytes poking out from the mounds of green, the more I welcomed this myopic view of the world. And when the smallest bit of gold glinted from the thickest section of moss, I reached to see what gift awaited.

Pinching the sun-warmed metal, I tugged, and as I made little progress, I whispered, "Thank you, wee mosslings, I can take it from here." With those words, the green softened its hold, allowing a hair clasp to slide upward. The narrow oval the length of my longest finger had pointed ends and was set with tiny freshwater pearls.

I stared, breathless. Because who could breathe when a piece of their long-ago past appeared in such an unforeseeable way?

Pressing the soil flecked piece of jewelry to my lips, I whispered more thanks, more promises that I would listen, that I would no longer forget.

Chapter 18

NO ONE LOOKED at me askance as I emerged from the stand
of oaks with bits of moss and smudges of dirt marking the fronts
of my jeans and blouse. I claimed my damp towel for depositing
the basket of empties under the table set with platters and bowls
and baskets of food and went to wash my hands.

"Is there anything I can do to help?" I asked Jilly. Recovering
the gold clasp had shaken me to the bone and I needed a chore, a
task, something to ground me in the present.

"Everything's under control, Mistress Barleywine," she said,
all bustle and business. "Give us ten more minutes, then I would
be pleased if you would sound the horn for lunch. I know our
menfolk are ready to raid the offerings and I want our guests to
serve themselves first."

"Ten minutes it is." Staring at a timepiece. That could work
—if I had a timepiece to wear. "Have you seen my horn?"

Jilly faced me, her harried exasperation turning to concern.
She held my wrist, stepped up onto a bench, and centered the
moonstone at my forehead. "Are you alright? Something's
happened, I can see it in your eyes."

I unfurled my fingers, showing her the clasp and the red lines indented into my skin.

"Is that yours? If it's yours, you should be happy you found it, m'lady."

"It's not mine," I said. "It belonged to one of my acolytes."

Jilly clucked her tongue and smoothed away the tears spilling from my eyes. I was grateful my back was to the faerie-folk and guests milling closer to the laden table. I neither needed nor wanted anyone to see my sorrow, to see what it cost to not remember—at least until a more convenient time when I could be alone, or with Baubo, and plumb the depths of what lay buried in moss and marrow.

The urisk fumbled in her apron pocket, then hopped to the ground. She ducked under the tablecloth and popped back out, a jar of honey in her hand. She undid the lid, scooped out a spoonful, and raised it to my mouth.

"Take this," she ordered, "and keep taking it, one teaspoon every five minutes. Hawthorn and motherwort will ease your suffering."

I warmed the sweet, viscous liquid on my tongue before letting it slide down my throat. "Thank you, Jilly."

"The Woodsman's looking for you." She pointed behind me. "Don't forget to take the honey and don't forget to come back and eat."

Rhys stared at me. My sex clenched around nothing, and I wished I had the freedom to drag the Woodsman somewhere more private and ask him to stroke away the ache and the unshed tears. Those moments staring at the moss— Why did I stay? Why didn't I push myself off the ground and get up, get away? Iona, whose mother was a nymph and whose nature it was to be a friend to all, had grown up on the banks of a similar river. She had come to me at thirteen, newly finished shedding her first moon blood, her long, black hair braided in her clan's distinctive style marking that joyous occasion. And because a few unruly curls were always breaking free, especially when she lost herself working amongst the herbs, I had gifted her the pair of matching gold and pearl clasps.

Iona was not favored more than any other acolyte. Each received physical gifts; I had more jewelry and baubles than I could ever wear or use, and I delighted in sharing my riches. Iona simply shone, lit from inside by a flame I thought no one could ever put out.

FURIOUS AT THE CRUELTY OF ZEUS' *actions and words, I left Iona to the healer's ministrations and retraced my steps to the temple's hearth. Holding a bundle of dried herbs in one hand, I stripped the stems of their leaves and watched as they fell into the ever-present flames.*

Hestia, Daughter of Rhea.

Hestia, Mother of the Flame.

Hestia, Heart of my Hearth.

Hestia, Virgin unto Herself.

Desperate for counsel, I waited for Hestia to appear, and when she did not, I poured wine into the fire and repeated the invocation.

Hestia, Daughter of Rhea.

Hestia, Mother of the Flame.

Hestia, Heart of my Hearth.

Hestia, Virgin unto Herself.

"HABONDE. *HABONDE.*" Rhys' voice called me back to the present. "You look distraught. Did something happen?"

Clutching a spoon and the jar of honey in one hand, I twined my fingers through his and searched for Baubo. I found her perched on Demeter's carved armchair, speaking with Persephone and Astrape who were sitting cross-legged at her feet.

"Come with me." I pulled Rhys toward the trio and interrupted their conversation. "Baubo, can you see that everyone gets what they need for lunch? Something's come up that I need to take care of before we meet again."

Before she could answer, I turned my attention to Astrape. "Will Zeus be a problem?"

"Not today. But I've summoned more of my team to enhance security. They'll be here throughout the afternoon."

"We've got additional guests arriving, Habs." Baubo uncrossed her legs, patted Persephone's shoulder, and motioned me aside. I followed, holding tight to Rhys and dragging him with us.

"Who else are we expecting?" I asked.

"You *did* say that if anyone thought of others who might wish to know about your idea, that we could invite them."

"Yes, I did say that." The fact that Baubo had maneuvered us out of earshot of the others and was now chewing at her lower lip did not bode well. "So, who's coming?"

"May I first say this is not my fault? Persephone's got some group goddess chat thing going and she might have mentioned—"

"*Might* have, or did?"

"Did. She definitely did, and now we have more goddesses arriving than we have tents and so after lunch Finn will supervise building bunk beds."

I pressed a hand to my stomach. "*Bunk* beds? As in goddesses accustomed to having entire temples and palaces at their disposal will be sleeping one on top of the other?"

Baubo cracked a lascivious grin. "If that's what they want."

I sighed hard. I did not need this complication in my day. Though I did need a laugh. "Give me their names."

She pulled out her notepad and flipped through its numerous pages. "Due to the constraints of preparation and travel times, everyone is fairly local. Thus far we have Scáthách coming in from the Isle of Skye. I believe Astrape suggested her. Saulė's daughters, Meita and Aušrinė, coming in from the Baltic region. Epona. Airmid. Bé Chuille. Creirwy. Oh, and a representative of the Lake Maidens."

She flipped to the next page. I'd heard enough. "Assuming Epona and others might bring their horses and beasts, I'll inform the stable masters to prepare a couple of stalls. I'll be back in an hour."

"Are you passing by the orchard? If so, could you station someone at the portal with directions to the stream and the tents?"

"I can do that," I said. "And could you blow the horn for lunch? I hung it on one of the awning poles. Jilly asked me to let everyone know the food is ready, and I forgot."

"Sure. See you in an hour." Baubo headed back to the gathering.

"We're going to your house?" Rhys asked. I loosened my grip, pressed my palm to one cheek, and the other, and took my second dose of the honey infusion.

"Stables first, then past my house to another section of the croft."

"Lead the way."

The barn for horses and farm animals was situated in the middle of the croft's Eastern quadrant, with access to open meadows and a stream-fed pond. We walked in silence. My mind buzzed with questions, and I felt certain Rhys could tell I wasn't terribly present. I again found his hand. He slowed our pace to a stop and turned me to face him.

"Can you give me a clue as to what's got you worried?"

"I'm not so much worried as I am confused," I confessed. Anxiety welled up my limbs from my knees and elbows. "I'm remembering things, Rhys. I'm not able to control when the memories come, or the order, and each one feels like it's one small piece to a much greater puzzle."

"Would it help if I recounted more of what I recall of our first Beltane together?"

I nodded. "I think it would. Though first things first. Let me pass the message on to the stable masters, and we can talk in the orchard."

We entered the cool, dark barn to the nickering and bleats of horses and goats. Bailoch and his husband Bodhi ran the barn with organized efficiency. The once randy satyrs professed to be excited at the prospect of guests. Rhys introduced himself, and clasped Bodhi's hand in both of his.

"I know you," he said, a wide grin splitting his face. "Both of you."

"Top or bottom?" Bodhi asked. Rhys roared with laughter and pulled Bodhi into a hug.

"Neither. You were entertaining naiads and dryads the first time I came to Bone Fire Croft for Beltane."

"Those were wild times, Woodsman. Wild. Times."

From the barn, another looping path brought us to the backside of the orchard. Hours of sun had warmed the apples, pears, plums, and cherries and the air was redolent with scent. My mouth watered at the thought of sharing fresh picked fruit with Rhys.

"The portal's over there." I shook off the desire to feel his tongue lick pear juice from my skin and pointed to an ancient apple tree. We'd long ago stopped trimming its branches and the sprouts at its trunk. From a distance, the portal had the wild air of a gnarled, bearded druid readying himself to speak. Benches had been positioned beneath nearby trees for travelers just arriving or waiting to depart.

I led Rhys to the bench directly across from the old tree. Rather than sit beside me, he chose the ground. Sitting back on his heels, with his knees framing my feet, he slid his hands behind my calves and held me, grounding me.

I spooned more of the soothing honey infusion into my mouth and let it trickle down my throat.

"You can tell me now," I said.

Gentle squeezes massaged my calves. "I remember a tent draped with gossamer cloth. Your acolytes bathed me, and I was told to await you, face up, on the altar inside the tent. The bonfires cast shadows on the walls and my skin heated as I watched you approach. I was hard and ready before you parted the panels at my feet.

"When you entered the tent, you stole the breath from my body, Habonde. So regal, so beautiful, it took everything I had to remain still. We were not lovers, not yet, and there were protocols to mind and your followers to appease."

"Did we put on a good show?" His recounting teased me away from my anxious place, and his words were every bit as sweet and healing as the honey warming on my tongue.

"I gave no show, my goddess. I gave them the truth."

The ferocity in Rhys' words pressed me against the bench's slatted back. Though fear announced its presence with a whisper in my ear, it was not brought on by the Woodsman. No, that fear resided within me. I exhaled slowly and waited for him to continue.

"You parted the front of your gown, straddled my hips, and coated me with liquid from a bottle left by the attendants. And when you invited me to touch you, my fingers went right to your center." Rhys rose on his knees as he spoke and slid his hands up my outer thighs. I set the jar of honey on the bench. "You needed no lubrication, my goddess, for you were as wet and slick as the morning grass and warmer than the sunrise. You lowered yourself onto me and I stayed still, so very, very still. And though you would not let me enter you, not that first time, a link was formed that I feel to this day. From that moment on, I gave those watching outside the tent a lesson in reverence."

Seeing only bare truth in his eyes, I grabbed Rhys' lush hair and pulled him in for grateful kisses at the sides of his mouth. Gratitude melted into unabashed desire, and I had to push myself away before I asked him to undo my pants.

"Then help me remember, Woodsman. Help me find that link you say we shared."

Chapter 19

RHYS AND I LOCKED EYES. I knew my face broadcast the
conflict playing out within my body. Like me, the Woodsman had
known loss, and lust, and love, and the depth and breadth of his
past thrummed underneath his skin. Drawn to explore, I touched
his jaw, his throat, his wrist, ending at the bands circling his
forearms.

"I will help you," he whispered, and his voice broke a little.
Pulling his arms away, he touched the moonstone resting on my
forehead. "But this is not the place and now is not the time for
dredging up either of our pasts."

Someone cleared their throat, breaking the spell and forcing
the tree at my back to open its sheltering branches and straighten
its trunk. The Woodsman again sat on his heels, and I looked into
the laughing eyes of the Isle of Skye's famed Shadow Warrior.
Her loose black pants likely concealed a lethal arsenal of muscles
and weapons, and a snug, bright pink T-shirt emblazoned with an
upward-pointing spear hugged her hardened curves.

"Scáthách! Welcome to Bone Fire Croft." Rhys and I stood,
and he quickly positioned himself slightly behind me.

"Habonde! It has been far too long since we last broke bread and shared your ale. Astrape said I should come, that you had a proposition I might be interested in hearing."

We embraced, and I inhaled horse sweat and sea air, and leather and metal and the oils the warrior used on both materials. "This is Rhys," I said, stepping aside. "He's one of the Woodsmen and he's here with two of his brethren and Hekate."

"Scáthách."

"Rhys." They clasped the other's right forearm and pressed their foreheads together.

"Did you bring a horse?" I asked. She spun around, confused at my question.

"I *thought* I brought my pony. Hold on a moment." Scáthách's arm disappeared into the portal and reappeared with a set of reins attached to the head of a clearly terrified animal. "Shh, shh, it's alright, Nixie, it's alright. One more step and you'll be here, not there, and we'll get you a treat."

Her skittish beast danced through on slender legs and jerked her head up twice before accepting the apple Scáthách plucked from the portal tree. Nixie ate it in one chomp and promptly scarfed another one from a nearby branch.

"Nixie's a Giara from Sardinia. She was gifted to me, and I thought this trip would be good for her, get her used to portal travel while she's young."

"Bailoch and Bodhi are going to love her. Follow this path to the barn and they'll show you to her stall."

"I'll leave my things there too. She's new to the reins and liable to cause a fuss."

"If you would like, there is room aplenty in my home. And if you'd prefer to sleep in a tent by the stream, that's also an option. And lunch is happening right now."

Scáthách patted Nixie's back and the two trotted off, side by side.

"Looks like the proxy program's going to include classes in weaponry and self-defense," I mused.

"Your what program?"

"I'm likely going to be opening a school and training acolytes. I'll tell you all about it later." I circled my arms around Rhys' waist. "Before you distract me again, let me explain why I brought your here."

"I'm all ears," he teased, drawing me closer to his chest.

"I want to show you what I found yesterday. And we need to hurry because I can't be late to my own party."

"Lead the way."

Inspired by Scáthách, I re-secured my sandal straps and took off at a jog. Running loosened some of what felt stuck inside, and without putting much effort into it, I picked up the pace. Rhys ran alongside me, through the orchard and down the path until I stopped at the outer perimeter of the exposed hearth. The air was still and quiet except for the sound of me catching my breath. The Woodsman didn't seem at all winded.

"I wanted to know if you remembered this place." I crouched and pressed my hand on a squarish paving stone. "Until yesterday, it was hidden under a brush pile."

"I don't," Rhys said, "though its shape feels familiar. Perhaps your Beltane temple was laid out in the same fashion." He began to walk the spiral. Like me, he crouched at one point and dug at the ground with a short knife pulled from the sheath at his thigh. "I'm sure there was a temple here, with corner posts of yew wood. One was here." He rose, followed the spiral, and crouched again. "Another was here, and it's likely we'll find the other two there" —he stood and pointed— "and there."

I joined him. "I started to uncover a hearth. I found bits of wood and rusted nails. The priest who extinguished my fires ordered the hearth boarded over."

"I can rebuild this for you, same as the Beltane temple." He put his knife away and scuffed the toe of his boot across the burnt wood. "I know exactly where the posts should stand. I remember the shape of the roof and the hole at its peak that let out the smoke. I remember where the wood was stacked before it was blessed. I—" His words trailed off as he ran his fingers through his hair and turned in a slow circle, surveying the vine-clogged trees surrounding three quarters of the clearing. "Though I do not know this place, I remember that festival like it was yesterday. Your acolytes guided townspeople in from the dirt road. Showed them where to set their blankets and baskets of food. Everyone worked together to erect the May Poles and braid wreaths of flowers."

I didn't try to stopper my tears. "And I can barely remember any of it, Rhys, except that I know in my bones that this bowl of dead ashes right here was my primary hearth. What does that say about me, that that's all I can recall? Did something happen here, beyond the little bits I've gathered? Do I deserve this obscurity, if my own past is as dark to my own eyes as the far side of the moon?"

He didn't answer. Instead, he traversed the paving stones, pulled a sickle blade out of thin air, and hacked at the chest-high wall of vines and brambles clouding the spaces between individual trees on the opposite side of the spiral. He kept swinging his blade until he'd made a hole he could pass through. The shadows absorbed him, sickle and all.

"Rhys," I yelled. Waited. Called his name again, adding, "I've got to go back to the tents."

Silence settled around me. No droning of insect wings, no birdsong. I approached the hole in the bramble and ducked through. Trunks of near equal size rose from the ground in rows like chiseled stones in a forgotten graveyard. Branches thick with needles joined overhead, filtering out sunlight and keeping the air cool and somber . Chills raced along my arms as the species of tree and the purpose of the ordered rows became clear. Yew trees, each marking someone's final resting place.

Heart in my throat, I moved toward the nearest tree and traced the vertical lines of peeling bark. I saw no words or symbols carved into the trunk, no stones, or shells, or vases for flowers at its base. I moved to the next tree, and the next, and at the fourth, I found what I both needed to see and dreaded. An agate cabochon with swirls of deep orange and greyish white, enclosed in a silver setting, it's chain nearly absorbed by the tree's growth.

I placed my palm over the agate and willed my memories forward.

Eilidh.

Fia.

Leith.

Lilidh.

Maesie.

Kenna.

Iona.

Every acolyte received a polished stone to wear on their forehead or around their neck. Gathered on walks through the highlands or along the coast, the agates were as different as their wearer, worn as a sign of their connection to the land. I wrapped my arms around the trunk and pressed my check to the bark.

Eilidh loved brambleberries and wearing yellow stockings she dyed herself from turmeric. As the acolytes studied the ways of herbs and plants, some chose to follow the Healer's path; others were drawn to use their knowledge to enhance cooking and baking, or for creating beauty compounds. Eilidh loved pulling color from plants. She was forever experimenting on her sistren's undergarments, using flowers, herbs, and roots, and I suspected she was drawn to adding as much color to her world as she could after surviving the drabbest of upbringings.

If what I suspected was true, every tree might hold an embedded gemstone. My task on another day would be to find each one, and to remember the young woman to whom it belonged.

I left the well-ordered copse with a heavy heart. Rhys' footsteps sounded behind me. "I was drawn to see what lay behind the mess of berry vines," he said, "and once I was through, I kept going. I heard you call, and I answered."

"I— I didn't hear you. Did you walk through?"

"Ay. The stand of yews is not that large." He quickened his pace and as soon as he drew up beside me, he wrapped his arm around my shoulder. "They were planted as a burial ground."

"Was that obvious to you?"

"The Woodsmen speak with trees, Habonde. I knew right away."

"And did the trees say anything I should know?"

He squeezed my upper arm and let me go. "Only that most of them are missing the bones of their dead."

THE WALK back to the stream and the tents gave me time to tuck Rhys' discovery into a compartment and seal it away until I could deal with it. By the time we made it back to the food table, lunch was no longer being served. Jilly waved us over and lifted the cloth covering a round tray, revealing wide bowls of spicy vegetable tagine. "I saved the last of the stew for you," she said, "and a pitcher of iced tea. Though I'm afraid the ice has melted."

"Thank you, Jilly." Suddenly, I was starving. "This smells divine."

"I was going to make a coupla cold sandwiches, but when I saw your face from afar you looked like you needed something warm in your belly."

I carried the tray to a shaded spot away from the bustle of urisk crews clearing the cooking and serving area. Rhys brought over the pitcher and two glasses and settled his back against an oak. We made our offerings to the ground below and the sky above and began to eat. Though the cold, heavy sensation I'd had since leaving the grave markers dissolved, the voices inside my head urging me to share more with Rhys would not quiet.

"I've been having dreams," I began. "And the meaning I've gleaned from them thus far is I must look deeper into the past, into *my* past, while simultaneously making plans for the future, for all goddesses' futures." I stabbed at a chunk of roasted aubergine and lifted it from my bowl. "I'm not the only one in the world having these dreams, but I seem to be the only one from these islands and northern Europe." I popped the dripping bite of savory stew into my mouth and chewed.

"You mentioned acolytes, and a school?" Rhys asked. Swallowing as I nodded, I eased the tightness in my throat with a long drink of tea, followed by a spoonful of the herbal honey Jilly had added to the tray. I'd forgotten the first jar at the bench in the orchard.

"I trained acolytes before, and I hope to be training them again. If I am to regain my stature, I will need help." *So much help.* I set down my spoon and focused on the Woodsman's openly curious face. "I am a builder of community, not of… of buildings, and if your offer to reconstruct the temple of the hearth was genuine, I'd like to take you up on it."

"It was genuine, Habonde. And what of this school?"

I breathed deep. I'd eaten fast, my belly was full, and my chest continued to feel constricted by the day's unexpected events and revelations. "The school would teach Magicals the ways of serving the Goddess. Selected students would go on to receive further training to then act as a proxy for a particular goddess. There are fewer of us, and so many more of them, and—"

"'Them,' as in humans?'"

"Mm-hmm, especially non-believing humans."

Rhys set aside his empty bowl and settled against the tree's trunk. He closed his eyes, and I seized the opportunity to gaze at him unabashedly. Fragmented images rose and faded, of other meals shared beneath these trees, beside this stream, in my home, followed by dessert and other treats in my bed. At times his hair was longer, his strong jawline covered in a beard. Always his arms were decorated with tattoos, not these wooden bracers.

He'd brought me pleasure then, yet there was more to these flashes of the past besides the handsome man leaning against a tree. When he was still, as he was now, melancholy cloaked his shoulders. In that moment I sensed—no, I *knew*—that the work ahead, the emotional work, carried the potential to hurt us both.

Chapter 20

BAUBO SNUCK up behind me and pressed a demitasse cup of steaming hot espresso into my hand.

"Thought you might need this," she whispered. "Everything's just about ready under the awning."

I unfolded my legs and stood to shake out the stiffness. Rhys' breathing had turned into a soft snore, and I wasn't about to wake him. "You are an absolute *goddess*. What did you do, haul your fancy machine all the way down here?" Baubo complained about my "country kitchen" and its lack of modern amenities nearly every visit. Though I didn't mind her good-natured ribbing, I'd added a couple expensive accessories to keep her happy. The food processor was one, and an espresso maker that did everything but wash the cups afterward was another.

"Such blasphemy! No, Jilly had her stovetop pot going."

"Anything you want to fill me in on?" I asked, sipping carefully as we made our way to the awning. Many of the arrivals had their backs to me, and most had claimed the wooden seats built the day before. I counted nearly thirty, including Jilly and

June Bug, and other urisk in their teens and upwards. "I'm thrilled to see so many locals are interested."

"Me, too."

"Any signs of trouble between our guests?"

Baubo snorted, then stopped me with a tug at my blouse. "Let me go through who's here. And by the way, everyone who was invited, accepted. Okay, there's Hekate, her Lampedes, Demeter, Persephone, and Brigid. No sign of trouble there, and Brig's practically adopted Junie, so I think the girl's a shoo-in for her first proxy."

I raised my empty cup in the direction of the tall goddess in the bright pink T-shirt. "I met Scáthách as she and her horse came out of the portal. And I think I recognize Airmid."

When I'd entertained the goddess of healing and herbs in times past, she'd often taken on the physical qualities of whatever plant or plant family currently held her attention. If her proclivity still held, her brown, ankle-length wrap dress with its shaggy surface signaled she might be exploring mushrooms or tree barks.

Airmid had spoken often of her lifelong quest to catalogue the curative and destructive uses of every known plant. Instead of traveling the worlds and doing all the work herself, she enlisted the help of healers and herbalists from every tradition. I would tap her for details about the cooperative they'd created, as well as the possibility of her teaching a course.

"Epona's next to Scáthách," Baubo whispered. "Persephone is sitting between Flidais' daughter, Bé Chuille, and Saulė's daughter, Aušrinė."

Bé Chuille was a skilled enchantress, who'd turned her ability to transmute trees and rocks into monsters, into the more lucrative and life-affirming profession of landscape gardening. Aušrinė I knew little about, though her mother might be interested in being part of the training program. Either that or starting her own. The beloved sun goddess had tremendous scope to her power and influence.

My gaze was drawn to a young woman sitting on a low bench off the to the side. Wearing modified safety glasses and a leather apron, she was extremely focused on whatever project lay in her lap.

"Who's that?"

"Creirwy. She's become a renowned jeweler . Her work is gorgeous. Persephone promotes it all over Magical social media."

My fingers sought and found the moonstone on my forehead, and my heart twinged remembering the agate cabochon I'd found embedded in the yew tree. There could be—no, *should* be—a place for learning the art of adornment and understanding its importance in ritual.

"We need her," I whispered in Baubo's ear. "We need them all."

"Our girl Persephone has her finger on the pulse of the world outside Bone Fire Croft."

"She certainly does," I agreed, tucking the empty cup into my back pocket. "And it's time for me to call this meeting to order. You ready to take more notes?"

"Always and forever."

I entered the shaded area. Conversation stilled as I stopped within the clear patch in the center and turned a purposeful circle to collect everyone's attention. Awash in anticipation, I swiped my palms on my jeans and quietly cleared my throat.

"Welcome." I turned another circle, this time greeting each attendee one by one, be they goddess or denizen of Bone Fire Croft. Speaking their names aloud, seeing nods of acknowledgement and faces light up, brought me to my own center. Beyond the awning, Astrape's guards waved as I acknowledged their roles, and the unexpectedly clear blue vista at their backs gave me hope there would be no more interruptions from the skyward realm.

"Bone Fire Croft has seen many gatherings, yet over the past few centuries, things have gotten a lot quieter around here," I began. "At some point, I stopped questioning why our gatherings had grown smaller and smaller. Why fewer and fewer acolytes showed up on my doorstep, eager to serve their goddess and their communities. It took me awhile to even notice the old ways were disappearing and with them, the old ones." Smiling, I paused to add, "Technically, I am an 'old one' and though I am very much here" —I patted my thighs, butt, and breasts— "I am not well known out there."

Gesturing outward, I shrugged. "It is time I take responsibility for my part in the losses I can see, and for the losses I've yet to uncover."

I explained to the newcomers the worlds-wide spate of dreams and their common themes. I reviewed the conversations flying between me and our kith and kin, and expounded on why I thought these dreams were happening. Finally, I painted the morning's proposed respite and training propositions in broad strokes. No one interrupted, and when I finished, I was ready to roll up my sleeves and start digging the foundation of the Bone Fire Croft School.

Goddesses weren't known for waiting their turn to speak, and it seemed like the majority had something they wanted to say. Demeter raised her arm and shook the bundle of hammered gold wheat sheaves she'd pulled from her bag. When that didn't quiet the crowd, she whistled.

"Habonde, thank you for your lengthy and detailed introduction. So that we may all have the opportunity to air our thoughts and opinions, I propose that the one who holds the sacred wheat, speaks, and leaves the chaff for later. Agreed?"

I read the bobbing heads and moving lips as consent and added my own.

"Good. Our generous host presented a smaller group of us with some of this information earlier today, which means I have had time to ponder the broader scope of her proposal." She rose and joined me in the center, twirling the wheat stems in her fingers. "Not only do I applaud the idea of a training program, but I also pledge my support. I shall donate coin to ensure teachers are paid a good wage for their knowledge. And I shall use the powers I was blessed with to boost these hectares' output of fruits, grains, and vegetables."

Facing me, she beckoned me closer and kissed my moonstone. "Who would like to speak next?"

Persephone's hand shot up. My surprise nearly knocked me on my butt. Demeter passed the wheat to her daughter and returned to her chair.

"Habonde. Mother," Persephone said, planting herself in the circle's center with an actress' sense of timing. "Quite a few of you are here because I asked you to come. And the main reason I requested your presence was because you each have skills I would like to learn, skills that any being gifted with magic and the desire to train as a goddess' proxy should have.

"I also asked some of you here because we are the daughters of primal mothers and often our desires are overshadowed by their light." She turned to Demeter. "I mean no offense, mother. It feels safe to speak here, and as you know, I've got a lot going on."

"No offense taken," Demeter said. "And know that I am listening, beloved daughter."

Tears glistened in the corners of Persephone's eyes, adding sparkle to her remarkable beauty. "I also asked some of you here because you, like me, weren't always given choices in your lives about who you were to become or who you were to be partnered with.

"I, for one, am a work in progress and I am beyond ready to rewrite my current chapter. I think that if I had a proxy who could share the obligations I have to Hades, to Hekate, and to the underworld, I would stand a better chance of rebuilding my mental health. A *much* better chance."

Persephone shoved the wheat into my hands and launched herself into Demeter's wide-open arms. I heard Demeter whisper to her daughter, over and over, "I'm so proud, I'm so proud."

Scáthách rose and made her way forward. I handed over the wheat and she examined the stems until Persephone's sniffles quieted. "I train all manner of Magicals in self-defense. I see the need for these proxies to be well-versed in the use of both defensive *and* offensive techniques, as well as the use of weapons. Traditional and modern weapons—as in *this* century modern," she added. "I cannot completely abandon my school to be here full-time, but I could see committing to up to four, five months out of the year. Habonde, you have my support."

Airmid was already making her way towards us. Scáthách passed the bundle of wheat over, then lifted Persephone off her feet and into a hug before finding her seat near Epona.

"Like others here," Airmid began, "I consider a portion of the knowledge I hold to be essential for any potential trainee or proxy. A *portion*, not all, as that would take *for-ev-er*." Airmid drew out the word's three syllables. "And like others, I already have apprentices I am committed to working with."

She tapped one palm with the wheat. "I have questions, Habonde, and concerns. Many, many concerns. The medicine contained within plants needs knowing hands to draw it forth, and discerning minds to direct in the appropriate ways. Plant medicine goes far beyond easing menstrual cramps and headaches.

"In the wrong hands, plant medicine becomes a weapon, much like Scáthách's blades and Astrape's lightning, that can be used to control, maim, even kill. And so, I would ask, who will elucidate the general guidelines and unbreakable rules by which these potential proxies conduct themselves by? And what of punishment, should they take what we teach and use it against others that are weaker or uninformed? Or even against us?"

The ever-elegant goddess ended her turn by giving the wheat to me and taking hold of my elbows. This close, I noticed the tiniest of mushrooms that had taken up residence in her hair, and how she smelled like the forest floor after a cooling rain.

"Habonde, you have my *conditional* support."

Chapter 21

WHILE A COUPLE of those who hadn't spoken waved their arms, Jilly and June Bug stood. She mimed pouring drink into a glass, and I shook my head. Motioning to the others to wait, I waved the urisk forward, reminding Jilly once she was closer that she was here as a potential teacher and Junie as a potential trainee. They hugged me at the same time, and I handed Jilly the wheat. Her eyes went wide and round.

"You want me to *speak*, m'lady?"

"There's no running a training program without you and your amazing squad. Seriously, Jilly, look around at what you've accomplished on extremely short notice."

"In that case, I *do* have a few things I would like to say." Jilly squared her shoulders and lifted the wheat.

"This is for those in the back who can't see me." She projected her voice as though "those in the back" were a passel of faerie-folk children trying to sneak fresh baked cookies into their pockets.

"My name is Jillian, and I supervise the cooking and serving of food for gatherings such as these here on Bone Fire Croft. I may be short of stature, but I am not short of opinions and the means to express them. Just ask my husband Finnock."

Her laughter invited the others to join with her, as well as shouted thanks for the food. Jilly patted the air with the wheat. "I've watched this place age, and it's not been a graceful passage. The magic I hear tales of hardly exists here anymore, not in the ways the stories describe, and I for one would like to see our magic grow.

"Every urisk I know works hard. We teach our children to work hard—when they're not eatin' and playin' and sleepin', that is—and we teach them to love the land they live on. And though I hadn't thought of it until right now, when Mistress Habonde brought us up to speak to you, I realized I *do* have things I could teach. Such as how to feed the likes of all of you."

More laughter, and Jilly handed the wheat to her oldest child. Junie blushed and, like her mother, raised the wheat over her head. "Hello! I'm June Bug. I am fifteen years old, and today I learned I would love to train as a proxy." She darted a quick side glance at her mother. "And go to regular school of course. But mostly, I wish to serve Brigid Herself." She grabbed Jilly's hand for support and gave the wheat to Brigid as they returned to their seats. Brigid thanked her and handed the wheat to Hekate.

The Queen of the Witches unfolded long legs clad in black pants. She'd traded live snakes for ones of richly patinated gold, and leather for the cooling comfort of linen. Her sleeveless, knee length tunic was split up both sides to her waist and she moved with elegant precision. Standing in front of me, she lowered her voice for my ears only.

"I support the premise, Habonde. Before you make any concrete plans, you must come with me to the underworld. I have a task for you to complete, and I must speak to you of the Woodsman and his debt to me."

She shifted slightly enough I could see the fine lines in the corners of her eyes and mouth. She looked far better than she had the night of my journey, and with time and care I knew she would look and feel even more robust.

"When do you want to go?" I asked.

"Tonight. I will have you back by sunrise tomorrow."

Pressing my lips together, I nodded. "Tonight, it is. Where should I meet you?"

She stared for a beat before replying, "The graveyard."

I knew exactly which graveyard she meant, and her words sent a chill down my spine. The golden wheat sheaths had grown cold in her grip and after she placed them in my hand, I couldn't rid myself of the bundle fast enough. Searching the crowd for anyone who had yet to speak, I chose Creirwy, daughter of my friend, Ceridwen.

She'd discarded the leather apron and safety glasses. Delicate chains draped her full, lush figure, every link an advertisement for her jewelry business, and bracelets lined her arms.

"Thank you, auntie Habs. Mum says she plans to visit soon."

"Tell her she is welcome any time."

"Ooh, I love your moonstone," she added, touching my forehead lightly and peering at the stone from different angles before turning it over. "Hmm, there's a story engraved in its setting. Did you know?"

"I did. And I'm embarrassed to admit I've forgotten the details."

"I get that a lot. I'll translate it for you whenever you'd like." Her kohl lined eyes stared into mine, and the next moment her back was to me. "Hi, I'm Creirwy. Most of you know my mother, Ceridwen. I design and craft jewelry. In the human world, I'm known as 'Ciri'. I love creating bling, as you can see by my attire, and it's been an excellent source of income from mundanes and Magicals alike. But I have two—"

Pausing, she tapped her chin and gazed skyward. "Fortes is

the word, I think. I create and imbue talismans for personal and corporate use, and I'm a whizz at using social media to promote myself and my products and therefore, increase my bottom line. Which is likely why 'Sephie invited me here."

Creirwy paced the edge of the open circle, emphasizing her words with gentle jabs of the wheat. "In order for this project to take off, we would have to get the word out, we would have to design a… a recruitment campaign. And that means we have to know exactly what it is we—as goddesses and mythological beings—deliver with our gifts, and what it is we want from a potential proxy."

She pointed at me. "Auntie Habs, I predict there will be many lists in your future."

That got a laugh, and she added, "I am willing to get this particular ball rolling, so before anyone leaves, please see me. I need to know the best way to reach you, whether it's email, dm's, scrying, what ev." Creirwy stopped again. "Oh, wait, is there someone else who'd like to do this? I have a habit of walking into meetings and volunteering to get shit done if it's something I know I can do."

She tossed the wheat to me and once the resounding quiet answered her question, she sashayed back to her seat near Persephone.

"I am more than willing to hand this aspect of the Proxy Project over to you," I said. "I hadn't even gotten to the recruitment aspect yet, so yes, everyone, give Creirwy your contact information and start answering the questions, what do you do and how do you do it, and what qualities do you think your proxy should have."

I hadn't called an end to the meeting, and already heads were bowed over phones and paper. I whistled lightly and waved the wheat. "Anyone else like to speak?"

"I would say a few words." Bé Chuille stood. More than any

other attendee except Airmid, she looked the part of a magical being. A confirmed witch, sorceress, and enchantress, everything about her swirled, from her hair to her garments, to the wildflowers floating toward her from the field beyond the awning. She stepped around the seats blocking a straight path to the center and accepted the wheat. The stems, leaves, beard, and plump kernels came alive, winding around her forearm like golden bracelets Creirwy might have crafted.

"Similar to my dear friend, I have adapted over the centuries. I too derive a great many clients, and therefore a great deal of income, from being active on social media. While there's more I could add to what Ciri said, this is not the time. What I *would* offer is my knowledge as a landscape designer. I would be honored to work alongside Airmid to design herb gardens, and with anyone else looking to maximize every bit of Bone Fire Croft. There is not much we can do about climate changes, not with our diminished powers. I'll work with what's already here, plan for the worst, and hope for the best."

She gently disentangled the wheat from her arm and returned it to me. As far as I could tell, everyone who wanted to speak had taken their turn, all but the representative sent by the Society for the Protection of the Lake Maidens. Though the Maidens weren't goddesses, they worked with water magic and illusion, and I was aware they had long ago reformed their penchant for using humans against their will.

The representative shook her head and drew her diaphanous scarf over her face when I looked at her.

"I think it would be good to get up, stretch your legs, wander the meadows or swim in the stream and let this proposition stew. Everyone is welcome to spend the night, and I have been informed that my head groundskeeper and his crew have been hard at work building more beds for the tents by the stream." I couldn't think of anything else to say, until I noticed Jilly waving her arms and pointing to her mouth. "Oh, and Jillian would like everyone to know an evening meal will be served at seven, and you should speak with her if you have specific dietary requests."

Jilly gave me a thumbs up before being surrounded by Persephone and her crew.

"I thought that went well." Baubo elbowed my side and showed me her stack of notebooks.

"How many of those did you fill?" I asked, mouth agape.

"Oh, not all the pages for sure. I used my enchanted pens, which lets me write in more than one place at once."

"Do I need to get you a laptop?"

"Pfft, the old ways have always suited me and besides, enchanted pens never run out of ink," she said, grinning proudly. "And enchanted paper self-duplicates."

Chapter 22

I FOUND RHYS, Hades, Minthe, and the two other Woodsmen sharing glasses of ale and lemonade underneath my pergola. I walked to the opposite end of the table, poured myself an ale, and downed half the glass before I dared speak.

"Hades. Minthe. The two of you showing up here, together —" Holding my glass near the rim, I swung the bottom in Minthe's direction. "With you obviously pregnant. Why go public here, now? And before you answer that, hello, I'm Habonde." I offered my hand to the nearest Woodsman. He brought my fingers to his lips and kissed my knuckles while rising from the bench. He stood a head taller than Rhys, with a muscled body and other generous assets his snug pants and T-shirt did nothing to disguise.

"I'm Siggi, and that's Pim." He tilted his head on the direction of the third Woodsman.

"Have we met?" I asked, forcing my eyes to stay on his and not wander downward.

"I believe you might remember me. Pim is newer to our clan and has not participated in group work with either me or Rhys."

I took another swallow of the cool ale. "'Group work'? That's an interesting way to phrase it."

Siggi didn't blush. "We raised an abundance of energy that evening, and for that your land was grateful."

"As was I, I hope," I said, swallowing back my discomfort. "I'm afraid I'm having issues with my memory."

Turning from Siggi, I shook hands with the somewhat shy Pim, then addressed the King of the Underworld and the pregnant nymph. "What's going on?"

Hades clenched his hands together and leaned in to speak. Minthe squeezed his arm. "I needed to meet with Hades, and I needed somewhere safe. The clutch of naiads living upstream of your croft has given me a place to live for the duration of this pregnancy. Though Kokytus is my home, the River of Misery it is not where I wish to birth this child."

Minthe was employed by her father, the River God, Kokytus, to use her bright-scented magic to ease the pain underlying the lamentations. "Who has taken on your duties?"

"Hades. And others."

"If I may I speak." Hades continued without waiting for me to answer. "Charon will ferry the souls to the underworld once they have received a proper burial in the aboveworld. I am working day and night to see those burials happen. I have help, and though it is not enough, it keeps me busy and away from Persephone's tiresome complaining."

Rhys tapped Hades' arm. "If I may interrupt? It appears this conversation doesn't require our input, and my men and I are needed elsewhere. I wish you both luck."

I reached for his sleeve. "Rhys? Could we talk at dinner?"

He nodded and left with Siggi and Pym. I took a seat and addressed Hades. "You've put me in an awkward position. The naiads do not require my permission to provide shelter for Minthe, but at this very moment, Persephone is on the grounds of Bone Fire Croft. Not only is she my guest but she is also likely to be an integral part of a school I plan to build here." I crossed my arms. "Have you and Persephone talked about just divorcing? Because she's miserable, and I can't see how hiding a baby from her will help."

"It's… complicated." Hades shrugged. Minthe glared.

"It's only complicated because you and your brothers *like* it complicated," she said. "One of my conditions in agreeing to go through with this, was that you apologize to Persephone, be honest with her about my situation, and ask her what *she* wants. It doesn't seem to me you've done *any* of that."

Hades studied his fingernails. "I've tried to talk to her."

"'Tried'? Godsdamnit, Hades. I took a risk coming here, and you—" The nymph buried her face in her arms.

"I think the two of you, and maybe all three of you, need a therapist, or a marriage counselor, or at the least, a… a moderator."

Minthe lifted her head and looked up at me. "Would you—"

"Absolutely not. Though I would consider creating a neutral place for you to meet."

"That would be a start." She kicked Hades under the table. "The sooner we have these conversations, the sooner I can get on with figuring out how I'm going to do this," she added, rubbing her belly. "This child is due at the end of October, and I refuse to live my life as a potted plant."

As touching as the scene before me was becoming, I had to set ground rules. "Until I hear that you've spoken with Persephone, please go back to the naiads and ask them to situate you across the stream and closer to the Lake of Secrets."

Though I had vague memories of buildings and such beyond the stands of trees, I couldn't recall any particulars. I knew, however, that the naiads maintained a small encampment near the lake's bank.

"Am I welcome to stay there when I visit?" Hades asked.

"As long as you meet my conditions, yes, including that you wait to speak with Persephone until after our meetings have concluded. And Hades," I added, "the sooner you stop thinking of Persephone as your wife and treating her as a thing you can control rather than an autonomous woman deserving of happiness, the sooner you'll be free to create the life you profess to want." I whistled for my birds and instructed them to bring Hades and Minthe to the section of the stream closest to the orchard.

The two departed with their avian escorts. I closed the screen door behind me, and the heavier wooden door, and blew out a breath. Keeping a balanced sense of power between goddesses and gods and Magical beings in general took a lot of energy, and I had an hour to recharge before I would again be on hostess duty. There were many things I could be doing, and the only thing I wanted was to soak in my tub. Alone.

I turned on the faucets and pushed in the plug. A hefty cup of Epsom salts would soothe muscles sore from clearing my hearth. Perusing my shelf of bath oils, I chose a wake-me-up blend heavy on the rosemary for its connection to memory and wondered if I should book a session with Mnemosyne. I stripped off my clothes, gathered my hair into a thick bun atop my head, and lowered myself into the water until I was nearly submerged.

Snippets of conversation and scenes from the day flooded my mind, especially once I closed my eyes.

Bathing Brigid, and later, swimming with Demeter.

Rhys. Bending my knees, I sank lower in the tub and traced lines up the front of each leg, and down my inner thighs. Cupping myself, I massaged gently as if to will my body into remembering more of this… thing the Woodsman and I shared in the past. Instead, others intruded on the intimate moment I might have had with myself.

Hades and Minthe.

Iona and Zeus' henchman.

Zeus again, riding in on his bundle of angry clouds.

Persephone and Astrape holding each other in the field. 'Seph contributing to the success of the meeting by having the foresight to invite other daughters of strong goddess-mothers. She navigated a more public world—one I rarely interacted with anymore—and if what I'd witnessed today meant she was finally throwing off her paternal yoke, I was all for it.

Hekate. The way she spoke to me, and only me, during the afternoon meeting. What did she mean when she said she had a task for me to complete? And what was Rhys' debt? Speculating would get me nowhere, so I left that question alone and focused again on the Woodsman.

He'd noticed I wasn't in my present-mind when I'd returned from the stream, Eilidh's hair clip clutched in my hand. He had come willingly to my outdoor hearth; spotted things I had not as I uncovered the stones; knew to uncover the yew trees and investigate further.

Stretching my leg so my toes could reach the faucet, I added more hot water to the tub and closed my eyes.

Eilidh.

Fia.

Leith.

Lilidh.

Maesie.

Kenna.

Iona.

A chorus of girlish voices raised in laughter and camaraderie met my ears. I entered the bathing room to the sight of the naturally heated, spring-fed pool filled with joyous, naked acolytes. Their plain linen robes hung from hooks pounded into the cave walls, their deerskin sandals had been tucked under the stone benches—and that was where order ended, and chaos began.

Flower petals in a riot of colors littered the floor, the girls' hair and shoulders, and floated on the surface of the pool. Hanging from more hooks were stockings in the same shades as the flowers: pink, blue, lavender, violet, orange, and red.

"What is the cause of such exuberance?" I had to yell to be heard, and while I waited for an answer, I counted heads and sets of stockings, and came up missing Eilidh and her meadow buttercup-colored favorites.

"And where is Eilidh?" I added, once the pool had quieted.

Each acolyte spun in place. Two dove beneath the steamy surface and bobbed back up, shaking their heads. Maesie slowly raised her hand, and all eyes turned to her as she spoke.

"A man came to the temple and Eilidh spoke with him. She said he had need of a hearth log for his new home, and she offered to bring it to him."

"Did she give you any other details, this man's name, or where he lives?"

"She said he was rich, and had clean hair, and that he offered to buy her a gift if she brought the fire this night."

I gazed at the innocent faces, pink-cheeked from the water's heat and the joy they found in each other's company, and I knew with cold certainty Eilidh was in trouble. "I shall go and find your sister. I want all of you to stay inside until I get back." Squatting near the pool's tiled edge, I added, "No one is to leave the safety of this temple, am I understood?"

"Yes, Mistress Habonde," was repeated by one and all. Rising to my feet, I left the bathing room for my private quarters, where I dressed as a man and armed myself for battle.

LUKEWARM WATER LAPPED against my breasts. Resting my arms on the curved rim of the tub, I waited for my racing heart to slow before I sat up, swept aside the bubbles, and cupped my hands below the surface. Lifting the water closer to my lips, I spoke the lines that would summon Mnemosyne.

Mistress of memory, speak to me.

Help my ears hear the songs of this land,

The voices of the beings who have lived and loved
And died while under my care.
Mistress of memory, show me what I cannot see,
Ease my fear and open my eyes.

"I AM HERE, dear Habonde. You may open your eyes."

"Thank you for answering, Nemmie." The goddess' face hovered below the surface of the water, and I struggled to keep my body still. She blinked and nodded, and almost disappeared.

"I'm staring into a teacup," she explained, "hence the blurry reception. You have a question?"

"I have so many questions."

"I'm afraid I have a scant few minutes. I'm in Istanbul in a tea house overlooking the Bosporus, waiting for my sisters."

"Then I shall begin with the question pressing heaviest against my heart." I breathed in through my nose, and out. "What happened on Bone Fire Croft that was so consequential that I have lost my memories of it?"

"Why is this question important to you?"

"Over the past two days, I've had flashes of memories. They come when I am bathing, or near water. They come when I am with this man, this Woodsman, touching him, breathing his scent. They come in bits and pieces, and I feel ill-prepared to see the event in its entirety."

My tears fell into the tiny scrying area. Frowning, Mnemosyne tilted her head, pressed her fingertip to her lips, then touched the tea in her cup. "I feel your pain, dear friend. And for that to happen with this distance between us, the weight you carry must indeed be great.

"Memory retrieval is not work any of us should do alone. Usually, I would send one of my assistants, or invite the questioner to my estate. In this case, I shall come to you. Every living thing on your croft has the potential to hold memories. Having a look at theirs should help us recover yours."

Mnemosyne disappeared and returned with reading glasses perched on her nose. "How does tomorrow afternoon sound?"

I nearly pressed my face into my palms in relief, an act which would have severed our connection. "Tomorrow afternoon is perfect."

"Good. My sisters are here, and I must go. Oh, and Habonde, if that Woodsman is around, ask him to stay."

———————————————————

Chapter 23

———————————————————

THE NIGHT AIR was cool for this time of year. I added a
cardigan sweater to my T-shirt and loose linen pants, and socks
for my feet, and slipped into my gardening clogs on my way out
the kitchen door. I'd not yet used the wooden ring Rhys had
loaned me, but tucked it deep into one of my pockets. I was
tempted to turn the ring, to see how quickly the Woodsman could
get to me, but we were about to have dinner together and then I
would leave with Hekate.

I glanced down as I walked. I wasn't sure how one dressed for
a visit to the underworld. Winter jacket and boots? All-black
attire? And aside from the moonstone now hanging around my
neck, I carried no protective crystals, no talismans of personal
power. Standing taller, I continued up the hill where I'd planted
my laundry lines and paused to soak in the hustle and buzz
below, and to remind myself that above all else, Hekate and I
both were blessed with weighty duties.

The dead would suffer if she shirked her duties as I have mine.

After losing Eilidh to the sickeningly violent man who
presented himself at my temple, pleaded for a hearth log, and left

with a trusting young woman in my stead, I'd become incandescent with guilt-fueled rage. I canceled all celebrations, refused to consider all petitions for blessing new hearths and new unions, and hired a sorceress to construct magical wards around the outbuildings where the acolytes lived and studied.

Lifting my gaze to the present time, I saw Demeter with her arms around Persephone and realized the mother and I had more in common that I'd ever thought to consider. My lands, and the humans and Magicals who populated these hills and valleys, had suffered because I went into a mourning so profound that I lost track of night and day. And rather than tend to my hearth fire with care, I threw logs on it at will, causing flames to light the sky for days on end and smoke to lay thick overhead.

A year passed before a sense of normalcy returned to Bone Fire Croft, and that was only because Hestia had saved me. Hestia and the remaining acolytes. With their help, I had come to my senses. I had been made to understand the effect my actions were having on those to whom I was bound by their faith in me, and the powers granted me by the great goddess herself.

There was more to this memory's backstory, I was sure of it.

"A pint for your thoughts?"

Without realizing it, I'd wandered into the grove of oak trees. Goddesses mingled with dryads, naiads, urisk, and others. Baubo placed the cool tankard in my hand and planted herself in front of me. Her gaze darted from my face to my clothes.

"You look like you've seen a ghost," she commented, "and your sweater's inside out."

I twisted my arm and noticed the seam. Baubo was right. I handed back the beer and quickly fixed my sweater. "I've been seeing lots of ghosts, and I'll be seeing more tonight."

"Tell me why and tell me quick. I have a date to dine with Pim."

Wrapping the halves of the sweater across my body, I sipped

the ale and waited for its coolness on my tongue to travel down my throat and become warmth in my belly. "Hekate's taking me to the underworld after dinner. She said there's something I need to do, and things I need to know about Rhys."

"Interesting."

"Interesting?"

"Well, not everyone gets a post-prandial visit to the kingdom of the dead with Keeper of the Keys as their escort." Baubo's mirthful eyes studied me over the rim of her tankard. "Let's just hope you can find your way back. I'm not running your school for wanna-be goddesses by myself."

Rocked by giggles, I couldn't safely raise my glass, or I'd end up wearing the ale. "What would I do without you?"

"Let's hope neither of us ever has to find out. Tell me true, though. Are you okay?"

This wasn't the moment to share the full scope of my pervading sense of disconnect, not even with Baubo. She deserved to enjoy herself with Pim, unencumbered by any worries about my mental state.

"I will be," I assured her. "I scried for Mnemosyne, and she's promised to be here tomorrow afternoon."

"I was planning to go home once all your guests had left, but I'll stay on if you want me to."

I pulled my best friend in for a one-armed side hug. "I'll be fine."

Baubo left me and set her drink beside Pim's. While I scanned the crowd for Rhys, I noted who was still here, and how those who lived on the croft and those who were visiting had chosen to congregate. Persephone, Creirwy, Bé Chuille talked animatedly while passing around phones and shiny baubles Ciri kept pulling from her bag. Demeter, Brigid, Hekate, and Airmid gathered closely and kept their voices low. Scáthách, Astrape, and Epona held their horses' reins, readying to depart, or perhaps race. The long tables had been rearranged and platters of food were out, buffet-style. My stomach reminded me I hadn't eaten lunch.

I finally found Rhys and Siggi ensconced in conversation with the dryads of the oaks. I looped around their backs, caught Rhys' eye, and gestured to the empty end of the table. Rhys excused himself and headed my way. I pointed to the food, and my mouth, and reached for the empty plate at the top of the stack.

"I've been waiting for you," he said, coming up behind me with his own plate in his hand and two bundles of cutlery rolled into napkins. "You're welcome to share my dinner."

"I took a bath," I said over my shoulder, and perused Rhys' choices. I added a scoop of a grain and vegetable salad seasoned with fresh herbs and lemon to his plate. Though I was hungry, and everything looked and smelled delicious, the agitation in my stomach meant I'd have to watch what I ate. Rhys led us back to the table and I chose the bench across from him.

"What have you been up to?" I pushed back my sleeves, offered my first bite to the ground and the sky, giving silent thanks to Bone Croft's bounty and to those who tended the gardens and orchards and animals.

"Listening." Rhys cut into a piece of roasted meat and speared it on his fork along with a piece of potato.

"To whom, or for what?"

He chewed, swallowed, and drank some of my ale. "To Finnock and others who live here."

I clenched my teeth. "And what did they have to say?"

Rhys stared at his plate, cut another bite, and paused on the way to delivering the food to his lush mouth. "They are worried about you and concerned about the amount of physical labor involved with building a school."

Guilt added to the agitation I already felt, and I murmured my agreement. "I know Finn and the rest of the faerie-folk already work hard, and I know how much their families mean to them. It is not my intention to burden anyone with my dreams, or what may come of them." I tried to take another bite, and set down my fork. I forced myself to stare at the grains, to count the colorful flecks of chopped vegetables, because I knew if I looked at Rhys, I would choose a path of lesser resistance.

"Tell me more of what you remember of me, of us." Sliding my gaze forward, I held my breath and waited. Rhys rested his forearms on the table and opened his palms. The lacing on his vambraces faced upward, and in the dim spaces between each crossed tie, I glimpsed scarred skin.

His fingers beckoned. I placed my hands on his armor and slid my fingers under the rolled cuffs of his shirt. He touched my elbows, light and gentle, simultaneously grounding me and threatening to send me into the vortex of memory. In this moment, I needed to stay present. I withdrew and clenched my hands in my lap.

Rhys cleared his throat. "After you chose me and mounted me on the altar; after we climaxed and returned that energy to the earth, you left the tent. I… I found my clothes and drank the wine that had been left for me. And when I rejoined the festival, I was invited by one after another to partake in other couplings in whatever configuration I desired. It seemed that to be chosen by you shone a light on me I did not want, for I had pleasured a goddess, and been pleasured by her, and I could not imagine having another lover. At least not on that night."

"And so, what did you do?"

"I left, and I returned to Bone Fire Croft on the next ritual night, Lithas, and at First Harvest, and the Equinox. Each time I returned, I disguised myself, and each time, you chose me. And finally, on Samhain, on the night when the veils between this world and the underworld are at their thinnest, you recognized me.

"That night, you also invited my two companions into your tent. Siggi was one. The three of us worshipped you by making a throne of our bodies. And when we finished, when you were sated, when the ground overflowed with so much… *life,* with enough to store for the following year and even the ghosts passing through the veils responded to what flowed between us, *that* was when you invited me across the threshold to your home and into your bed.

"Just me, Habonde."

Rhys finished speaking. Reaching for the sinews holding the vambraces snug, he untied one, wriggled that arm out, and followed with the other. "We made love, and when we finished, you brought me to your favorite bathing pool in another temple."

I AM FALLING in love with him, and he cannot know.

The Woodsman sauntered naked out my kitchen door and stretched in the moonlight. Twisting to see if I followed, he extended his arm and with his other hand, stroked the front of his chest.

"You look well satisfied," I said, sliding one sleeve of his shirt up his arm and admiring his nipples on my way to covering them. "And I would have no one's eyes but mine see what gifts lie beneath your clothes."

"I am quite satisfied, Habonde. Are you?" The corners of his kiss-bitten lips curled upward. He found his shirt's empty sleeve without breaking our connected gaze. "And what of my pants?"

"Your pants are here." I handed over his trousers. "And I would say I too am well satisfied and very much in need of a soak." The possibility of enjoying the Woodsman's gifts in the naturally heated pool brought a matching grin to my lips.

"Are there duties you must attend to this might? Any spirits you need to consult, any villager's bones in need of settling?"

"My acolytes are more than capable of seeing to the celebrants' needs." I

waved my hand as though brushing away a moth. Sounds of the Samhain celebrations had quieted. We would have the temple baths to ourselves.

The night air was cold. I tied the belt of the quilted robe Rhys had gifted me. Its pinkish-rose color deepened in the moon's light and though I already adored the luxurious sensation of silk draping my skin, it was the Woodsman's body I wanted covering mine.

"Come."

RHYS TURNED HIS ARMS OVER, palms facing up, showing me his scarred skin. "We were in your private pool inside the cave, when we heard screams." He traced the irregular outlines of the scars with his finger before clenching his fingers into fists. "I got burned pulling your acolytes from the building where they slept."

I leaned away, as though that would put distance between Rhys' retelling and my unfinished memory. "Why didn't you tell me all this when you showed up at my kitchen door?"

"Your eyes don't lie, Habonde, and I could see you had no memory of me. Of us." He slid his forearms closer and relaxed his fists. "Of this."

Before I could respond, before Rhys' words had time to sink in, Hekate was behind him, her lions at her sides.

"Habonde, it's time to go." She glanced at the table. Her eyes widened when she noticed Rhys' forearms, and the unlaced vambraces lying to either side. "You told her?"

"Some, not all. The ban on me speaking lifted when Siggi, Pym, and I arrived to pull your portal tree from the ground. The rest of the story I left for you."

I slid both feet forward until I could feel Rhys. Pressing against his ankles, I addressed Hekate. "Must we leave right now? Rhys and I, we were just—" I gazed up, into Hekate's intractable features, and understood the Woodsman and I would have to finish our conversation later.

"There is a time and a place for everything, sister goddess. Tonight, it is your time to finish the task awaiting you, and the underworld—not this idyllic setting—is the place." The Queen of the Witches turned her attention to Rhys and squeezed his shoulder. "Two weeks more, Woodsman. That is all."

Chapter 24

HEKATE GAVE me no chance to ask what was meant by "two weeks more." She waited for me to extricate my legs from under the table, then headed in the direction of her yew. Rhys reached across the table and caressed my fingertips.

"I will not leave the croft until you return."

Trepidation grabbed my ribs and shook me hard, and I had to say… something. "We will finish this conversation over breakfast."

I managed a weak smile and headed for the dark, looming dome of the distant yew.

Beneath the great tree's branches, the Lamp Bearers had vanished along with their gauzy red tents, leaving behind bare patches of ground. The lions preceded Hekate into the gape in the folds of the massive trunk. I entered the lightless space behind them and waited for the tug in my gut that announced the portal would soon suck us in.

The sensation never came. Lights, neither open flames nor electric bulbs, flickered to life. Most likely the glow came from bugs or worms or other creatures clinging to the walls. My thigh muscles tightened in response to the ground's sudden downward slope.

"We're walking?" I asked.

"For a bit. I am gathering my thoughts for what I want to say and so I have chosen a slower route."

I tented my fingers against the cool, earthen walls to either side. "I'm listening."

"Tell me what you know of the Woodsman, what he has shared with you thus far."

Intermittent pale lights illuminated the top and back of Hekate's head. The little I could see of her appeared to be morphing and I wondered if it was conscious. Her hair and skin glowed like reflected flames on a shiny copper pot, as they had the night I met my ancestors. Yet during the earlier outdoor gatherings, sunlight managed to dull her metallic shine.

"Rhys showed up at my house the morning after I met you and Brigid during my ancestor journey. He said he'd come to the croft with two other Woodsmen and that they'd used the magic in the land to construct the yew tree for you. Later that day, he explained he and I had met in the past, and that we had been sexually intimate. At that time, I had no memory of being with Rhys and I told him so."

"Did you ask Baubo if she had known of you and him in the past?"

"I did, and she did not."

"And has the Woodsman explained his relationship with me?"

"Not… fully," I said, stumbling at a turn that coincided with a steepening of the angle of the ground.

"He has been in service to me, Habonde. For two hundred years."

This time it was words that caused me to lose my footing. Hekate stopped and turned. Lit from behind, I could not see her face, just the coppery aura silhouetting her shoulders, her hair, and the crown on her head. "In two weeks, it will be First Harvest and Rhys' debt will be paid. Because relationships between the likes of us" —she touched my breastbone lightly— "tend to exist over the very long arc of our immortal lives, I wanted you to know what Rhys did to find himself in my debt."

She splayed her fingers and spoke an incantation. I felt myself being pulled toward her, even as she flew back through space. We landed on a mosaic floor, and I had to bend forward, prop my hands on my knees, and take deep breaths to fend off the nausea brought on by the sudden change of locales.

"Welcome to the underworld. This temple is used only for portal travel. Come, I have things to show you."

Hekate appeared to have no difficulty with the transition. Behind her, two Lampedes peeled away from the sculptural reliefs cut into the stone wall. I recognized Lumina and Incandia from the gathering. One walked ahead of Hekate, the other waited to get in line behind me. We passed through a tunnel carved of the same granite lining the temple and emerged into a landscape devoid of vibrant color.

If asked, I would have ventured the underworld was likely a lifeless place, every natural and hand-built element predominated by shades of gray, the air cold and damp. Though the vista in front of me wasn't a replica of the aboveworld, it wasn't as startlingly a contrast as I'd braced myself for.

Awed, I noted, "There's life here."

"Of course, there is." Hekate's response hinted my surprise was not unusual. "Though things are noticeably brighter when Persephone's in residence."

Sniffing the air, I caught whiffs of the lamps' burning wicks and, in the distance, the faint scent of brackish water. "Is there a river nearby?"

"Yes, more than one. The river Kokytos is our first stop. The river Lethe is our second."

Kokytos. That was the one Minthe mentioned, and in my mind's eye I perused the spines of ancient, encyclopedic texts gathering dust in my library. Their pages likely held maps of the underworld and its significant rivers. I would prioritize consulting those books once I was home and would invite Baubo to join me.

Hekate cleared her throat. "Are you ready?"

"I am," I said, lifting my foot to follow. My leg felt heavy, dense, and I was on the verge of saying something about it to Hekate, when she reached behind and took my hand. Lumina took my other hand and together the four of us travelled far faster along a road paved with square stones not unlike those spiraling my hearth.

We rounded a low hill. Sparse trees dotted the landscape. A soft sound, like murmuring or crying, met my ears moments before a river the color of my aluminum watering can came into view. Rolling ribbons of milky gray froth lined the shore.

"The River of Wailing." Hekate's pronouncement explained the low, indistinguishable sounds. "Minthe is in charge, though she has been sporadic and ofttimes absent in her duties. Now that I know of Hades, and the child, her behavior makes sense. Though I cannot condone or excuse it."

"The option of enlisting a proxy could be invaluable for pregnant goddesses and their partners."

My comment stopped Hekate in her tracks. She glanced at me, and in the pause the miniature reptiles and beasts adorning her crown shifted places. "That thought did not occur to any of us during the meeting, and it should have. And while I might take issue with Minthe's life choices, she should be given the same option offered any other goddess in her position."

"I agree."

Hekate sharply nodded her head and resumed guiding us closer to our destination. Wavering notes rising from the river separated into distinct tones. I cupped my hands over my ears to soften the disturbing noise. "What's making that sound?"

"Souls that Charon cannot ferry wait here until their bodies have received a proper burial in the aboveworld. Only then are they able to cross the river Archeron and find peace."

Dread dropped its heavy arm around my shoulders and my feet stuttered to a stop. "Why have you brought me here?"

"Because some of these souls are yours to bury, Habonde. I struck a deal with Charon, that I would guarantee your actions in the aboveworld, if you would row the souls across yourself."

"And after I row them across this river, I return home and bury their bodies?" Hekate nodded, and she and the Lamp Bearers tugged me forward. "What if I cannot find their bodies?"

"You shall. You uncovered your hearth. You have seen the rows of waiting trees. All you must do is dig deeper."

With my hands clutched in others', I had no way to wipe the tears flowing down my cheeks. "Then I should begin. Where is the boat?"

"Come." My trio of escorts guided me off the stone pathway and down the slope toward the river's bank. Matted plants underfoot transitioned to short-bladed grasses, then sand, and the mist clinging to the river's surface parted to reveal a long, weathered dock. Water lapped at the pylons. A simple skiff waited, secured to a cleat with a thick rope and a neat knot, its oars tucked under the middle seat. I lifted my foot to step onto the dock. Hekate held me back.

"First, we retrieve the shades of your acolytes from there," she said, pointing to our left. A low-lying spit jutted into the river; its distal end faded into the fog. "And then you ferry them across to a dock much like this one. Charon, or one of their representatives, will take them from there."

We talked as we walked. "Will I be able to speak with them?" I asked.

"Not with words," Hekate said, sighing. "Your actions will have to convey your thoughts, Habonde. The fact that you have come here and are willing to do this—" Her voice tapered off. "Be strong."

The land around us narrowed, and the river's bank grew closer. We came to the peninsula, and the two Lamp Bearers stood with me.

"Lumina and Incandia will light your way. When you have finished, they will escort you back to me."

Nodding, I strode forward, pouring strength and determination into every labored step. The gray mist hovering above the Kokytos grew darker and more turbulent, though the air around us remained unaffected. Six figures emerged where the shore met the river, standing in a straggly line and facing the other side. The closer I got, the more I recognized each individual acolyte, first by their hairstyles and then by their voices.

Fia, daughter of weavers, with multiple plaits streaming down her back to her waist.

Leith, the tallest of them all. Two low pigtails stuck out from the back of her head.

Lilidh, who kept her black hair shorn close to her head.

Maesie, tiny, incandescent.

Kenna, with hair redder than mine worn in two plaits she used to try to hide her breasts.

Iona, her wild waves uncharacteristically slicked against her head and wound into a tight bun.

Blessed Mnemosyne, guide me.

Stepping into the shallows, I faced the shades. Their skin tones had run the range from pale white to dark brown when they were alive; now, the young women's features, from their hair to their eyes and lips, even the nightdresses they'd been wearing at the time of their deaths, were shades of gray.

Both my fortitude and my mask threatened to crumble; all I wanted was to gather the girls within my arms, stroke their heads, soothe their troubled souls. On instinct, I sloshed through the ankle-deep water to the far end of the line, to Fia, and linked her hand with Leith's; Leith's to Lilidh's; Lilidh's to Maesie's; Maesie's to Kenna's; Kenna's to Iona; and Iona's to mine. The laments spilling from their cold lips quickened and the shades balked.

"Shh, shh, it's going to be alright," I said in my softest voice. "It's going to be okay. I'm taking you home."

Chapter 25

TUGGING GENTLY, I led my charges along the narrow
peninsula's sandy shore. Lumina and Incandia followed at the
same, slow pace. Hekate waited near the boat, and once I'd
stepped onto the dock, she crouched by the cleat.

"You get in first," she instructed, "and set the oars in the
holders. Two will sit behind you in the bow, four in front of you
in the stern. Row steady, row strong, and do not stop, not for
anything."

I stepped into the boat and quickly sat. I didn't trust my legs
to keep me upright. Though the water looked calm, it didn't feel
calm. Submerged grasses moved this way and that, their dark
green strands stroking the boards below my feet, adding an eerie
swish-swish to an already otherworldly experience. I gripped the
gunwales and steadied my breathing. One by one, the shades
stepped down and took their places on the benches. Incandia
pulled the stern toward her, then hooked her lamp to a slender
post and added Lumina's lamp to the bow.

"For their comfort," she said, her voice low and soothing.

"Thank you."

Hekate loosened the rope and tossed it into the boat. Incandia pushed us off. Gripping the oar handles, I turned the blades to the correct position and dipped them into the water. I fumbled the first stroke, and the next, and the girls' collective voices rose like a flock of frightened birds.

I ignored the urge to drop the oars and gather the girls into my arms. Inching one foot forward, I touched Maesie's toes. If she felt my presence, it didn't show. Her gaze, like the others', remained fixed on the shore at my back.

We're... running down a stormy sea
And rolling through the thunder
'Way, haul away, well, haul away, ho

I sang the first chorus of the sea shanty. The pace helped me row more steadily and keep my emotions in check.

It's... every lass aloft my loves or we'll be driven under
'Way, haul away, well, haul away, ho
'Way, haul away, you're bound for better weather
'Way, haul away, well, haul away, ho

I stopped trying to make a connection with the shades of my acolytes and concentrated on rowing. A quick glance over my shoulder showed me we were halfway across. I spotted the other dock, and a figure standing at the end holding a tall pole in one hand.

Relief was followed immediately by the sensation of something with far more mass than river grass sliding against the side of the boat. Gripping the oars tighter, I hauled them in and wedged them under the seat. Steadying myself on the gunwales once again, I peered into the river.

Sand. We'd coasted over a sandbar. Tension locked within my limbs abated, replaced by shaking. I let the river carry us off-course until I could regain my hold on the oars with confidence, and whisper-sang my way through another round.

'Way, haul away, well, haul away, ho

'Way haul away, you're bound for better weather'
'Way haul away, well, haul away, ho

At a shout of, "Steady now," I slowed my strokes and took a quick look. The boat was headed right for the dock. I pulled in the oars, found the rope, and turned in my seat. The fresh-faced figure who extended the pole and hooked the metal ring hanging off the bow was far younger than I'd expected.

"Are you Charon?"

"I am Moros. I was named for my uncle and thankfully, inherited none of his nature. I help my father whenever I can, as this is no job for just one."

"Thank you, Moros. I am Habonde, and these shades were once my acolytes."

"I will take utmost care with them," they solemnly promised.

Maesie stood, and the rest followed. The ghostly girls stopped their keening, leaving the air still and quiet. Moros reached out their hand and helped the shades one at a time to step onto the dock. When the six were lined up, I grabbed the edge of a board, expecting the young escort would assist me as well.

"I'm afraid this is where you leave them," Moros said. "These shades are where they need to be, and I know what to do."

I tried to hold back my tears and could not. "Would you do me one favor? Could you join their hands one to the other, so they are together through whatever comes next?"

They nodded, linked the young women's hands as I had, and stepped to the front of the line. Moros waved to me, I lifted one hand in farewell, and remained in the rocking boat, knees locked and cheeks wet, until Fia, Leith, Lilidh, Maesie, Kenna, and Iona melded with the gray.

RECROSSING the River Kokytos went quickly, though a boulder-sized lump of grief weighted down my heart. I pulled up to the dock, secured the oars under the seat and the rope to the cleat. Incandia lifted the lamps off the posts and returned with me to Hekate's side.

"Where do we go next?" I asked. Hekate brushed away my tears. She did not offer an embrace.

"Lethe. The River of Forgetfulness." She and I and the two Lamp Bearers again joined hands. The terrain did not change; this path too was paved with carved stones, and every tree, every rock, every surprising flower was still a grayer version of what it would be in the aboveworld. The smell of a body of water grew stronger, and another sluggish river came into view. The closer we got to its shore, the more prickles coursed painfully under my skin. I wanted to run, and I couldn't. My legs were like lead weights, I was sandwiched between Hekate and a nymph, and neither seemed inclined to pause.

"I think I've been here before," I murmured.

"You have. Rhys carried you to the underworld in his arms and brought you here." Hekate released her grip and turned to face me. She cupped my head in her hands; stormy gray-blue eyes gazed into mine. "He wanted to do something to help you forget the tragedy that befell your acolytes.

"You were burned, unconscious, and likely near death. He carried you from the croft to a crossroad and bargained with me to allow you both access to the underworld. Once our deal was struck, I brought the two of you here. He walked into this river with you in his arms. And he bargained again, this time with Eris to ease your mind of the burden of the memories left by the fire.

"When he bargained with me to allow him to bring you to the underworld, and back to your croft, I agreed on the condition that Rhys serve those bound to this place for a period of two hundred years. Eris agreed to Rhys' request on two conditions. First, only one of you could have their memories erased, not both, and whomever retained their memories could not tell the other for the same duration—two hundred years."

"Is this why I cannot remember what happened, why Rhys stayed away from the croft until now?"

"It is a partial reason. Eris' second condition was that you could not drink Lethe's waters without giving your express consent. Though you are immortal, and a goddess, your entire memory bank would have been erased forever. Plus, had you imbibed, others in the underworld would have insisted your corporeal form remain here and your soul be sent back to inhabit another body not yet born."

Hekate relaxed her grip on my face. "Eris suggested a compromise."

"Which was—?"

"She offered to still the coursing river and allow Rhys to carry you in. He agreed, though in doing so he risked losing his footing. He held you tight until the waters were chest high, keeping one hand over your mouth and nose, and kept you under until your burns disappeared."

I stared at the river. Pushed back the sweater's sleeves and touched the lightly freckled skin on my arms. "I don't remember," I whispered.

"Do you want to remember?"

I gazed out over the river again. Did I?

Fia. Leith. Lilidh. Maesie. Kenna. Iona. They deserved to be remembered. Shaking in the chill air, I shook out my sleeves and crossed my arms. "Yes, I do."

"Then you shall."

Hekate raised her fingers to her mouth. A clear, sharp whistle pierced the rising mist. Moments later, bellowing dogs, black-furred and intent, poured toward us. Hekate crouched to accept their affectionate kisses and rubbed their ears. Rising, she quieted the quartet with a mere gesture.

"Guide Habonde to the temple." Four tails stood upright as four alert faces mapped her every word. "See she does not fall, and do not let her stray. Be swift, my beautiful beasts."

Hekate rose and rested her hands on my shoulders. "Speak with Rhys. Know that though his actions cost you your memories, they could have cost him his life. How you go forward with him, should you choose to, is very much up to you. In two weeks' time, the Woodsman will be one unto himself again."

The goddess relaxed her grip. "On a separate topic, I wish to bless this proposed educational endeavor, Habonde. I will help in any way I can. All you need do is ask."

"Thank you." Holding Hekate's wrists, I leaned forward, hoping to kiss her goodbye. I did not expect her mouth to find mine, nor did I expect the rush of sensation in my feet and legs as a kiss between friends became something far weightier. The snake at her waist wove its way around mine and tightened. Dogs whimpered, closed in, pressing their bodies against my legs.

Hekate pulled away. Her gray-blue eyes had gone silvery white. "Visit me again, Goddess. My kiss bestows protection throughout the realm of the dead. I do not give it lightly."

"You have my gratitude, Liminal One." Stunned at her gesture, I could not think of what else to say, what I could possibly offer in return, only, "And you have my friendship."

"I shall see you at Samhain at the latest."

Part Three

Chapter 26

HEKATE'S dogs took their escort duty seriously. They stayed close, the tails of the two in front tapping my legs in time to their steady gait. At the temple, one dog entered; the other three stopped between the two squat, Doric columns at the entrance and turned to face outward.

My guide padded ahead, toenails clacking on the stone. I caught details in my peripheral visions that I hadn't noticed on arrival: the way the ceiling doubled in height once we were further inside; the half-columns carved from the stone walls and the acanthus leaves adorning the top third. The dog barked at my slow pace, and again when we entered the round room at the far end where the portal's shadowy door waited. Rather than risk another canine lecture, I pet the creature's head, thanked her, and pulled the swirling cold around my shoulders.

My diaphragm froze. I did not breathe until my feet met packed earth and I flung out my arms on instinct. The walls of the passageway curved against my palms. Breath returned to my body, and I began the long ascent from the yew tree's underground heart.

Green-soaked light greeted my eyes at the final threshold. My hands caressed the gap in the trunk rubbed smooth over the years by the elements, or perhaps by travelers like me. I reached up, feeling the sides narrowing inward. My fingertips almost met at the apex, and when I brought my arms back down, I realized the opening resembled a vulva.

The symbolism of the moment was not lost on me. Heart rubbed raw, I was poised for a rebirth of sorts. I took my time shedding my sweater and shirt; my shoes, pants, and underwear. It took me a few minutes to undo my braid and finger-comb through the worst of the tangled strands. When I finished, I slipped my moonstone necklace over my head and hung it on a broken branch. The adornment had served me well, but it was time for me to wear another stone, one infused with fire and better suited to a goddess of the hearth.

Dew dappled the meadow beyond the reach of the yew's lowest, twisting limbs. My time traveling to and from the underworld, chaperoning the shades of my acolytes, visiting the river Lethe, had taken the entire night. In this moment, I was content to watch the incremental shifts of morning's light as the sun rose higher and the minutes flowed by—and to wait.

And when I was ready, I decided I would walk the path to my home naked as the day Hestia drew me from the fire. I was a goddess after all, and it was time I re-embraced my duties. My magic. My powers. All of it. And though there was more to remember—Blessed Mnemosyne, *so* much more—and more to make right, the time for me to rise and reclaim had arrived.

I passed from cool shade into bright light. Warmth bathed my skin. A vivid blue sky sang my eyes open in time to witness a murmuration of birds swooping and dancing across the blooming field toward the horizon. All was quiet in the shaded area where tent tops shone like bright white mushrooms among the oak trees. Lack of woodsmoke signaled most, if not all, of the guests had departed the night before—unless revelries had gone late, and everyone was sleeping. Veering to the right, I made my way to the bend in the stream where Demeter and I had conversed. I stood on the same rock as before, set down my pile of clothes, and dove in, kicking and stroking until I could no longer hold my breath.

Surfacing, I swept droplets from my eyes. Naiads and dryads came into focus among the trees and plants bordering the river, all gazing at me.

"I'm back!" I yelled, treading in place. "I'm back!"

My joyful proclamation must have confused a few of the younger fairie folk. They bent their heads to listen to those who'd grasped my meaning. Accompanied by hoots and trills and slapping fins, I gave myself over to the river's slow current and kept an eye out for a clear spot to emerge.

I am back.

I FLICKED bits of river weed off my frontside and arms on my homeward stroll. An occasional bee hitched a ride on the wildflowers I couldn't help gathering. My hand met the wooden gate to my garden, and I stopped to soak in the view and the sensation of arriving home. From here to my door, the contents of the pots and urns lining the pebbled walkway appeared larger and lusher. Further to my right and beyond a somewhat tamed hedgerow lay the orchard; I swore I could feel the fruit ripening. To my left grew the hedgerow's feral cousin, its rock wall claimed by wild, five-petalled roses and fuzzy brambleberry canes. Hidden behind its seemingly impenetrable facade were ancient hawthorns, stone benches, and moss-filled bird baths. That way also lay the front of the oldest section of the house, its entrance known only to the elves.

I closed my eyes and smelled grape skins thickening on the vines crisscrossing the pergola. Beyond the pavers running between the trimmed and cultivated, and the orchard... well, that section of the garden had been slowly taken over by undomesticated flowers and shy faeries. I left it mostly alone.

Within one prolonged, exquisite moment, I smelled, heard, and felt every living thing within a wide radius of the gate: birds perched atop trees; insects plying their way through underground networks of unseen roots; hops and barley ripening in summer's heat. If I was to dig my toes into the ground and spread my arms, I could have sensed further, to the stables, to my uncovered hearth, to the ordered stand of yew trees where my acolytes would be given a proper burial once I had recovered their bones.

Fia.

Leith.

Lilidh.

Maesie.

Kenna.

Iona.

An overload of sensory input slammed my body. My fingers twitched, sending stems tumbling from my hand. Too much coupling between me and my croft, too soon, after decades and decades of cleaving myself from sensation and connection. Stooping, I re-gathered the wildflowers, fumbled with the iron latch, and stepped onto the pea gravel. The comforting sound of little stones rolling beneath my feet welcomed me home, as did the simple movements of reaching for a vase, filling it with water, and snipping the flower stems with scissors.

I exited my kitchen and entered the first of my houses, bare feet again marking my place in time as they *slap-slap-slapped* against the long hallway's cool stone floor. I left the vase outside Baubo's door.

I am back.

. . .

ONE SHOWER LATER, with a fresh cup of coffee in hand, I claimed the same chair Rhys occupied the morning he arrived and dried my hair in the sun. The freckles on my face and hands would multiply, but the heat felt glorious and though I'd donned a robe, I wore nothing underneath and wouldn't until it was time to dress to meet Mnemosyne.

Golden light stroked my inner thighs. My mind wandered to my recollection of Rhys sprawled in the same position, long legs spread, head tilted back and a grin playing at the corners of his mouth. The memory provided a temporary balm for all that ached within my heart.

"Is this how you wait for all your appointments? Or were you expecting guests other than me?"

I slammed my legs together and crossed the halves of my robe so fast I toppled the coffee cup I'd set near my foot. "Mnemosyne, you're early!"

"Am I?" Holding a hardcover book to her chest, the Goddess of Memory twisted left, then right, searching for something she seemingly expected to find. "What time is it? Have you no sun dial?"

"It's barely ten in the morning and I wasn't expecting you until after lunch." I bustled forward to embrace her. She wrapped an arm around my upper back and pecked me on the cheek.

"I'm famished, and I'll have whatever you're having, as long as it has no meat or eggs, just vegetables and herbs. Oh, and grains are fine. Served warm. And perhaps a bit of olive oil. My digestion does better this early in the day when everything's a tad cooked."

My rumbly belly reminded me I'd had coffee on an empty stomach and should probably eat as well. "I'll go make us something. Can I get you tea or coffee or a cool drink while you wait?"

She waved me off, picked up the satchel by her feet, and headed for the pergola. "I'll sit out here and speak with the bees."

There was leftover gazpacho in the refrigerator, but all the ingredients were raw. I cranked open the window over the counter to ask Nemmie if goat cheese was okay.

"Love it," she said, "especially if it's made with milk from your goats."

"It is."

Perfect. I set a cast iron pan on the stove, breathed the banked coals into life, and fed the flames a few sprigs of hops. I selected a rectangular serving tray and set out napkins, plates, and carved wooden utensils for two before returning my attention to the heating pan and selecting a couple of perfectly ripe pears. Those I sliced thin and added to the pan. Pulling a baguette from the cloth bread bag, I cut diagonal slices and dropped them into a basket. Spoonsful of goat cheese went into a serving bowl and once the pears released their juices, I drizzled them with balsamic vinegar. Honey from the croft's hardworking bees and a handful of crushed walnuts finished the dish, and I added the pears to another bowl.

Drinks. The day was perfect for brewing sun tea. I found and filled a big glass jar with heated water to hurry things along, added a bag of rooibos stems and leaves mixed with dried raspberries, and placed the jar in a spot I knew would receive the sun's brightest blessing.

I carried the tray outside and set it on the sunnier end of the table. Mnemosyne's book and bag were in one of the chairs and the goddess was nowhere to be seen. I called her name.

"Coming, coming." She reappeared, cheeks flushed, from the overgrown end of the garden and plopped into her seat. "What a spec*tacular* garden you have, dear one. There's nothing I love more in the natural world than seeing vines and flowers and herbs overrun themselves." She fanned herself with her hand, then leaned forward, eyes on the tray.

"All this was produced on the croft?" she asked, hovering her spoon over the goat cheese.

"All of it, from the wood the urisk used to make the tray and utensils, to the clay in the bowls, the ash in the glaze, and the flax used to weave the cloth for the napkins."

Sometimes, it took a guest to remind me of my land's bounty. Mnemosyne's delight did exactly that. She and I apportioned first offerings to the sounds of birds and bees, gave thanks to the earth and the sky, and traded the matching bites we'd fashioned.

"*Mmm,*" she groaned. "So, so good." She kept her eyes closed as she savored each mouthful, sitting up and opening them again as she prepared her next serving.

"Why do you close your eyes as you eat?" I asked, surveying the tray. Together, we'd devoured half the bread and most of the pears and cheese.

"This is a working lunch, and I am on a fact-finding mission."

"What do you mean?" While I'd been playing host and half-hoping to prolong the moment Mnemosyne started to ask about my memories, she'd been on the clock. Tricky goddess.

"Here, in your garden," she began, tucking her napkin under the edge of her plate, "and throughout Bone Fire Croft, everything with roots has a story, be it flower, herb, fruit, grain, or tree. Each of those stories has its origins in the soil, in the collected residue of the sun and the rain and even winter's frosty cloak.

"To find those stories, I must soften all my senses and rely on my nose and taste buds for details." Mnemosyne sat up straighter and pivoted in her chair to face me. "What I don't taste, is you, and that is something I think we should talk about."

"You don't taste… *me?*" I echoed. "I'm confused."

Mnemosyne pointed to the jar of purplish red tea. "If you'll fetch us glasses and ice, I'll pour. And then I'll explain what I mean."

I hurried to the kitchen, got the glasses and the ice cubes and a plate of lavender shortbread cookies. "These are egg-free," I promised, setting them next to her elbow. "I made them myself."

My guest filled our glasses. Thinking I should demonstrate I did indeed have a connection to my land, I waggled my fingers in the direction of the flower fairies and pointed to our iced tea. Two sets of whirring, iridescent wings buzzed over, and the wee ones released bright pink rose petals onto our drinks.

"Thank you," I crooned, and blew them a kiss. Mnemosyne used her spoon to push the petals below the cubes in both glasses.

"Exactly the flower I would have chosen."

I sipped at the tea, the delicate floral flavor rising above the fruitier rooibos. "Tell me more about what you taste. Or don't."

"It all begins with water. None of this—none of us—would be here without it." She grinned into her glass as she drank. "Though of course Zeus and every other sun god would tell you nothing would exist without light. And I cannot argue their point.

"But for today, for *this* conversation, we're going to talk about water, that life-giving fluid." Mnemosyne sighed. "I really should write a book," she muttered, smoothing the folds of her caftan.

"Should I be taking notes?"

The Goddess of Memory arched an eyebrow. "No, my dear, you should *listen* to what I have to say and *absorb* it, and then I shall help you listen for the parts of your past that appear to have lost their voice."

Oh my. I needed a few moments to collect myself. Where was Baubo, queen of perfect timing and saucy one-liners?

"Before we start, you should know I spent last night in the underworld with Hekate."

"Ahh, *that* explains why you were splayed out for all the world to see when I arrived. I am well acquainted with the underworld, and I understand exactly why you would seek the sun." Mnemosyne shuddered. "Tell me, what were you doing there, escorted by the Keeper of the Keys Herself?"

"Hekate had a task for me to complete. Though I didn't know I would be visiting the underworld when I asked for your help, that task was connected to my missing memories." I took a deep breath, folding my hands together to warm my cold fingers. "The last of my acolytes died in an event I cannot fully remember. Unbeknownst to me, their souls could not move on because their shades had been stuck waiting on the shores of the Kokytos for… for decades, unable to be transported by Charon because their bodies had not received a proper burial here in the aboveworld."

Mnemosyne reached across the table and surrounded my hands with hers. "Oh, Habonde. Do you know where their bodies are now?"

I shook my head. "I do not. Hekate suggested I dig deeper, yet how am I to 'dig deeper' when I don't know if she was speaking literally, or metaphorically?" Rising agitation settled behind my breastbone. "I'm hoping this time with you will pinpoint where I should start, but I don't think I have much time. Charon agreed to let me escort the shades across the river on the condition I find and bury their bodies as quickly as possible."

"You were granted an extraordinary dispensation. Did Hekate bring you to any of the other rivers?"

I fussed with my robe. I really should have dressed while the pears were cooking. "She did. The Woodsman, Rhys, carried me to the underworld after the event I can't remember, and bargained with Eris for the chance to float me in the River Lethe's waters."

Mnemosyne *hmm*'d. "Were you given a vial and instructed to drink?"

"According to Hekate, I was not. She said Rhys took care to keep my nose and mouth covered while he held me underwater."

Creases furrowed Mnemosyne's forehead. "Yet you say you have recovered *some* memories, correct?"

"Yes."

The goddess studied my face, then tugged on the heavy gold chain dipping below the bodice of her caftan and withdrew a stoppered glass vial. "Lucky for you, I always carry water from *my* river." She held the slender container up to the light before tucking it back under her clothing and rising to her feet. "I want you to show me every important body of water on your croft, bathtubs excluded."

"Let me just change my—" The sinking feeling in my gut was me realizing for all I wanted to know the truth, I also wanted to delay the inevitable. Next thing, I'd be telling Mnemosyne I had to put the food away and wash our dishes; or offering to take her on a tour of the croft; or asking if she wished to visit with Demeter or any of the other visiting goddesses.

Self-preservation was a double-edged sword.

"You're fine," she assured me. "It will be easier for you to get naked if you haven't much to shed in the first place."

"I'm ready." Hadn't I reclaimed the glory of wearing nothing at all this very morning? I pushed away my chair and stood, even as my tender, vulnerable skin shrank at the thought of facing more tasks akin to rowing boats in the underworld without some sort of protective outer layer.

"I'm sure you think you are. On to your waters."

CROSSING one arm under my breasts, I led Mnemosyne to the covered birdbath. Together we shifted its heavy lid to the side. "Here is where I do most of my summoning."

The goddess leaned over the bowl, trailed her fingertips across the surface, and lifted them to her lips. "Hmm," she murmured. "You've chosen excellent spells for seeking and connecting."

"Thank you."

"I've seen all I need to see here. Next?"

Most of the croft's larger bodies of water lay in the northeast quadrant: the stream, Brigid's newly dug well, the lowermost section of the Lake of Secrets. Even as I enumerated them to Mnemosyne, I knew I was missing other, important locations.

"I sense there are more," I admitted, "and that those are the ones connected to the memories I wish to retrieve. Oh, I just thought of something you might find useful."

I left Mnemosyne under the pergola and quickly made my way to the kitchen. A section of the croft on one of the maps Baubo discovered puzzled me. I showed the aged parchment to my guide and pointed to the markings on the side of the river shielded by living walls of marsh plants and moss-draped branches.

"I think I need your help remembering what all this… means." The legend listed caves and temples and other structures I would be hard-pressed to locate on my own.

"Then accept the help I offer." She pocketed the map and un-stoppered the vial she'd shown me earlier. "Open your mouth and press the tip of your tongue to the back of your upper teeth. One drop taken sublingually should do it."

I did as she asked, relaxed my tongue and jaw when told, and closed my eyes. Mnemosyne took my hands. "I am here, Habonde," she whispered, "though it is you who must let go. Leave your fears in my hands."

The inside of my mouth dissolved.

"Let yourself go."

My body dissolved, starting at the top of my head and continuing to the bottoms of my feet.

"Let yourself…"

ARMED *and armored and praying aloud for Eilidh's safety, I ran from the temple, across the bridge, to the stable. Once I had my horse saddled, he carried me down the long lane to the border of the croft. I paused at the wider, heavily travelled road. My beast danced a nervous circle as I contemplated which way Eilidh had taken.*

I looked to my right, narrowing my gaze, and noted the lack of light. To my left, random yellow sparks flared along the packed dirt like night-blooming flowers. I recognized remnants of Eilidh's magic, as it was yellower than most. I sent my gaze further in that direction and spied firelight behind curtained windows. The newest of the village's inhabitants had leased the cottage and the surrounding farm from a recently widowed shepherd.

Taking hold of the reins, I urged my horse forward, certain I would find

Eilidh inside the lone cottage. My beast turned off the main road without my asking and sailed over the gated fence at the end of the lane.

I brought my ride to a stop. Dropping the reins, I dismounted and tore for the front door. More splashes of yellow littered the stones at my feet. I tested the door handle, found it locked, and banged my knife's stag horn pommel on the wood.

"By the will of the Goddess, open this door." Muffled thumps and screams met my ears. Stepping back, I aimed my booted heel above the handle and kicked and kicked until the door banged open.

Eilidh lay on her side on the floor, bound and gagged. Cuts on her naked chest, belly, and thighs welled with bright drops of ruby blood, and the pattern of the lines suggested the stranger knew something of exorcism rites.

The man who'd taken Eili stepped between me and my acolyte, a blade in one hand, a hank of black hair in the other. Sweat poured down his bare, heaving chest. "This is my house. And I bought the girl's time, so you had best be gone or I'll be buying your time too, though not with coin."

While he spoke, I had pulled magic from the soil beneath the house's foundation, magic and secrets I would look at once Eilidh was safe. Gripping my knife, I let my fury sharpen its blade before I made a move.

"You bought her fire, and nothing else. Step away."

He laughed, and when he charged, I had no choice but to draw my knife across his gut and send him toppling to the floor. Ignoring his screams, I stepped over his body, cut the ropes binding Eili's wrists and ankles, and removed the blood-soaked gag. Her eyelids fluttered. Blood and spittle drained from her mouth.

I felt for Eilidh's magic. For that bright, buttercup light she shed with every step, every giggle, every waking breath. The palest of threads met my inquiry.

I had to get her back to the croft. My horse knew to fly and not falter. Once Eili was safely with the Healer, her wounds treated, her pain met with poppy's gift, I gathered the acolytes and explained what I had found, and what I had done.

"That man will not bother us again," I reassured them, "but for now, no

one leaves the croft until I am certain all routes in are protected and her attacker has been dealt with."

"THE CAVE OF POOLS," I whispered, clutching Mnemosyne's fingers.

"Where else, Habonde. Where else?"

AFTER THE FIRST *priest doused our hearth fire, boarded it over, and declared himself in charge of my acolytes' spiritual development, I moved the location of the ritual temple to the other side of the stream. Hestia Herself gifted me another log, the acolytes slipped the priest's clutches and returned to the croft, and our fires burned again.*

After a second priest repeated the first's actions, I paid for a coven of witches to spell an entire field from the prying eyes of non-believers. Those spells were refreshed regularly, especially after the incident involving Eilidh and the newcomer. Secure in the knowledge the old ways of marking Samhain were protected, and the croft would not be bothered by unwanted intruders, I led Rhys past the circle of celebrants departing the communal fire in small groups on their way to visit the graves of their dead.

"My temple and the cave of pools are not far," I said, guiding my lover left at the fork in the path.

"Pools?"

"Mm-hmm, they're fed by hot springs and the water is perfect for soaking."

"Soaking and other activities?"

"Oh, most assuredly."

"Then why are we lollygagging?" Rhys took my hand, I lifted my robe and bared my legs to the night air, and off we ran across fields dusted with frost. We came to a narrow bridge and crossed the stream, giggling at the sound of our feet hitting the uneven boards. Up a hill and around the cairn, we reached the

hidden temple complex where I trained my acolytes. At the back of the empty rooms lay the entrance to the cave with the pools. Most of the wall torches were unlit. I lifted one from its holder, flicked sparks from my fingers, and led Rhys down a short corridor, past the naturally changing area to the first pool.

"This one is my acolytes' favorite, and it's the hottest. We're going to my private pool."

I pressed my palm to the slice of druzy agate embedded in the curved wall. A tall section of stone slid back, revealing a round room with a pool at its center. I dipped my torch into the ditch ringing the pool. Flames flared behind natural crystal inserts, illuminating the water with bluish-green light. I dropped my robe, lowered myself into the water, and floated on my back. I loved the feel of my hair spreading out around me, and I was aware of the picture I presented to my insatiable lover.

Little waves lapping at my sides let me know Rhys had joined me. He surfaced between my legs, drew my knees over his shoulders, and steered me closer to the pool's edge.

"Hold tight," he whispered, before parting my lips with his tongue. His hands kept me afloat while he licked and laved and groaned. It had been nearly an hour since my last release, and I was as hungry for another as the Woodsman's tongue desired to provide it.

I was still pulsing when he drew my hips below the pool's surface and plunged his cock into me. I let go of my handhold and curled forward, wrapping my arms around his neck and holding tight. Water splashed out of the pool and onto the rocks and I yelled out my pleasure, urging Rhys on until another orgasm claimed us both. Completely spent, I let go of his neck and again floated, a fire goddess transformed into a limpid water nymph, connected to reality by the presence of his still-hard cock.

Our cries continued to echo off the walls of the chamber and though I knew there was magic in this place, it wasn't magic I heard accompanying our fading voices. It was fear. Abject, horror-filled cries of fear. Feminine. Masculine. Animal. I pushed away from Rhys and lifted myself out of the pool.

"Something's wrong," I said, extending him my arm. "Come. I have to see what it is."

We flew out of the room and through the corridor, me struggling to pull my robe over wet arms, Rhys stopping to jam his legs into his pants. I exited the cave first to the sight of flames reaching for the sky. I ran without thinking in the fire's direction.

"Habonde, wait, what is burning?"

"I think it's the acolytes' quarters," I yelled. "There is a well nearby, they use it every day, and buckets. Surely others are on their way to help."

Rhys and I ran hard, along the path and through a stand of aspen to the small field behind a long, single-story building. I didn't stop moving until I reached the well. Light from the flames illuminated the immediate area, and deepened the shadows cast by the trees. Frantic, I searched for the wooden buckets that were always stacked nearby.

Always.

"Rhys, I can't find them, I can't find the buckets." I stumbled. My heel landed on something sharp, and I yelped. Crouching, I felt along the ground and found a curved piece of rusted metal.

Goddess help us. I scrambled to my feet. Rhys stood at the well. He spun toward me, his hands in his hair. "The rope to lift and lower the buckets has been cut."

I held out the piece of metal. "And the buckets have been smashed. Come."

We got as close to the fire as we could. Samhain celebrants and members of the croft arrived with similar stories about broken buckets and disabled wells.

"Do we know if anyone's inside?" one asked.

"My acolytes. I have to see if my acolytes escaped or if they're—"

A guttering scream I would never forget shredded the air. I tore forward, leaving my robe in the trodden grass, and tried to enter the building. The iron handle burned my hand and Rhys pulled me back.

"I'll go," he yelled above the wind-whipped flames. "You figure out how to get water here. Go, Habonde, now!"

Paralyzed, I couldn't leave, couldn't uproot my feet and work my legs, even after Rhys kicked the door in and disappeared into the smoke.

I KNEW I was sobbing as I said to Mnemosyne, "The well at the site of my acolytes' quarters, and the one at my hidden temple."

"Where else, Habonde?"

Desperate to be rid of the fire, the smoke, the… the sounds, and to stave off what was coming, I shut my eyes and shook my head. "I don't know," I moaned. "I don't know."

"This is the hardest work you will ever do. Let your memories guide you, let them in."

"I'm done. I can't. I—"

"You can and you will." Mnemosyne let go of my arms. A determined hand clenched my jaw. Glass touched my bottom lip. "Open," she commanded. "Open and drink. Open and remember. Open, Habonde. *Open.*"

Chapter 28

I LAPPED at the water from Mnemosyne's vial and tasted salty tears.

Fia.

Leith.

Lilidh.

Maesie.

Kenna.

Iona.

Rhys stumbled from the burning structure, a barely-clothed body draped across his arms. He lay the girl on the ground and sprinted back inside the building. I couldn't follow him, and I couldn't stop him, so I knelt by the body —because it was a body, Fia's once vibrant, magical, joy-filled body. Frantic, I undid the knotted rope pinning her wrists behind her back; covered her limbs' nakedness with my own; wet her burnt face with my tears.

Rhys laid another body beside her, and another, until five acolytes, all in their smoked-stained nightclothes, all with wrists bound, were laid out in a line. The others, those who had come to celebrate Samhain around a contained fire, not a conflagration, placed the yew boughs and flowers meant for their loved ones' graves around us, boxing the bodies with a low wall of green punctuated by spots of white, pink, and red.

The fire had consumed what I loved most in the world, and nothing could persuade me to leave until every acolyte was accounted for: Fia. Leith. Lilidh. Maesie. Kenna. I waited for Rhys to lower Iona beside me and when he returned, empty-armed, I pleaded with him to search again.

"There is one more. Iona. Her name is Iona, and she has long, wavy black hair."

The whites of the Woodsman's eye had turned red from the smoke. Dead cinders and clumps of ash coated his bare shoulders and chest. "I… I don't know that I can go back in." Rhys agonized over my request. Ripping his gaze away from the line of bodies, he thrust his blackened arm at the voracious flames. "The roof is about to fall, Habonde, and I——"

I rose to my feet like a somnambulist and faced what was left of the wood and stone building. Iona was in there, I knew it, and though I doubted she was alive, she deserved to be found and buried alongside her sistren. Step by painful step, pulling magic from the croft's deepest reservoirs, I limped toward the building; shook Rhys's hand off my arm when he tried to stop me; shoved him away when he put himself between me and my objective.

"I am the Goddess of the Hearth," I growled, to him and to any other who would stand in my way. "Fire is my element. Fire is my ally."

One end of the roof collapsed. "Habonde, you can't——"

I ignored Rhys, stepped onto the live coals, and turned right. Iona's room was the second one in. Her door was closed and hot to my touch. I set my shoulder to the wood and pushed and pushed, fire sizzling against my skin, until the door opened enough that I could see inside.

Glowing cinders cascaded from the beams overhead. Iona was on her bed, eyes open, trussed and gagged as the others. I pushed again, squeezing between the door and the frame, aware of splinters tearing at my skin. The bed was one short step away, then I had Iona in my arms, held tight against my chest, but a few steps from safety.

The opening I'd passed through was too narrow to accommodate us both.

I struggled to pull more magic to me, magic to feed strength into my arms and legs, magic to keep my lungs clear, magic to share with my girl. And Rhys was there, adding his physical strength to mine. The door opened wider, and I pressed Iona into his arms.

"Take her. She's alive."

Our eyes met and the gods-awful groan of beams letting go filled my ears.

"HABONDE. *HABONDE.*"

I arched my spine. Gulped in clean, cool air and opened my eyes. Mnemosyne stood at my feet. Scáthách, Epona, Astrape gathered at my head, grave concern flooding their upside-down faces.

"I'm here," I whispered. My throat was bone dry, painfully so. "Water."

Astrape helped me to sit and supported my back. My screen door slammed, and a tall glass of hibiscus tea appeared from above. I drained the contents and thrust the glass into waiting hands.

"More."

Another tea appeared, sweeter, with ice added, and I finished that one too. "Nemmie, I remembered. Not everything, but— ." My body curled inward, knees to chest, damp hair clinging to my backside, as the last image from within the burning building repeated and repeated inside my head: Iona cradled between me and Rhys; the overwhelming sounds of everything collapsing in an unstoppable wave; the roar of insatiable flames; the dreadful, resigned look in Rhys' eyes; the sensation of my skin catching fire—

That was then. This—my cool skin, the crushed yarrow leaves clinging to my cheek, the comforting hands at my back— this was now. And I was okay, Rhys was okay, Iona was—

Oh Goddess, this hurts. This hurts.

"I think I can find the bodies now," I whispered, the weight of Iona's body still present along my forearms.

"We've got horses," Epona volunteered. "Would that help?"

"Yes," Mnemosyne said. "I don't think Habonde's in any shape to walk."

She was right. My legs would not hold me upright. I raised my arm and felt for the caftan covering her legs. "I want to get this done."

Scáthách mounted her pony. "Hand her up. Nixie can bear us both." Epona lifted me as though my grief weighed little and set me firmly between Scáthách's thighs. "Lean back, relax your legs. Let the horse do the work," she counselled, adding, "I've got you" as she slid her arm around my waist.

"Where to?" Epona asked. She insisted Mnemosyne take her horse.

Closing my eyes meant seeing those last seconds between me and Rhys on a never-ending loop. I shook it off. "Mnemosyne has a map. There's a path behind the stables that will take us to the foothills. Follow that path over the stream to the two cairns. Just beyond is my temple and the opening to a cave. We'll start there."

Astrape took off, her mount's great wings beating at the heavy air. Epona jogged alongside her horse, her hand on the saddle. I kept my gaze on Mnemosyne's back the entire way to the stable, where we stopped to get another horse for Epona. Bailoch and Bodhi offered to lend their help with the solemn task of locating the bodies of my girls and Scáthách nodded gratefully.

"We need shovels." My raspy voice disappeared inside the cavernous barn. I patted Scàthàch's arm and repeated my request. She rose off her saddle.

"Habonde wants you to bring shovels."

"And scythes," I added. "In case the path is overgrown."

"And scythes."

We set out again, with Astrape circling above and Bodhi joining Epona at the front, followed by Mnemosyne and Bailoch.

Nixie seemed content to bring up the rear. Safely wrapped in Scáthách's arms, I shoved my hand into the robe's pocket and felt for the wooden ring Rhys had given me. I realized I wanted him here, that he should be part of this expedition. I slid the ring onto my thumb and turned it three times. Closing my eyes, I pictured the Woodsman as I had last seen him, when he had removed his armor at dinner and shown me the scars on his arms.

I now knew how he'd come by those scars, and that I was responsible for his injuries. Guilt threatened to topple my fragile state. I focused on Scáthách's support and the figures in front of me; on controlling my breath through waves of nauseating impatience brought on by intermittent stops while Bailoch and Bodhi tackled the clogged sections of the path with wide sweeps of their scythes.

"I see the cairns!"

Epona's shout jostled me out of the apprehension encroaching on my mind. She leaned forward over her horse's neck, spurring her on. The sun we'd been graced with the past few days had handed the sky over to thick clouds threatening rain. A fine mist covered my cheeks. I licked the moisture off my lips.

And slid right back to the scene of the fire.

Rough rocks and dried stalks of grass biting into my damaged skin. Hushed voices, crying voices, scattered left and right. The yelling in the background coming closer and closer on ominous, thundering hooves.

"Run!"

"Run!"

I couldn't run. I couldn't move. Until I was lifted by familiar arms and fainted into a place where all I knew was unending pain.

"WE'RE HERE."

I did not know where "here" was. Though I knew I was

wearing my favorite robe, the faded silk one, and sitting atop a horse. Whoever was behind me slid to the side and I almost toppled. Nixie. The horse was Nixie, and it was Scáthách helping me dismount and replacing my robe's missing tie with one of her own leather belts.

"Can you walk?" she asked, threading one end of the belt through the buckle and pulling it snug to my waist.

"I think I can." I stepped out from between Nixie and another horse. A bank of mist was setting in, making it harder for me to see beyond the start of an upward slope collared with swaths of heather and lichen-spotted rocks. I let my feet find the narrow, once-familiar path; the others with me followed.

I rounded a tall rock and pressed my hand to its craggy surface to steady myself and catch my breath. Ahead, the empty, levelled ground hollowed my gut. My temple was gone, any remnant of its footprint consumed by the elements. Mnemosyne came up beside me and touched my lower back.

"I don't know what happened to the temple and the teaching rooms, if I had them destroyed or—" I lifted my limp arms and let them fall.

"Are the bodies in there?" she quietly asked, gently holding my shoulders and directing my gaze to the next hill, and the opening in its smooth face.

"I— I don't know."

"There is only one way to find out."

This time, Mnemosyne led the way and I followed. She paused before the cave and stepped aside to let me pass through first.

"Hekate said I should dig deeper," I said, more to myself than the others. "But it's all rock in there. Rock and water." I slipped into the cave and waited for my eyes to adjust. "We need light."

"You can make fire, my dear," Mnemosyne reminded me.

I could, but I rarely did, and the movement I used to make with my fingers came awkwardly at first. A handful of tries brought flames to two fingers and my thumb. It would have to suffice. I raised my arm and entered the circular room.

"This is the antechamber." Traversing the space, I added, "and that leads to classrooms, and this leads to the changing room where we washed and rinsed before entering the pools."

I brought everyone through to the largest pool. The last time I remembered being in here, flowers littered the floor, laughter bounced off the surrounding stone—and I learned that Eilidh had gone off with the man who'd intended to keep her for his own terrible purposes.

"Habonde?"

I shook my head. The clues I needed didn't lie on the rocks' slick surface or within the heated water. "There's another pool, more private." We returned to the antechamber, and I took the corridor to the pool where Rhys and I— "The night of the fire, Rhys and I came here. I should have stayed at the bonfire, with the celebrants. I should have known retribution was coming. I should have—"

"Retribution for what?" Astrape asked.

"A man who was new to the village had come to the temple the year before and asked to have his home's first fire lit by... by me, as was customary. I wasn't at the temple and one of my acolytes offered to do it. Her name was Eilidh, and she was radiant as the sun."

My raised arm trembled, and I almost doused my hand in the pool. Shining light on the past was both a relief, and terribly humbling. "Eilidh went with the man. I only found out because I came here, to the big pool, where the rest of the acolytes were bathing. As soon as they told me Eili had left, I knew something was wrong.

"I got my horse, and I rode to the village road and beyond,

up a hill to a cottage glowing with light. With Eili's light. I kicked in the door and found her on the floor, bound and gagged with cuts on the front of her chest… her belly… her thighs." My unlit hand stroked the front of my robe as I remembered her wounds and the smell of her blood.

"I was enraged. The man who'd hurt her wore only his pants, but he had a blade in his hand. I had a blade, too, a goddess-blessed blade and I swung it at him." I mimicked the movement, sweeping my arm in a waist-high arc. "I thought I gutted him. I didn't stop to check. I just cut Eili free, picked her up, and rode her home as hard as my horse could manage. I left her with our healer—"

Oh Goddess, Great Mother Hestia. I dropped to my knees as I remembered what happened in the early hours of the following morning. "Eilidh died from the uncommon poison the man had rubbed onto his knife. I mourned. For months, I mourned, punishing everyone and everything around me in my grief. And when the wheel of the year turned and landed on Samhain, and the Woodsman appeared as he had been since Beltane, I gave myself respite from my anger, my pain. I chose to be with him, over remaining by the fires until the last ember cooled.

"Only, the man who took Eili returned to the croft that night. He brought others with him, others who saw the Goddess as a whore to be plundered, and after I left the field, they scattered those who had come to celebrate.

"They cut off access to our wells, smashed all the buckets, and set fire to the old building where the acolytes lived. And every single one of those innocent young women died. They died because of me."

I stopped speaking. The cave held me, held us, with only the sounds of our breathing breaking the silence. Until Mnemosyne spoke.

"Where are they, Habonde? Where are the girls?"

Chapter 29

WHERE ARE THE GIRLS? I collapsed onto my side, one hand landing in the pool, and closed my eyes.

Where are the girls? Warm water lapped at my fingers. Fia, Leith, Lilidh, Maesie, Kenna, Iona. Eilidh's bones rested beneath the small yew tree near my hearth.

Where were the others?

The young women's faces rose in my memory, flushed and happy. Their beautiful bodies moving through the pool, petals scattered like celebratory confetti: lavender cuckoo flowers for Fia and violets for Leith; tufts of orange hawkweed for Lilidh; red poppies for Maesie; pink thistledown for Kenna; blue harebell for Iona.

Lavender, purple, orange, red, pink, and blue. Eilidh's favorite color was yellow. The droplets left by her waning magic had led me to the old sheep farmer's cottage that horrible night. Goddess willing, remnants of her sistren's magics might now lead me to them.

I pushed to my hands and knees, then to my feet, and stumbled out of the cave and down the rocky slope. Once, many,

many decades past, I had known how to find my acolytes. I called for Mnemosyne and like a baby bird, opened my mouth at her approach to accept another dose from her vial.

Rhys and I had crossed the stream on our way to the temple and the secret pools. Following the map Baubo found, Scáthách and I and the rest had crossed the same bridge in search of the two cairns marking the way to the cave.

Mnemosyne's drops worked their magic. A net of magic floated above the heather, sparkling with drops of lavender, purple, orange, red, pink, and blue.

"North," I said, facing the direction of the moving net. With Epona's help, Mnemosyne and I remounted our horses. Our group stayed close as we rode over rolling hills toward the site of that long-ago fire and what might remain of the destroyed building. Ahead, Bailoch raised an arm and slowed his pace as the leafless gray limbs of a towering oak formed within the light gray mist. I saw Rhys, his tall figure dressed in black and framed by the oak's wide trunk. He pushed off, took one step forward, and stopped.

Both Epona's horse and Bailoch continued their cautious walk forward. The satyr grabbed Epona's reins and signaled her beast to stop. She dismounted, disappeared in the tall grass, and rose with a worried face.

"Leave your mounts here and watch where you step," she cautioned. "The grass hides debris that is not safe for hoof or foot."

Between the satyrs and the reverberations underfoot as Astrape landed her winged horse, the twang of metal as Scáthách unsheathed two blades, and the company of other immortals, the unfolding moment could have happened yesterday, or two centuries ago. I moved along the cleared path with care, bending here and there to touch bits of blackened boards and intact sections of stone walls.

Rhys accepted a sickle from Bailoch and without a word from me, began cutting handfuls of grass and tossing them aside. Scáthách joined him, as did Epona and Astrape and within minutes, the hulking form of the building's remains rose from the cleared area in a rough rectangle. I slowly wound my way across the uneven ground until I found what was left of the building's entrance. My toes bumped against the stone threshold. Rhys came up beside me, his sickle hanging between us.

"The last thing I remember of the fire was the heat, and handing Iona to you, and everything falling around me. And then I remember you lifting me off the ground."

"That was when I called for Hekate," he said, his voice tight, his features grim, "and made the bargain that would grant us safe passage to the Underworld. She escorted us herself, all the way to the river Lethe where I made my bargain with Eris."

"And you decided I should be the one to lose their memories of what transpired that night."

He switched the sickle to his other hand, found my fingers, and held tight. "I— I loved you, Habonde, as my goddess and as my lover, and your rage over those young women's deaths would only have grown had you remembered. Your people, this land, they needed time to recover. They would not have survived another round of your fire."

In my heart, I knew he was right. The way I'd reacted to Eilidh's death had impacted every living being on the croft. "Do you know what happened to their bodies after you took me away?" I asked.

"No, and if I had, I would have told you, especially once I knew your memories were beginning to return."

I lifted my gaze to the dead tree, at the way two of its lower branches curved forward as if embracing the air.

Oh Goddess, the third Woodsman from the night Rhys and his brethren made a throne for me and pleasured my flesh.

"You lost a brother that night, didn't you?"

"I did." Rhys' voice broke.

"What was his name?"

"Darragh. His name was Darragh. As I carried you to the underworld, he sought to move the girls' bodies away from the fire and hide them until the ones who'd started the fire were off the croft. He was a giant of a man, and he had them all in his arms, ready to carry them to a safer place the moment it was safe.

"He was trapped by the villagers who had come to see you burn. Instead of fighting, he turned as a Woodsman is able to turn once in their lifetime. Darragh became the oak you see before you."

"Why didn't you tell me?

"I didn't tell you because I did not know, Habonde, not until Siggi, Pym, and I arrived here to raise the yew for Hekate and found bits and pieces of Darragh's story stored underground." He squeezed my hand. "You used the ring to summon me, and I ended up here. I pieced it all together as I waited for you to arrive."

"Did you find the bones?"

He shook his head. "Finding the bones is your task and I would not take that from you."

"What will happen to Darragh? Will he go the way of the elder oaks and feed the soil at his roots?"

"My brothers will want to bring him home. He has family, and they will want what is left of his heartwood. There are cases of finding living material even in one gone as long as he is."

I disengaged my fingers from Rhys' grip. Asking him to explain the ways of the Brethren of the Woods would only delay my task. "I need to look for the bones on my own."

"I understand."

Retightening my borrowed belt, I strode toward the old oak,

toward Darragh, and placed my hands and forehead on his bark in gratitude for his actions that night. Feeling my way around his trunk, I stepped over roots and rocks and searched within for my acolytes' bones.

At the back of the tree, out of sight of the others, one of the exposed roots stirred. I sank to my knees, slid my hand into the space between the root and the ground, and scooped out clumps of rich, damp soil.

Dirt jammed underneath my fingernails. Pebbles embedded in the skin on my knees. Leaning to one side, I yelled for a shovel. Bailoch arrived, followed by Bodhi and Epona, Astrape, Mnemosyne, Scáthách, and Rhys.

"I need your help. I think the bones are buried here, or near here."

There wasn't room for everyone to dig. I took the shovel Bodhi offered, Astrape joined us, and we took turns loosening the soil at the oak's base. Rhys paced behind me, then leapt and caught a low branch. Bits of bark rained onto my head. Shielding my eyes, I looked up to see him standing halfway up the tree, one arm looped around where the trunk had split, peering into great oak.

"I see light," he said, never lifting his gaze from Darragh's heart. "Keep digging. Try to pull the dirt away from those larger roots."

A few more big shovelfuls, and a space underneath this side of the tree opened up. I got onto my belly, lit my fingers with the smallest of flames, and stuck my arm into the hole.

"Rhys, can you see anything?" Bodhi called.

"I can," he called down. "I see bones. You're going to have to widen the hole to get the bones out."

Graves. Bones. I sat back on my heels and stuck my fingers into the loosened soil to douse the flames. Overwhelmed, I made fists, punched at the earth to anchor myself and absorb the discovery's impact. My heart slowed and I gradually loosened my aching fingers.

Epona dropped onto her hands and knees and peered into the hole. Bodhi kneeled beside me. I leaned against his warm, furry thigh and rested my head on his shoulder. "Let us help," he whispered, petting my hair much as I'd seen him comfort distraught animals.

"I can do this. I *must* do this. I just need something to hold the bones." Patting his thigh, I pulled away and started to undo the buckle, intending to use my silk robe.

"Wait, Habonde. I've got something in my bags. I'll be right back." Epona scrabbled to her feet and jogged off. Rhys and Bodhi conferred, and I agreed to let them take over for a spell.

Epona returned with a handful of scarves. "Will these do?"

Making room for my replacements, I stepped away from the growing pile of soil and spread out the silk, optimistic squares of color against the trampled ground. "They're beautiful. Are you sure about this?"

"I like to fancy up my horses. Use them, please. I have plenty more."

She hugged me tight, then left to stand as witness alongside Astrape and Mnemosyne. I watched Bodhi and Rhys dig until they agreed the hole was big enough. They waved me over, then stepped aside. I again lowered myself onto my belly and worked my arms, head, and shoulders into the hollowed-out cache at the base of the tree.

I stopped trying to skate through this part of my memory-recovery process. Feeling my way forward with deliberate slowness, I curled my fingers around the first bone I touched and waited.

Maesie. Shortest of her sistren and forever running to catch up. I felt her stride, and her frustration at being left behind, embedded forever in the bone's framework.

"I remember you," I whispered, and handed the tibia into the waiting hand at my back. "Please place this bone on the red scarf." I continued in the same manner, bone by bone, memory by memory, calling out one color or the other depending on what I'd learned, until my hand felt the smooth dome of the first skull.

Unable to stop the tears, I cried as I recovered five more skulls and many more bones, muddying my face in the process. Not once did my companions try to hurry me along, even as mist turned to rain and soaked us all.

Scooting forward, I lit my fingers and made a visual sweep of the cache. Though the light was low, and my eyes might have been playing tricks on me, I thought I spied a silver chain. Digging my finger under the short length of gleaming metal, I tugged, and tugged again. A cluster of chains broke away from the soil's hold.

Chains *and* agate cabochons, given to every acolyte on completing their first year. I dragged the precious handful to my chest and rested my cheek in the dirt. There were no more bones left to recover. Using my elbows, I pushed back and sat on my heels. "I think that's all of them," I said, swiping my fingers on my filthy robe.

"I'll tie up the corners of the scarves and we can help you carry the bundles home."

"Thank you, Epona." I pushed upped to standing and faced my helpers. "Thank you, everyone. I would like to take the bones straight to the burial ground and lay these girls to rest. If any of you need to leave, I understand."

No one protested the added task or seemed eager to say their goodbyes. Bailoch and Bodhi each picked up two bundles, Mnemosyne picked another, and I carried the sixth.

• • •

OUR SOAKED and somber party arrived at my newly uncovered hearth and placed the bundles under the yew trees' interwoven branches.

"This is where we'll dig."

Astrape made a quick trip to the tool shed for more shovels, providing us enough for each of the graves. I asked that the trees sheltering the girls be close together, in two rows of three, and include the yew where Eilidh was buried. Each of my helpers chose a tree, working silently to clear a hole big enough to accommodate one bundle of bones. Mnemosyne, who'd asked to borrow Epona's horse for an essential errand, returned with a basket of fresh herbs, flowers, the golden goblet I kept on my personal altar, a small bottle of oil, and a bottle of mead.

"I took a quick look through your kitchen and garden and brought a few things. There's myrrh and cinnamon oil for anointing the bones, and parsley, laurel, wormwood, and other herbs too."

With Mnemosyne's help, I opened each bundle. Together, we brushed the dirt from the skulls and bones, then shredded all the herbs, stripped the calendula flowers of their petals, and mixed those together. Once the holes were dug, the others sat with us and helped. The fragrant oil was rubbed into the skulls, and each of the burial holes was lined with a layer of the combined herbs.

When all preparations were done, I carried the first bundle to its final resting place and set Maesie's bones within the earthen bowl.

While we repeated the process five times more, Bailoch hurried back to the stable and returned with hand-forged iron nails. Bodhi hammered one into each tree for me to hang the silver and agate necklaces on. Rhys and I shoveled dirt over the bones until all six were covered and night had dropped its cloak.

There was more to be done. Centering myself within the

trees, I lit the fingers of one hand, lifted the mead-filled goblet with the other, and opened my arms wide and spoke.

"Beloved Fia.

May the light of your magic be forever lit.

May the song of your worth be forever sung.

May your soul rest knowing you are remembered."

I poured a stream of mead over Fia's grave, and proceeded to the next grave, and the next, until the cup was empty and Leith, Lilidh, Maisie, Kenna, and Iona were properly laid to rest.

Overhead, Fergus circled with the rest of his parliament, soothing the girls' bones with soft hoots and swishing feathers. I thanked Bodhi and Bailoch for their help, and they departed for the barn and its hungry inhabitants. Scáthách, Epona, and Astrape said their goodbyes and left with their horses, leaving me with Mnemosyne and Rhys. The Goddess of Memory took hold of our wrists with gentle hands and led us into the clearing.

"I have a gift for you," she said, stopping at my hearth. "For both of you. I will share it only if your desire to see it is mutual."

I looked to Rhys. He appeared every bit as exhausted as I felt, and equally as emotionally drained. "Is this a one-time only offer?" he asked.

"No. But I think it would help you heal from everything you have witnessed this day."

"I'll do it," I said, my arm limp in her hand. I was too drained to have a stronger opinion.

"Then I shall too."

Mnemosyne wiggled the chain out from beneath her caftan, and slowly untwisted the vial's stopper. "Hold each other's hands. As before, Habonde, open your mouth, place the tip of your tongue against the backs of your top teeth. Rhys, you too."

We followed her instructions. She poured a few drops under my tongue, then under Rhys', and shuffled back a step.

"My gift is a memory from your shared past. My wish is that

you take this memory and build on it, if that is what your hearts guide you to do. And if your hearts say no, that this memory does not reflect your truth, then you part as friends with sweetness on your tongues.

"Now, close your mouths and close your eyes and let the water of memory do its work."

Chapter 30
DARRAGH

TOGETHER AND WITH OTHERS, *Rhys and I had pleasured many a goddess—and god, and other mythologicals, and even a handful of humans —in our decades as Brethren of the Woods. I had seen his face buried between sweet, plump thighs; sucking fingers and toes; smiling in post-coital pleasure.*

What I had never seen, was longing. And as we exited the orchard portal at Bone Fire Croft, the mask adorning my fellow Woodsman's face fell away, revealing a depth of longing that speared me to my heart.

"You love her, don't you?" I asked. Rhys' usually sure footing slipped on the dew slicked grass.

"Darragh, my brother, I don't know who you—"

"Nice try. You know I mean Habonde. I have seen you with her how many times now? And every time, you fight against what your wise heart tells you."

We walked side by side in silence until we passed Habonde's gate and were on the path leading to the gathering ground.

"She is an immortal goddess," my clueless friend began, "and I am a Woodsman, bound to my brethren and their families. My roots are with you."

"*True. But were you to leave for love, you would not be the first of our kind to replant themselves in more… amenable soil.*"

Rhys snorted. "I have made my own inquiries, Darragh. This goddess does not take on permanent consorts."

"*Yet you disguised yourself on Beltane, and at each ritual since, and on every one of those nights, it is you she has chosen." I grabbed his arm and stopped him in his tracks. "Declare yourself, my brother. Declare yourself and open your heart to her. Riches await the man who is brave enough to love."*

RHYS MUST HAVE TAKEN *my counsel seriously. After darkness fell and the Samhain fires were lit, he and Habonde linked hands and left the rolling field clustered with celebrants preparing to honor their dead.*

Curious, I pulled my cloak's hood over my head and followed the lovers along the stream to Habonde's cottage. They kissed at the outer gate, and again at the humble door, and if the sounds emanating from the goddess' quaint home were any indication, they'd joined their bodies the moment the latch had fallen.

Smiling to myself, I settled on a stone bench hidden amongst a stand of hawthorn and holly. If Rhys was not brave enough to court the object of his affection on his own, I would help by feeding him words from the safety of the shadows. Pulling my cloak tight around my shoulders, I rested my eyes and waited.

And waited.

I had almost given up when the door opened. Rhys walked onto the path, naked in the moonlight and unaffected by the cold, and stopped. Habonde appeared in the doorway, looking both regal, and well and truly fucked. I was happy for them both.

Sinking further into the shadows, I thought to listen in on their conversation for signs Rhys had bared his heart. Instead, I was completely taken with the look on the goddess' face.

Rhys could not see her. He was busy stretching himself in the moon's light, unaware Habonde stared at him with glowing eyes, and glowing skin, and the same longing I had seen earlier on my brother's handsome face.

Their unspoken feelings could have fueled a chapbook of poems, a roomful of paintings, a concert's worth of songs. I could not say how long Rhys stood there, eyes closed and face lifted to the stars; or how long Habonde gazed at his backside, her eyes glittering like those very same points of light.

What I came to know from my vantage point was that I would do everything in my power to ensure these two stayed together.

MY FINGERTIPS BRUSHED RHYS' pulse. His ever-present warmth emanated outward, wrapping my exposed skin. I anchored myself within the rhythm of his breath, flowing in, flowing out.

"I don't know what to say," I confessed, licking the stream of tears pooling in the corners of my mouth. Rhys squeezed my hands and drew me against his chest. I wedged my head under his chin and breathed in his vetiver-laced scent.

"I don't know what to say either. I… I had no idea Darragh was watching us that night."

Neither of us seemed willing to separate, or open our eyes, or discuss the memory culled from Mnemosyne's repository. But I had one more task to complete before I could assume the mantle of Goddess of the Hearth.

"Would you help me with something?"

"Do I need to wash up first?"

I shook my head. "No. I need you to gather dried grasses and twigs and whatever pieces of wood you can find, to set a fire which I shall light."

Night sounds filled my ears. The scents of grasses and grains, and the flowers and herbs we'd shredded, wove their way into my nostrils. I was beyond exhausted and though I craved a bath, and my bed, and a deep, dreamless sleep, I had to do this.

"Your wish is my command." Rhys kissed the top of my head and extricated himself from our embrace. While he gathered the makings for a fire, I walked the perimeter of the space I'd cleared, staying off the stones and inviting the magic I sensed moving under my feet to rise.

Soon, the soft *ssh-ssh-ssh* of brooms on stone greeted my ears. Short bundles of dried straw, bound with wild vines, followed the spiral from the center outward. No Magical guided the bundles, just magic. I choked on a muffled sob and whispered, *Thank you.*

The bundles finished their task and lay themselves down to the side of the spiral. Stepping onto the cleared stone, my bare feet met a cool, grit-free surface. I loosened Scáthách's leather belt and dropped it to the stone. The front halves of my robe fell open. Shrugging the dense, dirtied silk off my shoulders, I cherished the sensation of the fabric sliding down my arms. I caught the robe before it landed, folded it, and set it beside the brooms. To give this ritual my all, to bare myself to the magic within and without, required I enter the inward spiral skyclad.

Curious breezes raised the fine hairs all over my body, leaving tiny bumps of anticipation in their wake. I loosened my tangled braid and teased out my hair. It had been so long since I cut it, the wavy ends brushed the fullness of my bottom.

With arms raised outward and palms facing the moon, I began to walk the spiral path, setting down each foot slowly. Carefully. Deliberately. My body traveled by memory, not sight, because my eyes were turned inward, intent on finding the words to a chant lost in the winding warren of a goddess' interminable memories.

Sacred fire, sacred flame,
I call you by your sacred name.
I call you to awaken.

. . .

SACRED FIRE, *sacred flame,*
    You know my heart,
    You know my name.

    I am Habonde,
    I am Goddess of the Hearth.
    I walk the spiral,
    On my way to your heart.

    I am Habonde,
    I am Goddess of the Hearth.
    I walk the spiral,
    On my way to my heart.

While I walked, while I spoke the chant, my fingertips searched for remnants of another kind of magic. Invisible hands found my bodily form, lightly pinching the tops of my shoulders, along my outstretched arms, and around each wrist. Hands swept downward from the back of my neck; from my collarbones and shoulder blades; over my breasts and belly, back, butt, and thighs to my ankles. Nearing the end of the spiral, I lowered my arms and looked down.

I was garbed in a sheer, long sleeved gown, simple in design and extravagant in the amount of magic imbued within every thread. To the human eye, I was a ghost in a nightdress, hovering above the ground. To the initiated and magically inclined, I was in my Goddess form. With a flick of my wrist, an egg-sized ruby appeared in my palm. With a flick of my other wrist, I conjured citrine and carnelians, garnets and cinnabar, coral and fire opals.

Curling my fingers, I crushed the gems and coral to dust and sprinkled it over my hair.

The ruby I pressed to my forehead.

"I am here, My Goddess." Rhys' voice penetrated the center of my back from where he stood outside the spiral.

"Do you have your knife?"

"Yes."

"Remove your shoes, your shirt, all of your weapons except for the knife, and follow the path to me."

I did not turn to watch the Woodsman undress, nor did I monitor his progress. I waited at the edge of the fire bowl, savoring the sensation of breathing in tandem with the surrounding nature, in and out, in and out.

The Woodsman stopped across from me. I gestured to the modest piles he'd gathered.

"Ready the wood."

Crouching, he waved his hand over the blackened bowl at the spiral's center, pulling the last of the dirt off what was left of the old embers. Atop those he laid the grasses, twigs, and sticks and lastly, three logs.

"It is done, My Goddess."

"Rise."

He stood, arms hanging at his sides, neither slack nor tense. Reaching for the back of my head, I parted my hair and brought it forward, over each shoulder, and held the long, wavy ends over the pile of wood.

"Use your knife to cut my hair."

A question flickered in his eyes and passed. I would have ignored him if he'd spoken what was on his mind. The Goddess knows what must be done, and those who follow Her know to do Her bidding.

His knife sliced fast and true. Each hair burst into flame as it was released. The particles from the precious stones glittered in the flames as they floated, slow as downy feathers, and landed on the wood. Not a single strand went out; each kissed the spot where it landed, waiting for its flame to take hold before becoming as one with the wood.

A voice rose from the stones and the wood and the fire and circled me and Rhys.

Hestia. I fought to not lose my composure when I saw her face within the flames and felt the fullness of her presence; there was yet more for me to do. I freed the smile I was holding back, then refocused my attention on the fire building at my feet. For this hearth to stand a chance at remaining ever lit, I had to take the flames ignited by the cutting of my hair and invite them into my body.

I held my forearms above the fire and spoke to Rhys. "Cut me once on each hand. Make it deep, clean, and fast."

Without hesitation, Rhys grasped one wrist, held it steady, and sliced the pad at the base of my thumb. He completed his task on the other hand and stepped back, absorbed into the shadows as my blood flowed downward in slender, dripping rivulets, creating a conduit for the flames to climb. As heat and light followed my blood and entered my body, the elements combined to create a pattern beneath the skin of my forearms. I kept my eyes open, my gaze steady, until my blood stopped flowing and the cuts had sealed.

Only then could I look at the agreement made between me and the flames and forever set upon my skin.

This flame lives on, forever afire.
Forever afire, this fire lives on.

THIS GODDESS LIVES ON, *forever afire.*
Forever afire, this goddess lives on.

• • •

YOU HAVE DONE WELL, *my daughter. Welcome home.*
Thank you, Mother Hestia. It is good to be back.

RHYS DRESSED. My magic-made goddess garb would last until I crossed the threshold at the side door to my house. Before we left the hearth fire, I picked up my folded robe. Rhys and I did not touch the entire walk, nor did we speak.

As in times past, the sheer gown covering me to my toes whispered away when my bare foot touched the wooden doorsill. The fabric's magic had not only kept me covered, it had kept me whole once the ritual was over and the hearth fire lit. Without it, the weight of the day's events cascaded through me in waves, battering my insides from every angle.

I stopped in the middle of my kitchen. The original hearth had changed over the centuries, from a fire pit to a multi-burner cookstove fueled by an ever-present fire. Rough shelves had been replaced with custom cabinetry. I no longer had to go outside to pump water. Indoor plumbing was a modern miracle, and my kitchen had two soapstone sinks. One was big enough for pots.

This room was the heart of my house, and the comfortable chairs scattered throughout spoke to its use as a gathering place when I had company.

I announced, "I'd like to bathe," to the kitchen and to Rhys, intensely aware of the Woodsman's quiet presence at my back and equally aware that we should probably talk before we went to bed. In fact, it would be best if I told him to help himself to anything in the kitchen, showed him to one of the guest suites, and said goodnight.

"I would like to bathe with you."

My spine softened at the tenuous hope in Rhys' voice. I flicked at a patch of dried dirt on the folded, faded silk robe still clenched to my chest.

"I'm not sure that's a good idea. We're both exhausted."

"I will do whatever you prefer, Habonde." He moved close enough I could feel his breath on the back of my neck. "Goodnight."

The screen door squeaked as it opened. I knew without watching that Rhys used care to see it wouldn't slam shut. I knew without watching that he had stopped and turned.

Could he see my heart clawing its way out the backside of my body? Because I could feel it, could feel my front growing cold and the sorrow and longing struggling to break free of the confines of my bones and skin because I was doing nothing to acknowledge how I felt.

"Rhys. Wait." I set the robe on a chair and held the screen door open, hoping the words I was about to speak would be enough to bring him back over the threshold and into my home, if not my heart.

"I… I think we need each other tonight. At least, I know that I need you."

Chapter 31

"AND I NEED YOU, HABONDE."

The man facing me hadn't moved a muscle, except for those required to speak. His face and his stance broadcast so many emotions I couldn't begin to sort them, especially not in the dark.

"Come in, then, and we'll start clean."

"With a bath?" he asked, passing between me and the doorframe.

"I was thinking we'd start clean by talking, but we can talk in the bath."

Rhys loosened the ties on one of his vambraces. "You have a tub big enough for two?"

"In one of the guest suites, yes."

"Then lead the way."

Rhys followed me into the first house I'd added to the original. I stopped at my bedroom to choose another robe and deposit the dirty one in a basket in the laundry room. I stared at the pile of stained, faded silk and almost started crying. For so long, I'd worn it without remembering it had been a gift from Rhys, and now the events of the past twenty-four hours were recorded in its numerous rips and stains. I shook off my tears and continued down the hall and into the covered walkway joining the two buildings.

"I rarely come in here, except to show guests to their rooms. We're going to the second floor."

Like other nineteenth-century homes, this one had dizzyingly high ceilings on the ground floor, which my winged guests always appreciated. Up the wide staircase was a central landing and two corridors, one with multiple guest suites, the other with a single, extravagant set of rooms. I pressed the handles on the latter's double doors and pushed them open. Rhys gave a low, appreciative whistle.

"I'm leaving my boots in the hall," he said, "and going right to the bath, which is—?"

"There." I entered the sitting room and pointed to the right. "The door's beside the bed. You can't miss it."

It delighted me to watch Rhys explore the sitting room and the bedroom, stroking the fabrics I'd chosen for the chaise lounges and ottomans. A sensual side I'd never expressed in home furnishings had come alive during a visit with Aphrodite. Though I wanted Rhys to share my bed, and knew there was a chance he wouldn't, I thought the soft colors and cushions would hold our fractured hearts and bodies more gently than the mattress in my bedroom.

"Where should I leave these?" Rhys asked, holding up his vambraces and his dirty shirt.

"On the bench. I can ask the house elves to clean everything tomorrow."

While the Woodsman finished disrobing, I started to fill the tub, then turned on the shower in the corner stall. "Rinse first. We're both a mess." My cheeks heated when I glanced at Rhys. We'd shared so much in such a short span of time, but this kind of intimacy felt different.

"I'm scared," I whispered.

Rhys checked the temperature of the water filling the tub, and gently pushed me toward the walk-in shower. "I am too."

We rinsed quickly, though my hair took longer. I turned my back to Rhys, and he squeezed out the excess water without me having to ask. I opened one of the standing cupboards, brought out a stack of towels, and set them by the tub. In another closet, I found a large, soft robe for the Woodsman to wear after.

When I first envisioned this bathroom, I knew I wanted comfort. I had the faucets positioned in the center of the clawfoot tub's side to give bathers room to relax into its curved ends. A nearby table held soaps, wash cloths, nail brushes, and other necessities.

"Goddesses first."

I finally felt like I could shine a smile at Rhys without forcing it, and I held his gaze as I stepped into the steaming water and chose which end I wanted. He entered after I settled, watching the water rise dangerously close to the rim. I opened the drain as he lowered himself.

"Thank you for not flooding the floor," I said. "The elves would be very displeased.

"I've seen the havoc angry elves can wreak." Rhys pretended to shudder, and my tentative smile widened. He pushed in the plug and closed his eyes as he leaned back and draped his arms along the tub's rounded sides. I relaxed enough to rest my knees against his and let the heated water work its magic on my sore and tired limbs.

"I had a memory of us," I began, once I felt I could speak, "from that Samhain night, before everything fell apart."

"Do you want to share it with me?"

Pressing my lips together, I nodded. "You were standing outside my kitchen. You were naked, because we'd made love, and I was wearing the robe you'd just given me."

"The robe you had on today."

"Yes, the same one. And I looked at you, standing in the moonlight, and I knew I was falling in love with you."

"How did that make you feel?"

"Scared. I had no idea what falling in love with you would mean, how it would affect my duties, if I was even capable of having a… a 'normal' relationship. I…" I had to stop and swipe my cheeks with the side of my hand as I gathered the words to shape my confession.

"I let myself be led by my desire for you, and so I neglected my duties at the Samhain fire, and at the graveyard, and took you to the pools in the cave instead. And that's when—" Sobs wracked my chest, threatening to turn me inside out.

"That's when we heard the screams. I remember it all," he said softly, curling forward to offer me a washcloth, "like it was yesterday."

I took the cloth, rolled its edges with my fingers, held it under the tap and soaked it with a thin stream of cold water. Squeezing out the excess, I pressed the cloth to my face. I wanted to stay hidden the rest of the night. Rhys stroked my wrist, encouraging me to stay present.

"You honored the young women well tonight."

"Did you know why Hekate brought me to the underworld?"

"I did not, though I suspected it was to show you the unsettled shades. Does she want you to go back?"

"She allowed me to cross the Kokytos in a boat and take the girls myself."

"That was kind of her."

"Then she took me to the River Lethe and told me what you did."

"I felt I had no choice but to take you there. You were… you were dying, Habonde."

"But you had the choice to cure me of my burns and save my

life, which also meant I would lose my memories, and you took it."

"I did."

"You were given another choice as well."

"I was."

"I should be angry at you for sacrificing yourself like that, first by following me into the burning building, and then by choosing to erase my memories of that night, of that… that entire era of my life. My mind has not been right since then, Rhys."

"I didn't know that would happen, and I'm sorry," he said, looking me straight in the eyes. "Once we left the pool, every decision I made that night came within seconds. If I had to do it all over again, I'm not sure I would choose differently. Would you?"

"I might have chosen duty to my acolytes and followers, over the pleasure of being with you."

"Does this mean there is no hope for us, Habonde?"

"I'm not sure."

Rhys soaped up the cloth I'd let drop into the water and took one of my feet. He cleaned me slowly, running the cloth between and around each toe, massaging my arch, scrubbing away the dirt staining my knee. He rinsed the cloth, soaped it again, and did the same on the other foot and leg.

"Give me your hand," he said, eyes on the water and table of supplies, everywhere but my face. He washed my fingers, hands, and arms with care, tracing the flames tattooed under the skin of my forearms.

"Whether or not there is hope, I wish to take you to bed, my goddess."

Rhys claimed a clean cloth and slid closer. He lathered it up and rubbed it across my upper chest, each shoulder, my jaw and ears. Every touch a quiet plea for me to reconsider—or to end all this with fireworks and memories we'd never forget.

Good memories, the kind we'd want *never* to forget.

"Then take me to bed, Woodsman."

Rhys watched me the entire time he scrubbed his own body. I washed his hair when he asked, and he washed mine. I told him I was getting cold. He finished rinsing, rose from the water, and stepped out. I held onto his shoulder to keep from slipping, assuming he would help me onto the waiting rug.

Rhys had another idea. He grabbed me by the waist, lifted me up and hoisted me out, leaving me no choice but to wrap my dripping legs around his waist. He cupped my butt in one hand and adjusted his cock between our bellies with the other.

"I want to have you right here, standing up, and I want to have you in that bed, and on those couches. I want to leave my mark everywhere, Habonde," he growled, his lips hot against my neck. "On your furniture, on your skin, on your life. I want you to never forget me."

I ground against him, squeezed his waist, and lifted my hips enough he could guide himself to my entrance. I was slicked from the bathwater, from arousal, and ready, so very, very ready to stop feeling past and present sorrows and rages, and to start feeling pleasure—toe-curling, mountain-collapsing, pleasure.

I bit my lip as Rhys entered me roughly, squeezing hard and pulling me down. He stayed standing, solid and strong, holding my hips with focused intent. I held tight with my arms and legs, my mouth buried against the side of his neck, unsure if this was punishment or a prelude to something rougher, more primal.

I wasn't ready for either. I needed the softer Rhys to surface.

"Take me to the bed," I said, licking the drops beading his neck, faintly tasting salt and soap. "Please."

He did as I asked and stopped by the side of the elevated mattress. Adjusting his hold, he freed one hand and fisted my hair. I tried to undo my legs. "Stay." His voice a ragged whisper, he repeated his request. I stopped clinging to him so hard and cupped his throat right under his chin.

"I understand why you might want to hurt me, why we might want to hurt each other. But that is not what I need from you this night."

He swallowed hard, his throat's cartilage bobbing against my palm. "Then tell me what you need, Habonde, because all I know is that I need you and there is a part of me that is dying."

Chapter 32

"START with taking off that coverlet. It's too heavy."

I thought Rhys would withdraw and set me on my feet. I thought I'd go to the other side of the bed and that we would draw down the covers like couples readying for sleep; toss off the excess pillows and keep our favorite; get between the sheets, face each other, and exchange the highlights of our day.

Rhys had another plan. He kept himself inside me as he shoved the heavy cover to the foot of the bed. I clung tighter. He tossed away pillows, brought one knee to the mattress, and lowered us both. Another maneuver or two and we were both on the bed, breathing short, hard breaths, and Rhys was still inside me.

I straightened one leg and felt for the sheet with my toes. "Cover us," I whispered. "Cocoon me."

He propped himself on his elbow and reached for the light blanket. "What else do you need?" he asked, stroking the side of my waist and hip. He continued down the back of my thigh and pulled my knee up, moving in and out of me so slowly I wanted to tell him to go faster, harder, until I realized I was getting exactly what I had asked for.

I was wrapped and pinned and free to go and there was nowhere else I wanted to be. And so, I addressed his question.

"I need to know I can be with you. Like this, when it's just the two of us trying to make us one." I rolled my hips and wet my lips and poured fire into my eyes. His gaze tracked everything I said, every movement my body made. "And also… like this." I relaxed my limbs and opened my arms wide. "I need to know you can be with me, when I'm out in the world doing all the things I want and need to do to make my amends for the past and build something beautiful and strong for the future."

Rhys had stilled as he listened. Lifting my head, I kissed the side of his mouth and spoke against his skin. "Once you've completed your obligation to Hekate, what comes next for you?"

I dropped back onto the pillow, struck by the realization I didn't have a clear idea what Rhys and his brethren did, what their responsibilities were, how their magic manifested. "I have so many questions."

He centered himself between my thighs and wedged his elbows against my ribs. His fingers brushed away the damp hairs sticking to my face and spread the rest to either side.

"A Woodsman prefers to live in the company of his peers," he began. "To put down roots where the air is clean, the soil is amenable, and the possibility for growth ever-present."

While he spoke, he shifted his weight to one elbow and explored my body with his other hand. "This Woodsman has lived with the longing to return to this croft, to return to his goddess, to return to you, for two hundred years." He bowed his head and kissed my breast. His cock swelled, and I drew in a breath as Rhys tongued my nipple and coaxed it into a peak. He shifted his weight and gave the same attention to my other breast.

"I knew there would be a reckoning between us," he

continued, passing his attention from one nipple to the other and back and sliding his knee up to wedge against my butt. "There had to be. I knew that if I was to stand even a slim chance of being back in your good graces, I would have to bare myself to you and accept the consequences of the choices I made."

His cock left me wanting as withdrew, kissing his way down the front of my body. I forgot to breathe as he settled his shoulders behind my knees, cupped my butt in both hands, and brought me to his mouth.

"I love you, Habonde." He licked me, used his thumbs to part my swollen lips, and licked me again. "I love your cunny," he murmured, sucking at my clit.

I tried to stay anchored on his words. "Is there more you have not told me?"

He lifted his head and looked into my eyes. "I have not told you my brethren support my desire to leave our enclave to be here, with you." He worshipped me with another long lick. "I have not told you Hekate has asked me to tend to the yew tree on this croft so that she may visit more often. Or that she has offered me the position of Head Keeper for all her portals."

"*All* her portals?" I asked, giggling at the double entendre.

Rhys nipped my inner thigh and grinned. "There is only one goddess I wish to serve in that way and that is the goddess who feeds me nectar I will never tire of tasting."

My Woodsman returned to lavishing attention on me, to the point where an orgasm lifted me in its swell and set me down softly once it passed. Rhys moved slightly, enough to rest his head on my leg.

"How did you do that?" Sated, I threaded my fingers through his hair.

"Do what?"

"Make me come with such… stealth."

He chuckled. "It's a gift."

"I have a gift for you."

"What kind of gift?"

"Forgiveness." My chest shuddered as I spoke. I had meant forgiveness for *him*, and realized it was equally important I grant forgiveness to myself. "I forgive you for taking away my choice about whether to keep or lose my memories. Were the roles reversed, I would likely have done the same."

"Thank you." Rhys kissed my belly and took his time returning his gaze to meet mine. "I'm grateful you thought to ask for Mnemosyne's help retrieving memories you knew were missing."

"Gratitude," I continued, pressing one finger to his lips. "I, too, am grateful you knew who to ask for help. Thank you for taking me to the Underworld, and for saving my life."

He nudged my finger aside with his tongue. "You are welcome."

We lay there, in the quiet. I wasn't sure what Rhys was thinking, but he seemed in no rush to speak. A hundred thoughts flew through my mind, and I invited the most important one to settle.

"I told you before that I've never lived with a lover," I began. I had to force my body to stay relaxed as I spoke. "When I had acolytes, and actively served my local community and engaged with other goddesses, I'm not sure I ever thought I needed a long-term romantic partner.

"Here. Now. I—" I pressed my lips together and turned my head. "I'm afraid to let you in all the way. I'm afraid to think I might need you."

Rhys rose, repositioned his arm underneath my back, and rolled us so I was on top. He even managed to bring the covers with him. Curling up slightly, he shoved a pillow behind his head and did that thing again where he tamed the hair sticking to my face and managed to coil it all in his hand. With me on my knees, he reached down and settled his cock below where I straddled his thighs.

He slowly released my hair, admired the change in view, and showed me his unarmored forearms. "These scars will never go away," he said, rubbing his palm over the wrinkled sections of pinkish white skin. "If they're ever too much, let me know and I'll cover them."

"They will never be too much, Rhys." I showed him my forearms, with their subcutaneous red and orange lines. "I fear you could tire of *my* markings, and what they mean."

He traced the lines of quiescent fire with his fingertip. "What do they mean to you?"

"They mean…" I sank more of my weight onto Rhys' legs and snuggled my toes between the mattress and the backs of his knees. "They mean I serve my spirit mother, Hestia, as Goddess of the Hearth. They mean I must remember it is my duty to serve others."

I spread all ten fingers and made gentle fists of my hands, and repeated the actions two times more, triggering the dormant insignia under my skin to reach a molten state.

"It's like your veins hold liquid fire," Rhys said. "What does it feel like, when they glow?"

"It feels like…" I closed my eyes and almost giggled when I found the words I was searching for. "It feels like love, Rhys. Potent, liquid, love"

He stared at me without moving, then raised his hand and placed his palm over my heart. "Do you feel your fire all the way in here?"

I closed my eyes again and centered my awareness under Rhys' touch. His heat warmed my skin; the coolness within my heart chamber needed more than surface touch. I couldn't answer, couldn't open my eyes, so I shook my head.

Rhys rubbed slowly, making soft, soothing noises deep in his throat. His cock hardened and I took him in hand, ran my thumb down the ridge. I rose just enough I could position him where I needed him most. Before I could ask, he whispered, "Yes."

I sank onto my Woodsman, my lover, my future, and grasped for something to hold. His hands found mine, our fingers locked together, and I rocked up and came down, up and down, met every time by Rhys.

Our pace quickened. He loosened his grip and pulled us both up to sitting. He made sure I didn't lose my rhythm as he rocked side to side so I could wrap my legs behind him.

"Hold on."

Grateful for my long, strong legs, I held on. He lowered me onto my back, again found my hands, and swept them over my head until I touched the bars in the headboard.

"Hold on."

Rhys cupped my face. I heard the slap of skin meeting skin, of body meeting body. The fire flowing through my arms heated. Fiery light bathed Rhys' features and every stroke of his cock inside me pushed me closer and closer to another release. This one was going to be far stronger and louder than the one I'd had earlier.

I could only imagine what Rhys' body was building up to. Sweat dropped onto my cheek. My shoulders and throat warmed; the curtains of the canopy, the curtains at the windows, and even of the walls seemed to melt away until it was just me and Rhys and our sex-slicked bodies.

My orgasm crackled along the tips of my toes and the roots of my hair. It licked up my legs and wrapped around my ribs, warming my bones. Emerald green tendrils twined through Rhys' thick locks and his eyes went from brown to black to the same radiant green.

We gasped, drawing oxygen from the same source. I lifted my head as he lowered his and our lips met. Finally. The kiss was worth the wait as two bodies shared one tree-felling, fire-starting, release, lips and tongues exploring through wave after wave of sensation. The cold space around my heart disappeared in a slow rush of molten emotion.

I let go of the bedframe and hugged Rhys to me, my arm muscles spent and languid. He buried his face in the side of my neck and kissed my jaw.

"I love you, Habonde."

"I love you, Rhys."

Epilogue

BEFORE I OPENED MY EYES, before I moved an arm or a leg
or rolled to my other side to test the feel of the day, I scanned my
body for remnants of my night with my Woodsman.

My Woodsman. I could imagine Baubo's reaction when I told
her my news. She would be delighted that despite my
reservations, despite the tragedy Rhys and I had shared, we were
together. I wiggled my toes under the covers and stretched my
arms. Paper crackled under my fingertips and my eyes flew open.
The curtains were closed on the window beside the bed, but the
ones at the farther window were parted. Seated in a comfortable
armchair, one leg crossed over the other, was Rhys. My
handsomely be-robed, smiling Woodsman.

"Good afternoon, Goddess."

"Good… did you say *afternoon,* Woodsman?"

"I did."

I waved the paper in the air. "And what is this?"

"I wrote you a goodbye note, but I couldn't bear to leave
without seeing you waken, so… here I am." He gestured to the
sunbeams illuminating the side of his face and shoulder.

Loosening the tie on his robe, he stood. More sun caressed his chest, his chiseled belly, his legs. The same strong, steady legs that had carried me from the bathroom to the bedroom and back again and would likely transport me between the two rooms any time I asked.

I shot up to sitting and smoothed the paper I'd inadvertently crumpled. "What does it say exactly?" I asked, pressing the bedsheet to my face to hide my watering eyes.

"It says I love you, and I will see you in two weeks, and should you need me before then, use my ring."

"Oh." I swiped away the unnecessary tears and used the sheet to muffle the sound of my relief. "Have you eaten?"

Rhys stalked toward me and took hold of the covers at the foot of the bed. I propped myself up on my elbows as he flung everything aside, reached for my ankles, and hauled me to him. I might have squealed.

"Spread your legs for me, Habonde." *Oh, mighty Aphrodite, that tone.* I would do anything for Rhys when he deepened his voice and spoke to me in *that* tone. There was no use protesting, or trying to resist, or offering to leave our sanctuary and make us tea. I scooted forward, let my legs dangle, and waited for Rhys to tell me what he wanted me to do next.

"Watch."

"Yes."

I watched him sink to his knees and part my lips with his thumbs.

I watched him lick me like a beast grooming its fur, his tongue broad and flat and all-encompassing. When I tilted my hips for a better angle, Rhys groaned and cupped the backs of my knees. On the verge of coming apart, I dropped back and gave in. I could handle one more orgasm. One, and no more because I had work to do and I—

"Rhys!" I yelped as he straightened, taking my legs into the air with him and hauling my butt to the edge of the mattress.

"What?" He wrapped an arm around my thighs, pinning my legs to his chest, and guided himself inside me. Thrusting slowly, he stared at me from between my ankles.

"I love you," I confessed, arching as my Woodsman came closer and closer to drawing one more orgasm from my sated body.

"And I love you." Rhys kissed the inside of my ankle. "I love this ankle." He licked my arch and sucked on my toes. "And I love this foot and these toes and—" The combination of him speaking his love and showing it sent me over the edge. His grip on my legs tightened, and he followed with his own release.

After, Rhys rested his forehead against my heels, in no hurry to withdraw. "I think I can safely leave you now," he murmured. His heavy-lidded gaze swept up my front and met my own very, *very* satisfied smile.

"Will you be my consort for the First Harvest festival?"

"I wouldn't leave the job to anyone else. And as it's your birthday too, expect extra attention." He eased out of me and set my feet gently on the floor. "Do you think a man could a get a cup of tea before setting off?"

I GAVE Rhys more than a cup of tea. I scrambled eggs and toasted bread and opened a jar of rosehip jam. We ate at the table underneath the pergola, I in a turquoise robe and Rhys in clean clothes I found in the guest closet. The pants might have been from the 'sixties, as in nineteen-sixties, but the silk shirt was all pirate and when I told Rhys he could swashbuckle me anytime, he almost did, right there in front of the bees and butterflies and nosy crested tits.

I recognized the yelps and yips nearing the front of the house as coming from Hekate's dogs. The same quartet that guided me in the underworld veered around the corner and paused in front of Rhys' chair, casting hungry glances at his plate. He tossed them what was left of his toast.

"My escorts are here. Hekate must be concerned I've reneged on our deal."

"Go." I lifted my face to the sun and his lips and once he'd kissed me fiercely and fondled my breasts, I bade goodbye to my Woodsman.

LONG AFTER RHYS LEFT, I was still in my robe, still sipping tea, still letting the sun multiply my freckles. Regretting *nothing*, I grinned into my mug when I heard footsteps approaching from the orchard. Baubo wasn't in her room—I'd checked when Rhys and I had passed her door—and I expected my prescient friend would want all the details before I shared them with anyone else.

"I hear you!" I called. "Water's hot for tea and I'm—"

Screams and growls sounded from the hedgerow to my right. I tore out of my garden and onto the path, to be met by Bruiser, another of Hekate's dogs, trotting toward me, carrying a human-looking foot in an expensive-looking shoe in her mouth. The foot's owner was close behind, waving his arms and staying stubbornly and angrily upright.

"*Zeus?*" I made no move to help the one known, amongst other epithets, as Mechaneus. I had no doubt he could invent himself a brand-new foot before he came anywhere near to bleeding out beneath my cherry trees.

"Gods-damn dog," he yelled, stopping to sit. He ripped off a strip of his button-down shirt, wrapped the stump at the bottom of his calf, all while glaring up at me. "And gods-damn you, Habonde."

"Are you going to tell me why you've come creeping into my orchard via the backdoor?"

"I came here," he said, crossing his injured leg over his intact one and affecting an imperious look, "because I've heard rumor of this school you plan to start, and I don't like it. Not one whit. There is no reason whatsoever for a goddess to shirk her duties for a single *day*, let alone an entire *year*."

Bruiser bumped against my leg as she positioned herself in front of me and growled at Zeus. The darling beast still had the foot in its silk dress sock in her mouth. Alas, the shoe must have fallen off. "My training program is happening whether you like it or not, Zee. Now, if you'll excuse me, I have a campus to design."

My new best canine friend and I turned as one.

"You try my patience, Habonde Barleywine. You, and Baubo, and Demeter, and even my own *daughter*. My patience and that of the other—"

I had no desire to let a maundering fool put a damper on this glorious day.

"The Goddess is back, Zeus, whether you like it or not. You had best get gone before I ask Bruiser to bring me your other foot."

THE END

(for now…)

Also by Coralie Moss

Join Coralie's mailing list

for news & ongoing short stories (www.coraliemoss.com).

Many of Coralie's stories are also available in "closed door" editions (meaning there is no adult content).

Visit her website for more information.

Coralie's latest books feature goddesses and other mythological figures navigating the modern world.

The Goddessverse Fantasy series includes:

The Goddess & the Woodsman - book 1

Persephone Lost & Found - book 2

Demon Healer - book 3

Pandora's (as yet untitled) story - coming in 2024

———

The Goddess by Proxy series includes:

- **Medusa's Proxy,** a paranormal romance novelette

———

The Shifters in the Underlands series:

- **Paper Dragon** (Jake Winslow Book 1)

- **Blood Dragon** (Jake Winslow Book 2)
- **Moon Dragon** (Jake Winslow Book 3)

The Sister Witches Urban Fantasy series:

- **Once Blessed, Thrice Cursed** is book #1 of the Sister Witches Urban Fantasy Series. Set in Northampton, Massachusetts, it introduces us to Clementine, Beryl, and Alderose Brodeur.
- **Demon Lines** (book 2) is the continuation of Clementine's story.
- **The Scarab Eater's Daughter** (book 3) gives us the sisters' continuing adventures from Alderose's point of view.
- **Beguiled, Bewitched, & Broken** (book 4) features the middle sister, Beryl.
- **The Sister Witches Urban Fantasy Series: Box Set 1** (includes book 1-4)
- **Witches Everbound** (book 5) completes the Sister Witches Urban Fantasy series.

The Calliope Jones series:

- **Magic Remembered** (book 1)
- **Magic Reclaimed** (book 2)
- **Magic Redeemed** (book 3)
- **Magic Restrained, a novelette** (book 3.5)
- **The Magic Series Box Set #1**

Acknowledgments

——

Two people knew Habonde's story had to be longer than the original novelette I had planned: author and beta reader Katrina Carruth, and my husband, Mr. Moss. I am grateful they ignored my protestations and sent me back to the manuscript more than once.

Two people are there for me every workday (and even on weekends): Authors Meka James and Lily Michaels. We met on Twitter, and we've been together through all the wild ups and downs of being writers and authors. Everyone should be so lucky to have cheerleaders like these two. I love you both.

Wordmakers. This group of writers/authors inspires me on a daily basis, through sharing the ups and downs and in-betweens of being creatives and entrepreneurs. Thank you, Tasha L. Harrison, for creating a space for us to learn and thrive.

Finally, the ancestor journey I took with the guidance of herbalist, ritualist, and homeopath Seraphina Capranos sparked the beginning of Habonde's story. I am grateful for Saera and Reed and the elecampane Mother Plant at Orchestra Farm; for Seraphina's plant wisdom; and for those I met with the help of her voice, her drum, and "a fresh nubbin of elecampane."

About the Author

Author Coralie Moss likes to start her fantasy stories with witches, goddesses, and other Magicals and plunk a surprise or five into their seemingly normal lives. She lives on an island in the Salish Sea - the site of much magical inspiration - with her husband and two rescue cats.

Join Coralie's mailing list for book news, giveaways, and the occasional homage to apples.